Tess

T.A. LEINEMANN

Copyright 2018 by T.A. Leinemann.

All rights reserved. Except as permitted under the U.S. Copyright Act of 1976 no part of this publication maybe be reproduced, distributed or transmitted in any form or by or any means, or stored in a database or retrieval system, without the prior written permission of the author.

This book is a work of fiction. Any references to historical events, real people or real places are used fictitiously. Other names, characters, places and events are products of the author's imagination, and any resemblance to actual events, places or persons, living or dead, is entirely coincidental.

ISBN-13: 978-1986342599
ISBN-10: 198634259X

ACKNOWLEDGMENTS

With love and gratitude, I thank Mark, Christina, Johanna, and Samantha, for their ongoing support and encouragement of me and my passion for writing.

Thank you to Christina Knittel and Johanna Leinemann for their creative and expert design of the front and back cover.

A heartfelt thank you to Robert, my father for his invaluable advice and keen eye for detail in helping me polish my story.

Author photo taken by Amagee Photography of Dawson City, Yukon. Thank you, Andrea.

Thank you to my family and friends for your continued support and encouragement.

ONE

Tess Douglas lived in Vancouver, a bustling young port city in 1905 filled with vitality and promise.

"Stop daydreaming. I am late as it is," said Anna, Tess's mother, as she tossed chopped carrots into the stew pot then wiped her forehead with her apron.

A Coastal spring downpour distorted Tess's view as she stood at the window, its rhythmic beat against the glass giving her solace inside their cozy kitchen. Startled by her mother's voice, Tess gasped and stared at the potato in her hand, blinking as her dream world faded away. The shift between fantasy and reality left her dazed, as if she had traveled through time. Her favorite memory, building sandcastles with her father was no longer enough to make her happy.

Through the kitchen window, raindrops spattered onto the landscape swirling blue, red and yellow into a muddy brown vista that flowed into the street like globs of paint dripping off a canvas.

"Yes, Mother." She peeled the last two potatoes quickly, nicking her finger in the process. Tess stared at the tiny drop of blood forming on the tip of her finger. Touching her tongue to the wound she licked the crimson droplet, scrunching her face at the metallic taste of blood mixed with potato juice. Dirt crunched between her teeth, a sensation both irritating and intriguing. She played with the tiny particles of grit, lightly grinding them with her teeth to create a grating noise that tickled her eardrums.

"For heaven's sake, Tess, rinse out your mouth before you ruin your teeth." Anna grabbed the peeled potatoes from the counter.

Tess rolled her eyes, certain her mother could hear a hatpin drop from across the street. She poured water into a glass, took a sip and swished before spitting into the sink.

"Young ladies do not spit."

"How am I supposed to rinse my mouth without spitting?" Tess stood at the sink and wiped her mouth with the back of her hand, frustrated with her mother's irritability.

"Do not sass me." Anna chopped the potatoes into bite-sized pieces and threw them into the pot. She stirred with a wooden spoon, and set the lid in place before putting dinner into the oven.

Tess gathered the potato peels and dropped them in the tin bucket by the back door. Despite a regular supply of nourishing kitchen scraps, the postage stamp garden struggled to grow in the shadow of the majestic oak tree.

If Tess had to choose between fresh vegetables or devoting her time to reading beneath the oak's protective branches, reading won over weeding every time.

As she washed her hands, the empty wood bin beckoned. She had forgotten to bring in an armload of wood for the demanding woodstove. A pair of gray woolen stockings hung on a thin rope strung across the top of the stove.

Tess knew her mother worried about the dwindling wood supply in the shed. Tess was concerned about the fate of her beloved oak tree, that they might be forced to chop it down to keep the woodstove radiating comforting heat from its black belly. Her stomach clenched as she wondered if her inclination to spend time reading instead of helping with chores might be the cause of her mother's irritation.

"I didn't mean to be rude." Tess wished she knew how to make her mother happy again. Her father's absence was taking its toll on them.

She ran out to the woodshed, grabbed an armload of wood and carried it into the kitchen, dropping the chunks into the bin with loud thumps to express her frustration.

Anna sighed. "I know it hasn't been easy without your father but we must work together and continue to be a loving family."

"Yes, Mother."

"Sweep the floors, and tend to the fire while I'm gone. My meeting could run longer if problems arise, but I should be home in two hours. We will eat then."

"Yes, Mother." Tess sat on a hard wooden chair with her hands clasped in her lap, squirming as she tried to find a comfortable position. An itch crawled across the skin of her nose but she ignored it, fighting to sit motionless while her mother spoke, fearful the slightest movement on her behalf would add extra chores to the list.

"Have you finished your homework?"

"Yes, Mother."

"Work on your lessons."

"But, school is almost over for the year. I learn while I read. I don't know why you worry."

"Silence. You may read when your chores are done. The parlor is off limits until you learn to sit properly. You are a young lady not an Egyptian princess reclining on her throne. I prefer to entertain guests in a room that does not look like it was hit by a tornado. I raised you to be well-mannered and…"

"Why bother keeping it tidy? We never have guests. What is the use?"

"Do not interrupt. We shall carry on as usual, and I expect you to help without question. I am dreadfully late." Anna glanced at the grandfather clock in the corner as she untied her apron and hung it on a hook near the stove. She pulled on her fitted cotton jacket and set a straw hat on her head, securing it to her hair with a hatpin. "Remember, no reading until your chores are done, and stay out of the parlor."

"I promise." Tess smoothed her apron and stood, extending her arms waiting for her usual hug before Anna left for work at the chocolate shop or her volunteer duties.

Tess's face dropped as her mother rushed past toward the back door slamming it shut with a bang.

TWO

Tess blinked and lowered her arms, dragging her feet back to the table, glaring at her school books piled on the end.

The fire crackled in the woodstove, reminding her she was not entirely alone. Rain fell harder, clanging on the tin roof of the woodshed. Tess loved summer storms when she and her father would sit in the parlor quietly reading books, amiable companions in silence. He was gone, and Tess struggled to breathe in the thick humid air.

Tess threw responsibility and duty to the side. After all, her mother tossed her aside. The fire and floors could wait. She had more important ways to spend her time. Reading the latest mystery story and enjoying two wonderful hours of freedom. She would finish her chores before her mother returned.

Tess checked the fire. Two pieces of wood crackled and popped inside the stove. Thunder rolled in the distance. Her mother had forgotten to take an umbrella.

She decided to dedicate an hour and forty-five minutes to reading. These moments had to be stolen whenever the opportunity arose. Sweeping could wait. She wanted to be adventurous and daring like the heroines in the stories and throw caution to the wind.

Since Tess's father left, her mother had buried herself in her work at the chocolate shop and volunteering at the downtown soup kitchen. Tess was not used to being alone, rarely venturing far from home without her mother.

Time flew by as Tess immersed herself in another world. Her muscles tensed as she followed the story's heroine down the worn, wooden steps of the abandoned house into the damp cellar. She shivered as the intrepid teen crept toward the menacing villain hunched over a motionless figure on the floor.

Tess gasped.

The new electric lights sputtered in the parlor then went out leaving the room in darkness. Thunder rolled and rumbled above the house.

Tess inhaled sharply, clutching her book with shaking hands.

"Stupid lights. Do your job, and glow brighter. Hiding in the dark won't solve anything. There is nothing to be afraid of." Tess sank further into her nest of blankets, waiting. Her heart pounded as the clock ticked. She breathed a sigh of relief as the lights flickered on, and then groaned as they went out.

Shadows leapt around the room, taunting her as they transformed the furniture into wavering ghosts.

"Stop playing around, I need you to be strong for me."

She was just a child, learning to live without her father, and trying to be a help to her mother, resenting both for thrusting her into a life of worry and responsibility before she was ready. She was tired of dealing with bossy Agatha in knitting group, and the stupid boy in her classroom.

Tess could see the fatigue in Anna's eyes, the hint of a tear held back behind a wall of irritability. She could see it in her mother's need to stay busy outside their fractured home, unwilling to face a bleak future without her husband.

The thunderstorm had darkened the sky despite the early summer evening.

Tess peeked through the lace curtains.

Rain poured onto the street, droplets bouncing back into the air from the force. The rain had washed color from the world replacing it with gray and black.

A vivid flash of lightning lit up the sky and silhouettes of buildings across the street appeared then disappeared. The burst of energy jolted Tess's heart, reminding her to breathe. In the flash, a glistening, wet figure stood outside in the street behind the iron fence, facing their house. She gasped, filling her lungs with oppressive humid air.

Tess flopped onto the couch, shutting out the mysterious scene. It was almost seven o'clock. Her mother would be back soon. The lights flickered and glowed to life, strong and steadfast. A sob of relief escaped her lips.

Anxious to flee the dreary rain and its unsettling creatures, Tess picked up her book. She picked up where she had left off, and ignored the storm raging outside the house.

The story's heroine had been hiding behind a dusty wardrobe in the cellar. She moved her arm against the wall searching for something big enough to wield at the villain's head. Her fingers touched a rough wooden handle, and, hoping it was a shovel, she tightened her grip and lifted it in front of her body. At that moment the villain whirled around…

Bang! Bang! Bang!

The book fell from Tess's hands as her mind was dragged from the dangerous cellar of the story back into the parlor. It took a few seconds for her to realize someone was at the door. Her heart leaped in fear, slamming against the confines of her ribs. A steam engine roared in her ears.

The clock in the kitchen chimed. *One.*

Tess frowned. Who would be out in this weather?

Soulful chimes, insistent and foreboding, continued to announce the hour.

Tess held her breath and counted. *Two. Three. Four.*

Who dared to show up unannounced? Maybe her mother forgot her key?

Another sharp knock rattled the front door. The clock chimed. *Five.*

The pages of the book crunched under Tess's knee as she peeked out the window above the sofa. The nest of blankets fell apart and pillows dropped silently to the floor.

She counted chime number six, and a sharp intake of air filled her lungs. She froze.

An opportunity to be the heroine of her own story had presented itself. Should she confront the mystery person, face-to-face? Confident and fearless, Tess could solve the mystery and save her family from whomever, or whatever was at the door. Fear kept Tess glued to the sofa but curiosity pulled her to the window.

A figure in a black rain slicker stood on the porch.

The boards creaked as the person shifted their weight and leaned against a railing as wind whipped rain sideways.

Tess chewed her nail. Was the door locked? What if he tried the latch?

Tess ran into the hall. She hesitated. Metal scratched against wood, the sound coming from the kitchen. Shivering, she turned her back to the noise and faced the front door, preparing to confront the distorted black figure on the other side of the bevelled glass.

Floorboards groaned behind her.

Tess was trapped, not daring to turn around as a sinister presence moved closer. Her spine tingled as if a thousand tiny spiders crawled up her back and she shuddered.

"Don't kill me." She screamed, as something cold and wet touched her arm.

THREE

Tess rubbed the spot on her arm as instinct possessed her to turn and see what horror lurked behind her.

"Heavens, Tess, you startled me. I thought you were in your room. The fire has gone out in the kitchen."

"I'm sorry, Mother."

"Why haven't you answered the door? How rude to keep visitors waiting, especially in this storm," said Anna. She hurried toward the front door, and despite scolding Tess for making their visitor wait paused to pat her hair with a dish towel and shake water off her beige summer suit before yanking open the door.

The black figure stumbled back a step as Anna moved onto the porch and pulled the door closed before Tess could follow.

Tess ran to the parlor window.

Anna greeted the boy who pulled back the hood of his slicker and tipped his cap, bowing slightly. She crossed her arms and glanced at the wilted telegram in his gloved hand.

Tess's fingers flew to her mouth, and she gnawed on her fingernail as her mother took the message from the boy who turned to leave.

Tess held her breath. The boy on the porch held the key to returning Tess's life back to the way it used to be. Or render it hopeless forever.

What if it was bad news? Her father hadn't written in a long time. Tess searched the movements of the telegram delivery boy for signs.

He glanced at his pocket watch and adjusted his bag.

Tess could tell he wanted to get off the porch as quickly as possible. Tess certainly would. He seemed anxious to put distance between himself and the fallout of his recently delivered message.

Her mother placed a hand on his arm in a silent plea of support and tore open the envelope. She quickly scanned its contents.

Tess closed her eyes to avoid witnessing her mother's reaction. Please, please, let it be good news. Tess summoned the mystery of magic to surround her. She knew it existed, as it did in her storybooks, and at the right moment it would grant her one wish. This was the moment she had been waiting for, and she clamped her eyes tightly shut. White light flashed behind her eyelids. Her fingers tingled. Please let it be good news.

Tess put her ear to the window but their voices were muffled. It had to be from her father. Who else would send a telegram?

The last message had upset her mother terribly with its official-sounding declaration that her husband, Tess's father had been declared MIA. Tess balled her fists remembering the anguished moans rising from her mother as she dropped to her knees on the hard wooden floor. Tess took the paper from her hands and read the message. *Missing In Action.* How could the army lose one of their men? Every soldier was vital to the team fighting bravely alongside each other in the Boer War overseas. Tess's stomach had tightened into a knot as she knelt beside her mother. How cold-hearted could someone be to misplace a person and send an unfeeling telegram to the family stating they were sorry, but they didn't know where he was? To Tess, it was plain irresponsible.

Tess knew her father was not lost. He knew exactly where he was and would do everything he could to find a way to return to them. It would take time, but her mother was losing hope.

"Please, please, let it be a message from Father," she whispered, feeling the fragile power of wishes disappear, and a cold, dull ache settle into her heart, an anchor securing her joy to the bottom of a black sea. She needed another chance to tell him she loved him. She would give anything to take back the words she had uttered the day he left.

The door opened. Anna came inside and stood motionless on the worn hall carpet with the wet telegram in her shaking hands.

"Have they found Father? When is he coming home?"

Anna's brow furrowed in confusion.

"Mother?" Tess pushed the door closed, shutting out the tempest.

Anna drifted down the hall, as if in a trance, toward the kitchen. Tess grabbed her hand.

Anna stopped.

"What did it say?" Tess had a right to know. Her life hung in the balance, waiting for the man who had left them to fend for themselves while he served their country with pride and courage.

Tess wished her mother would confide in her. She was eleven, but they had no one else. Tess's father had asked her to take care while he was away, but he forgot to tell her how.

"Tess, my sister needs our help."

"Aunt Molly? I don't understand. What does she have to do with Father?"

Her mother wrinkled her brow and stared at Tess for a moment. "It wasn't about Father. Molly is in trouble and she needs us. She sent the funds for our trip. We must leave as soon as possible."

FOUR

Tess let her mouth drop open. "We can't leave. What if Father shows up, how will he find us? Aunt Molly lives in the middle of nowhere." Tess brought her hands to her mouth. Tears filled her eyes, blurring her mother's face like the landscape in the rain. She was losing the tenuous grip on her father's memory despite her efforts to preserve it.

She had secretly taken his favorite grey wool sweater and kept it hidden under her pillow, breathing in the tobacco and peppermint each night before she went to bed. When the scent began to fade she had found a pouch of his pipe tobacco and tried rubbing bits into the fabric. It was not the same without the man inside the sweater, laughing and hugging his little girl who used to encircle his neck with her sticky fingers.

Tess sobbed, not caring about the giant tears splashing onto the linoleum floor and mixing with the puddle of rainwater created by her mother.

A storm was brewing indoors and Tess was powerless to stop the devastation. Why did her father leave? She had not understood then, and she did not understand now. She had been angry with him, for tearing apart their happiness, ripping it to shreds and expecting them to carry on a normal life without him, forever wondering whether he was alive or dead.

"Why don't we ask Aunt Molly to stay with us?" Tess pleaded, feeling childish for whining but willing to do anything to keep from leaving all that was familiar to her. "What if Father returns?"

"She needs help at the hotel. We can't stay here, Tess. Not a day goes by I don't pray for your father's return, but we must be realistic. He would have wanted us to be strong, to move forward. We have to help Aunt Molly. She has no one else. Family looks out for each other."

"Where's Uncle Beau? Why can't he help her?"

Anna hung her head in silence. "That is not possible."

"Why? What's wrong?"

"Never mind. Children do not need to know everything."

"That is not fair."

"You will do as I say." Anna picked up the kettle, held it under the water tap then placed it on the stove. She sighed as she held her hand over the surface then picked two logs from the bin and relit the fire.

"But, isn't it dangerous in the Yukon Territory?" Tess wiped her face with her handkerchief, standing at the door to the kitchen, refusing to enter or show agreement with the far-fetched plan.

"Dawson City has changed since the wild days of the gold rush. Most of the prospectors left. It is a respectable town these days." Anna opened the oven door and, using a folded dishtowel, lifted the steaming pot of stew onto the top of the stove.

The hearty aroma filled the kitchen, and Tess's stomach betrayed her by growling loudly. She refused to give in. "It is in the middle of nowhere. What about me? I don't want to leave my friends or our home. What if I don't want to go? I am almost twelve. I should have a say in the matter." As she spoke the words, she did not believe them. It was never about her. She was a child, not old enough to have a say in anything. Goodness knows she tried. She had thrown spectacular tantrums in the past. They never ended well, but she never thought that far ahead.

"You can't make me go. We cannot abandon Father." Tess's chin jutted out and her ears burned.

"Tess, please understand. I have tried to make a life for us here, but I cannot continue. We must leave, we have no other choice."

Tess's heart pounded as she turned her back on her mother and stomped up the stairs into her bedroom. She slammed the door, taking wicked satisfaction at the glass rattling in the window frame, and flopped onto her bed.

FIVE

A cavernous hole in Tess's stomach woke her the next morning. She had ignored her mother's knocks, pretending to be asleep.

Tess strained to hear signs of activity as she descended the staircase into the kitchen but her mother had left for work.

She checked the wood bin. It was full. Her shoulders dropped. Her mother had brought in the wood. Was she trying to make Tess feel guiltier than she already did? She clenched her teeth. Didn't she know dragging Tess thousands of miles from the only home she had ever known would traumatize her for life? Adults didn't care how their decisions affected their children, expecting them to stay silent and meek. Tess felt powerless.

She unclenched her teeth and rubbed the sleep from her eyes. Her mother told her everything looked better in the morning, but not this time.

A pot sat on the warming shelf. Tess peeked under the lid and inhaled the fragrant smell of meat and potatoes. Her stomach growled as she spooned the leftover stew into a bowl and sat in a chair at the table. Tess gasped as she spotted the magazine lying next to her. Her mother had bought the latest issue of *Adventure*

Girls Weekly for Tess. Tess groaned. Why did her mother make it difficult for Tess to stay angry?

She flipped pages and scanned the contents while she ate. In the middle of the magazine, the next chapter of the serial mystery she had been following sat in wait, in all its inky black glory. Tess had been on edge for weeks as she devoured each thrilling chapter within minutes then was forced to wait for the next issue. Maybe she could read it at school during lunch.

Tess washed the dishes and set them on the counter to dry. She cut two thick pieces of bread, slathered on butter and blackberry jam, clapped them together and wrapped the sandwich in paper.

She placed the magazine into her schoolbag, along with the sandwich, an apple and two cookies.

The bell rang when Tess entered the sixth-grade classroom, breathless from running the four blocks from her house. She poured into her chair and glanced to her left.

Sally, her best friend smiled at her. She touched Tess's arm in greeting but quickly sat up straight to face the teacher.

Tess felt a tug on her hair that yanked her head back and she whirled around in her seat. "Stop that," she hissed at the boy behind her who smirked and ignored Tess as he clasped his hands on his desk and stared obediently toward the front of the classroom. School could not end soon enough for Tess.

Tess knew he never missed a chance to bother whoever was within reach. She turned and narrowed her eyes at him as he snickered and opened his hands, letting Tess's crumpled blue satin ribbon drop to the floor.

Tess raised her hand to her head with a gasp before leaning over to pick up the ribbon. With both hands raised she tried to tie a bow, with frustrating results, and turned to glare at her tormenter.

"Tess Douglas, turn around, eyes to the front."

"Yes, Sir." Tess's face glowed bright pink as the rest of the students giggled. She tucked her ribbon in a pocket and clenched her teeth. The teacher's voice faded as her thoughts traveled to her magazine.

At Noon, Tess and Sally grabbed their lunches and ran outside, plopping down on the grass behind the school. Tess had brought her magazine, itching to begin reading, but it would be rude. Sally usually carried a book with her.

"This week is going to drag by," said Sally, taking a cookie from her lunch. "I cannot wait for summer. We can spread a blanket under the tree in your backyard and read. This summer we are going to build the biggest sandcastle ever. I have been making little flags out of scraps of material left over from Mother's quilt-making."

Tess leaned against the fence and let out a long, loud groan. "I won't be here."

"Why?" Sally's mouth dropped open, holding her apple in mid-air. "You have to be here. What will I do this summer without you?"

"Mother is dragging me north, far away from civilization, and I can't do a thing about it."

"When will you be back? Is it for the summer?"

"I hope so. We are city people. We would never survive a northern winter." Tess shivered as she imagined fighting her way through icy winds and ten-foot drifts of snow to get to school each morning, remembering a letter they had received from her aunt.

"You must be back before school starts. I couldn't bear it if you left me to face Agatha alone."

"I will. I promise." It felt good to say those words, as if saying them aloud made them valid and true, as if she had control over her life. Deep down she knew she had a monumental task ahead of her, convincing her mother, Aunt Molly, and Uncle Beau, wherever he was, to leave the Yukon for the warmth and safety of Vancouver.

SIX

After school, Tess and Sally attended a social group for girls, knitting socks for the needy. To keep her mind occupied, Tess imagined her father, somewhere in Africa, wearing the socks she had knit for him before he left.

The room was quiet except for the rhythmic clicking of needles, randomly interspersed with audible sighs from the girls who were refrained from talking by the formidable leader, Agatha.

Tess hated having her free time monopolized. Despite her assurances to her mother that she would knit socks at home, she was strongly encouraged to be part of the group and learn valuable social and domestic skills.

"So much for the social aspect," whispered Tess.

Sally giggled.

Tess preferred to read and learn how to be confident and brave like the characters in her stories. Someday she would solve mysteries and save the world from shadowy villains. For now, she practiced what she knew best, avoiding attention.

Unfortunately for Tess, attention was attracted to her despite her numerous attempts to evade it and blend into the background.

"What is on your lap, Tess?" Their self-appointed leader, Agatha asked with narrowed eyes, constantly on the lookout for someone to make a mistake.

"Nothing. It is none of your business," said Tess, as she moved the ball of yarn to hide the open magazine.

"It is my business, as a matter of fact. As head of this knitting group, I am responsible for the quality of the socks, and there is no possible way you are knitting to the best of your ability. I saw you sneaking glances at that magazine on your lap. Do not lie to me."

"I was not lying. I can do both." Tess lowered her chin intent on studying her hands neatly clasped over the yarn and magazine.

Agatha took pleasure in bossing others. She stuck her nose into everyone's business, finding fault. No one was safe from her bullying, and no one was brave enough to stand up to her.

"Give me that magazine this instant." Agatha moved to grab it from Tess's lap. "You probably stole it."

"I did not. My mother gave it to me." Tess slapped Agatha's hand away.

"How dare you?" Agatha took a step back as she rubbed her hand.

Tess jumped to her feet. The magazine and ball of wool fell to the floor. Before she could reach down to pick up her belongings, Agatha dove in front of her and grabbed Tess's magazine, ripping the cover as she stuffed it under her arm.

Sally and another girl sat motionless in their wooden chairs like porcelain dolls, with their hands and knitting needles perched in mid-air as they stared past Tess with widened eyes.

Tess tried to catch their gaze, silently pleading with her friends for help but they remained frozen in fear.

"That is mine, you… you…" Tess struggled to find the perfect word to sum up every feeling, every thought she wanted to say to this self-righteous, arrogant snob, to no avail.

Instead, Tess clenched her teeth as she stuffed the wool and half-finished sock into her bag. For a moment she contemplated fighting for the return of her magazine but turned and ran out the door.

The smug, satisfied smile on Agatha's face burned into Tess's memory as tears flowed down her cheeks.

She ran home, angry and humiliated.

Tess entered the house and pulled the door shut with a bang, momentarily disturbing the silence that hovered in the air. The clock welcomed her with its rhythmic Tick Tock that traveled throughout the empty house.

She dropped her schoolbag on the table in the center of the kitchen and went to the sink. Water soaked the counter and splashed onto the linoleum as Tess washed salty tears of frustration, anger, and sadness from her face, feeling slightly better as the tainted water swirled into the drain and disappeared.

Tears again formed at the corners of Tess's eyes.

"I'm home," Anna announced, placing a large envelope on the table before removing her straw hat and jacket. "I purchased tickets for our voyage. We leave tomorrow."

Tess rubbed the rough towel over her face before turning to greet her, hoping her mother would not notice her red eyes.

"I am sorry for the way I acted last night. I will try to do better." Tess turned away from her mother and hung the towel above the wood stove.

"Oh honey, it was a terrible shock to both of us. I do not want to leave our home any more than you do, but we have no choice."

"I understand. I truly do. I hope Aunt Molly will be alright until we get there." Tess forced herself to smile with eager eyes, torn between leaving a familiar life wrought with nasty, bossy girls and mischievous boys, and facing a new life. She could picture a life of adventure, or a life of peril. It was her choice.

Anna wrapped her arms around Tess who leaned into the warmth of her reassuring hug.

Tess gazed out the window at the majestic oak tree, beckoning to her with its vibrant green leaves swaying in the breeze, and felt another tear drop onto her cheek.

SEVEN

Tess shivered as she leaned her arms on the polished wooden rail of the riverboat heading to Dawson City.

Her stomach tossed and turned as she stared into the churning black water, watching it snake alongside the boat before joining the vessel's wake in a frenzied turbulence.

As they neared their destination, Tess mourned the loss of a lazy hot summer under the oak tree in their backyard.

Dense clusters of alder and birch jostled for access to the banks of the river, branches intertwining as they extended into the water. Leaves twirled and fluttered in the cool breeze.

Tess imagined the trees as spectators at a parade waving at the floats as they passed. She waved with a regal half-smile from her position high above the river.

Anna joined Tess at the rail, placing an arm around her shoulders and pulling close.

"How are you feeling?"

Tess shrugged.

"Is the fresh air helping?"

"I miss Father. I don't want to live up here, away from my friends, away from everything familiar."

"Think of this journey as an adventure, experienced firsthand instead of reading about it in one your books. How many young girls have the privilege to travel in a steamship from Vancouver to Alaska then ride a train through the magnificent White Pass Mountains in this day and age? Now we are on a steamboat navigating the waters of the mighty Yukon River. What wonderful stories you could write if you desired."

"I was content to read about others and their adventures, preferring a safe and loving home free from upheaval and change." Tess had read many stories in which the characters traveled and found danger at every turn. She had no desire to look for trouble.

"This upheaval is nothing in comparison to the troubles that have befallen your aunt. She is my sister, and I will help her as much as I can, despite the circumstances."

"What circumstances? You never told me what happened. Where is Uncle Beau? Why does Aunt Molly need us to help her run the hotel?"

"It is best you don't know the whole story."

"Why won't you tell me? I am not a little girl anymore."

"You are a child. I do not want to upset you any further." Anna kissed Tess's cheek.

"It is not fair for children to go through life knowing half the story." Tess pulled away slightly.

"It is not a child's place to know everything."

"My imagination fills in the gaps making me worried and anxious. You don't want that, do you?"

"Dear me. I hate to imagine what horrors your imagination would conjure up. I will never understand why you refuse to read lovely little stories suited to a young lady. Those awful mysteries fill your head with nonsense."

"I am expanding my world. Please, tell me what happened. Help me understand, so I can be brave for your sake."

"I want to protect my little girl from having to grow up too quickly."

"It is rather too late, I am afraid. You must tell me."

Anna's arm tightened around Tess.

"Your Uncle Beau drowned in the river. It was a horrible accident."

Tess exhaled as her mother's words hit like a cannon ball, and she fought to fill her lungs with cool air. Her legs grew weak, and she struggled to stand. Tess leaned against the rail until she regained balance.

As the grim reality sunk in a shiver crawled along Tess's spine. Dark clouds passed in front of the sun gripping the air in a sudden chill. She squeezed her eyes shut imagining the door to her childhood slowly closing with a soft click of the latch. The deadbolt slid across with a ghastly rasp.

"Uncle Beau? It's not possible. He is invincible."

"It was an accident."

"Why would you keep this from me?"

"It has been difficult enough already, with your father away."

"Were you and Aunt Molly going to sit me down at her kitchen table, hold my hands and drop the church bell on me?"

"I thought it might be best if Molly told you."

"What happened? Or am I too young to know that either?" Tess crossed her arms on the rail and rested her chin as she stared at the passing scenery.

"Your uncle tripped and fell off the dock. He was hit by a piece of debris. The current carried him downriver. A search party scoured the banks for miles but they did not find him. There is no question your aunt needs us now, more than ever."

Tess shook uncontrollably. Her heart ached for her aunt, imagining her sorrow cutting deeper and more painful than Tess's own loss of her father. She held out hope her father would return. Aunt Molly had no such luxury.

Tess shivered in her mother's comforting arms. She pulled away quickly as her mouth tingled and filled with saliva. Just in time she leaned over the rail and with one great heave sent her lunch flowing over the railing into the Yukon River, her uncle's final resting place. What was waiting for them at the end of their journey?

Whatever it was, Tess would figure out a way to convince her aunt and her mother to return to Vancouver as soon as possible. It would be best for all of them.

Tess remained in their cabin for the rest of the trip despite her mother's pleas to join her in the dining room. She could not concentrate on her book. Reading encouraged a swarm of disturbing thoughts to force their way into the story, as well as countless images of ghostly shapes swirling in black, murky water.

The wilderness of the North was no place for a young city girl. Tess was certain of it. What was her mother thinking?

EIGHT

Two days later, the ship arrived in Dawson City. Every passenger stood at the rail, calling and waving to people on the crowded docks.

Anna called to Tess to stay close as she made her way toward the gangplank.

Tess stayed by the rail a moment longer searching the crowd for her aunt.

It had been six years since Tess last saw her aunt and uncle. They had stayed with her family the night before embarking on their journey to seek their fortune in the Klondike. Tess had been five, a wondrous age.

"How is my little bear cub?" Uncle Beau leaned over and picked her up, settling her on his shoulders. They danced around the parlor; her fingers nestled in his wavy dark hair.

To Tess, he was a giant. She reached her hand toward the ceiling.

"Careful up there, my little Tessabelle." Tess's father, James held a lit match to his pipe. He pulled air through to light the tobacco and let out a swirl of smoke that rose to encircle Tess. He winked and smiled up at her.

"I am fine, Father. I can see everything from up here. You and Mother look so little."

Aunt Molly and her mother sat at the table in the parlor with cups of tea and a plate of cookies.

"I think I would like a cookie to eat while I am up here."

Aunt Molly picked up a sugar cookie and stood on her toes to hand it to Tess, her other hand placed firmly against her new husband's chest.

"Are you sure you want to do this?" Tess's mother asked. *"The Klondike gold rush is no place for a newly wedded couple."*

Uncle Beau brushed a cookie crumb off his nose and turned to face her. *"Don't worry. We know what we are doing. Our supplies are bought, and we have booked passage on the next boat heading north. Our fortune awaits us."*

Aunt Molly put her arms around Anna's shoulders and hugged her tightly. *"Anna, we will be fine. We are ready for an adventure."*

Later that evening, Tess watched her aunt brush her hair admiring the way it fell in shiny black waves down her back. *"Aunt Molly, where is Dawson City? Why are you and Uncle Beau leaving us?"*

"Tess, my darling, we must make our own way in this world. Dawson City is in the Yukon Territory far away from here. They say the streets are paved with gold. You can pick up a gold nugget right out of the creek. This is a great opportunity for us. Your Uncle Beau and I are young and strong; two ingredients that will help see us through the hardships we know we will face. And we have love, the most important ingredient of all." Aunt Molly

touched her finger to Tess's nose and kissed her forehead. "Time for bed. You do not want to miss seeing us off tomorrow, do you?"

"I will be there, but I will be sad."

"Try not to be sad. Imagine us happy to be following our dream, side by side as Mr and Mrs Beauregard Bruin. Someday you can come visit us."

They hugged, and Tess felt the softness of her hair within her fingers. She did not want to let go.

As Tess stood on the deck searching for her beloved aunt, she wondered what this city had done to her and Uncle Beau.

"Tess, come quickly." Anna motioned with one hand as she picked up her valise.

Tess adjusted her book bag onto her shoulder, picked up her carry case and hurried to line up next to her mother.

"Where is Aunt Molly? Do you see her?"

"No, I don't, but I am sure she is here. She promised she would meet us."

They picked their way along the creaky wooden gangplank.

Tess clutched the railing as she scanned the crowd of people milling about greeting friends and loved ones.

What a strange sensation to be on solid ground again. Tess felt the ground swaying beneath her. The motion of the boat stayed with her, and she staggered slightly, an eleven-year-old vagrant unsteady on her feet, smelling of lavender instead of whiskey.

The air filled with voices yelling, crying, and calling out to loved ones, and the commotion rattled her brain. To one side, men unloaded trunks and crates, and on the other side animated groups of people hugged and shook hands, talking over each other.

Tess followed her mother through the crowd to an open space where they could gather their wits.

"Oh dear, I cannot see Molly anywhere." Anna dropped her valise and pulled a dainty white lace handkerchief from her sleeve to pat her lips. "I do hope she is alright."

"I knew we should not have come. How on earth can we help Aunt Molly in a place like this?" Tess shuddered.

The main street ran parallel to the river. Buildings lined both sides of the muddy road, stores with false fronts, log cabins, warehouses and new construction. A faint scent of yeast and vanilla mixed with sawdust wafted through the air.

Tess sniffed, inhaling deeply as she spotted a bakery at the end of a block of buildings in mid-construction.

"Should we start walking?" Tess looked left then right with no idea where her aunt lived. "We could ask directions at the bakery across the way." Her stomach rumbled in agreement.

Anna clutched her wrinkled handkerchief with gloved hands, her brows knitted together in worry and fear.

Tess reached for her mother's hand with compassion, remembering her father's words. 'Take care of your mother.' Her mother looked lost and alone. Tess hesitated. Instead, she crossed her arms and frowned. She was too young for this nonsense. She should be home, reading under her tree, playing with Sally in the warm sand, while her mother looked after her. Not the other way around.

A man staggered toward them. His dusty, battered, wide-brimmed hat sat low over his eyes. Tangled white hair touched his shoulders, and a long, matted gray beard covered the rest of his face. He lurched forward with his dirty hand outstretched in greeting.

Tess and her mother stepped back, shaking their heads from side to side, searching for an escape route.

NINE

A man dressed in a dark single-breasted morning coat and black trousers strode towards them. He held a gold pocket watch in one hand, and its chain glinted in the sunlight as it hung from a button on his vest. Tucking the watch into his pocket he edged his way in front of the old man and pushed him aside.

"Madam. Miss." He tipped his hat and bowed. "Is this fellow bothering you?" The man waved his hand to dismiss the vagrant.

"No. I mean, yes. I do not know that man." Anna held her handkerchief to her mouth as she glanced at the figure who had wandered off to greet another new arrival.

"I apologize for Old Bert. He used to be a miner in these parts but lost everything and has taken to the drink to fill his days. He is harmless but a might overpowering to those who are new to these parts." With a wink, he continued, "If it isn't his breath that bowls you over, it will certainly be the ungodly smell of his beloved Mackinaw."

"My goodness, what an unfortunate man," said Anna, patting her forehead with her handkerchief as she searched the crowd.

"May I be of assistance?" The kindly man addressed them with a smooth bow and another tip of his hat.

"No, we are waiting for someone, my sister. She assured me she would meet us upon our arrival, but I do not see her. I hope nothing is wrong."

"You needn't worry about your sister. You and your lovely daughter are the reason I am here."

"I do not think so." Anna quickly picked up her bag and motioned for Tess to follow her toward the road.

"I beg your pardon, please forgive me, I did not mean to frighten. I am a close friend to Mrs Bruin. She is feeling poorly this afternoon and asked if I would be so kind as to bring you safely to her establishment. I have arranged transport of your trunks."

Anna stopped, then hopped forward a step as Tess bumped into her. She straightened her shoulders and turned to address the man in the impeccable suit and black bowler hat.

"My apologies, kind sir, forgive me. Our lengthy journey has caused a heavy weariness to settle upon our shoulders, and that frightening man scared us out of our wits. It was not the welcome we had been expecting."

"Understandable. Allow me to escort you to your sister who is waiting with great anticipation of your arrival."

Anna handed her valise to the man and gingerly placed her white-gloved hand on his arm.

"Where are my manners? The man nodded sideways toward my mother.

"Mr Frederick Barrett, at your service. Please call me Fred."

"Mrs Anna Douglas. This is my daughter, Tess."

Fred glanced at Tess and winked. He smiled and his perfectly coiffed dark brown mustache turned up at the tips. Tobacco-stained teeth peeked through his thin lips.

A lingering odor of tobacco smoke mixed with onions and peppermint accosted Tess's nasal passages. As a lump threatened to rise in her throat, she brought a hand to her mouth and coughed. She turned her head away quickly as the fragrant memory of her father became tainted with the unwelcome smell of onion.

The commotion of the dock faded as they walked toward the main street where voices competed to be heard over the sawing and hammering.

Tess and Anna followed Fred to a white horse and buggy parked at the side of the muddy road.

"My apologies for the state of our streets, Madam. Wettest spring on record this year. Summer's not starting off too well either. Not a welcome addition to the mud bog that Dawson City sits upon."

Fred offered his hand and helped them into the buggy. He jumped from the boardwalk and made his way around, pulling himself into the driver's seat with little effort.

Tess tucked her skirt around her legs and wiggled, stuck between the two adults.

Her head jerked as the horse pulled the buggy through the mud, along the busy road for two short blocks, and turned left twice before stopping in front of a two-storey building with white clapboarding and green trim around the windows.

Tess snickered.

Anna turned to hush Tess with her eyes, but a hint of a smile on her lips confirmed the humor she found in the situation as well. They could have walked the short distance.

Anna handed Fred her valise then took his hand as she stepped lightly onto the wooden boardwalk running the length of the street.

Fred offered his hand and helped Tess.

A large sign hung on the side of the building. Tess read it aloud. "The Golden Grizzly Hotel and Fine French Cuisine."

Tess scampered up four steps to the raised verandah skirting the front of the building. Her heart raced, and her palms grew clammy as she remembered her aunt's predicament. Poor Aunt Molly. Her life had been disrupted in the cruelest way possible. She was in mourning, possibly stricken ill with grief and worry, and in desperate trouble. How far removed from the Aunt Molly Tess knew and loved would be the woman she found inside?

"Slow down and walk like a proper young lady."

Tess stopped in front of two wooden doors, each inset with a delicate stained glass design of pink flowers and greenery. It seemed oddly out of place in the middle of nowhere, yet civilized and welcoming in a harsh environment. She hesitated, waiting for her mother to lead the way.

Anna turned to thank the man who had brought them to their destination, but Fred moved past her and took the steps two at a time toward the door. He grasped the brass door handle and pulled it open with a flourish, bowing as he waited for them to enter.

Anna had no choice but to nod and enter the cool, dark interior.

They stood in an open space, a mix of pink wallpaper and dark wood panels facing a large reception desk front and center. Brass light fixtures lined the wall and sunlight shone through two windows facing the street. A staircase to the left led to the second floor. Alongside the staircase ran a narrow hallway. To the right was a door into a large dining room.

A young man pushed his chair back, smoothed his straw-colored hair with one hand and stood to greet them from behind the ornate oak counter.

Anna stepped forward. "Good afternoon. I am Mrs Anna Douglas and this is my daughter, Tess. I am Mrs Bruin's sister."

"Welcome. We have been expecting you. If you need anything, please do not hesitate to call on me. My name is Theo." He smiled and nodded as he adjusted the black bands holding the sleeves of his shirt to his elbows.

Tess detected black ink stains on his fingers. She smiled and raised her hand in a slight wave, wanting him to like her for some strange reason. He had kind eyes.

Particles of dust floated across a sunbeam, and Tess sneezed.

Fred pulled a white handkerchief from his pocket and offered it to her.

"Thank you, I have my own," she said, forcing a smile as she pulled a delicately embroidered handkerchief from her sleeve. Tess glanced at Theo but he was already in his chair with his head down, busily writing.

"This way, please. Madam Molly is resting in her suite. This way to the parlor." Fred motioned for them to follow him down the narrow hallway past the staircase.

Anna walked behind him, clutching her valise, sighing noticeably.

Tess stopped to peek into the dining room.

Round wooden tables filled the large room. Faint conversation drifted from the kitchen. It was early afternoon and lunch was over.

Tess's stomach growled, and she wondered when dinner was served. She hurried to catch up to her mother along the soft, burgundy red carpet that muffled her footsteps. She ran her fingers along the smooth wood panels and flowery wallpaper as she continued along the hallway.

Delicate glass lamps hung at intervals along the wall, casting yellow light on the flowers, fading their cheerful colors to a weary sadness.

Tess had expected a rickety old building, built quickly and simply from the limited materials at hand, as a wild uncivilized town might be, but her Aunt Molly's hotel was elegant and richly decorated.

Tess raised an eyebrow in surprise as she entered a door on her left. A brilliant gold, green and red oriental carpet covered the floor. Two tall cabinets, filled with fine china, stood along one wall, and a round table, covered with a cream-colored lace doily, stood in a corner. A gramophone sat on a dark wooden table next to a plush, green horsehair chair.

Her aunt sat in a wooden rocking chair with a hand-stitched quilt decorated with embroidered pink flowers resting on her knees. A black lace shawl covered her shoulders. Soft ebony curls framed her face, and the rest of her glorious hair was pulled back into a loose roll, emphasizing sunken cheeks and tired, dull eyes.

Anna knelt beside her sister holding her hand and sobbing.

"We are here, my dearest. How I have missed you."

"Aunt Molly," said Tess, hurrying toward her.

Molly smiled and struggled to get up but Tess leaned down to hug her, feeling the hardness of the bones beneath her shawl. "I am so sorry. Mother recently told me what happened."

Tess glanced at Fred who stood next to the piano, one hand resting on the ivory keys, waiting, watching.

Why was he here? Tess wanted to ask her aunt but it would be rude and unbecoming of a young lady. When she was five, she had no qualms about saying whatever came to mind but as she grew older she quickly learned children's honesty was not appreciated.

Music books formed a precarious tower on a hard wooden chair beside the piano bench. Two piles sat on the floor beside the piano. The pale, pink rose-colored wallpaper was barely visible behind dozens of ornate frames hung close together creating a claustrophobic feeling. Pairs of unsmiling eyes followed Tess as she ran over to one picture to get a closer look. It was worn and slightly wrinkled.

"That's us," Tess exclaimed, examining the black-and-white photo of a little girl wearing a frilly pinafore and dress. A large bow held her long dark ringlets in place, and she sat on her mother's lap. Her father stood behind with his hand on her mother's shoulder and a serious look clouding his strong features.

"Yes, it is, my darling. I believe you were about three when that was taken. It was the only photo I could find to bring with me. You have grown since I last saw you. I have missed you dreadfully."

"I have missed you, too." Tess hurried over to kneel beside her chair. "We are here to help. Mother says family looks out for each other." She avoided looking at Mr Barrett by smiling sweetly at her aunt.

Molly raised her head, realizing he was in the room.

"Fred, my dear friend. Thank you for meeting my sister and niece at the dock and bringing them home. I do not want to keep you."

"Madam, you need not worry yourself. I have cleared my day to make myself available to you."

"You have done enough already, but I am in good hands, as you can see."

Fred strode over to her and bowed deeply, lifting her pale hand to his lips. "It has been my honor and privilege to assist you in every way possible. I will call on you tomorrow." He stood, turned to Anna and bowed. "Madam, I am at your service, as well. Good day to you all."

He strolled out of the room and down the hall.

Tess held her breath in anticipation of the click of the front doors heralding his departure. She jumped onto the settee in front of the window. After a few moments, she let out a sigh of relief as she heard the welcome bang of the door. Through the lace curtains she watched Fred jump onto the buggy and ride away.

Anna moved toward the window. "Who was that gentleman?"

Molly shook her head. "We can discuss it later, Anna," she said, glancing at Tess.

Thus began Tess's new life, expected to act like a young lady but treated like a child.

TEN

Fred tipped his hat to people on the boardwalk as he directed his horse and buggy through the mud.

The trip was slow due to the crowd of pedestrians crossing the two intersections, and he popped a mint into his mouth while he waited. He nodded at the waves from people who greeted him along the way, enjoying the recognition. As an upstanding citizen and businessman in town, he was particularly generous and kind to those who could advance his status in society.

Wooden buildings leaned against each other along the two blocks to his office. Sandwich board signs and banners advertised clothing, meals, haircuts, and lodging.

Fred shivered as he passed the mortuary and guided the horse to turn right, pulling to a stop next to a white clapboard building with red trim. Dead men tell no tales but living men have experienced the slip of the tongue now and then.

Men slouched against the outside walls, slapping their knees with laughter and coughing before taking another draw on their pipes and cigars.

Piano music floated through the hinged saloon doors.

A man ran out as Fred jumped onto the boardwalk from the buggy.

"See to it Daisy gets a thorough brushing. It does not reflect well on my stature to have a muddy nag pulling my carriage."

"Yes sir, Mr Barrett." The man nodded, clutching the stub of a cigar in his teeth.

"Where is Earl?" Fred clenched his teeth, the muscles in his jaw tensed as he snarled.

The man widened his eyes and swallowed. He jerked his head toward the entrance, hopped into the buggy, flicked the reins and urged the horse into a canter down the crowded road.

Fred narrowed his eyes as he regarded the noisy interior before pushing the swinging doors open. He blinked, waiting for his eyes to adjust to the smoky room.

The boisterous conversations faltered for a moment then rose to a fevered, drunken cacophony despite the mid-afternoon hour.

Fred fixed a broad smile on his face as he removed his black bowler hat and strode toward the bar where the bartender cleaned a glass while he watched him approach.

"Have you seen Earl?" Fred leaned against the smooth metal bar running the length of the polished dark walnut counter supported brass eagles at each end. He rubbed an eagle for good luck.

The bartender pointed to the back of the saloon with the towel then went back to wiping the glass, slightly lifting his chin in warning toward a man approaching Fred.

"Mr Barrett, how are you this fine day?" A customer accosted him as he headed for the office. "I was telling the good bartender here I will gladly pay for a finger of whiskey when I am compensated for my hard labor."

Fred swerved to walk past the man. "I am afraid, good sir, this establishment requires payment before refreshment."

The man manoeuvred into Fred's path and stood his ground, a sly smile flickered at the corners of his mouth. "Mighty tough to pay for refreshment when the boss neglects to pay his crew."

"Not my problem as far as I know. Take that up with your boss."

"Seems I am rightly doing so, at this moment. Boss." The man raised his voice and looked around as a few patrons glanced their way.

Fred crunched the rest of his mint, curling his lips into a smile but his eyes remained cold and steely. He shook the man's hand. "That is unfortunate. Which of my supervisors forgot to pay my workers? Please, sir, come with me and we will sort this out at once." Fred led the man to the back room as he nodded to the customers in the saloon. "Can't have a thirsty man unable to buy himself a drink, can we?"

Laughter drifted through the room mingling with the piano music and the patrons carried on with their conversations.

Fred opened the door, and the man followed him into a luxurious room with a massive oak desk in front of a window.

A man sat in the chair behind the desk, leaning back with his feet on the surface and his hands behind his head. As Fred and the man entered, he sat up straight and lowered his legs off the desk with a bang, then jumped to his feet.

Fred frowned, chuckling as he hung his hat on the coat rack. "Sorry to disturb you, Earl. This fine gentleman informed me he has not been paid for his loyal employment." He turned to the employee. "Where was it you said you worked?"

"Your new dredge out near Bonnet Creek. The men have not been paid in weeks, sir." The man lowered his head, clutching his hat, no longer courageous without a room full of customers watching their every move.

Earl removed himself from the chair and leaned against the wall with his arms folded. "That was Roy. He's in charge of payroll. I'll get it sorted out right away. We cannot abide our men struggling to pay their bills."

Fred nodded before addressing the employee. "You did the right thing coming to me. I admire a man who takes the bull by the horns and addresses an inconsistency. You showed a grand display of initiative on your part in representing your crew." He sat at the desk, pulled open a drawer and brought out a ledger. "What is the amount you are owed?"

"Twenty dollars, I believe." The man flinched as he glanced from Earl to Fred. "The others more, some less."

Fred stared at him for a moment, then wrote in the ledger. "I have deducted two weeks' room and board for your stay in camp, the rest to be paid in cash."

Fred went to the ornate steel safe in the corner, spun the dial and opened the heavy metal door. He pulled out ten one-dollar bills, turned to the man and slowly counted as he placed each in his hand. Fred waited as the man folded the bills and tucked them in a leather pouch then shoved it into a pocket. "Have a whiskey on the house, my friend." Fred shook his hand, with the other on the man's shoulder. "My apologies for the troubles you have experienced under my employ. It will not happen again."

The man shook Fred's hand vigorously. "Thank you, sir. I am much obliged to you."

"Tell the other men they can expect to be paid in full within the week. I look after my employees, remember that."

"I will, sir. Thank you." He rushed out of the room and hailed the bartender.

Earl ran his fingers through his curly black hair. "Think it was a smart idea telling him to run his mouth off about getting paid?"

"By the time he leaves this saloon he will have nothing left but his words. If he tells the others he got paid, they may not take kindly to the fact they didn't. We best get the situation under control before he ends up in the river."

"I'm on it, Boss." Earl grabbed his hat. "Won't the others come asking for their pay?"

"We will deal with each one as they arrive. I need time to soothe the worries of our investors. With Beau Bruin gone, they are hesitant to commit funds to the dredge company."

"What about Mrs Bruin?"

"Madam Molly is feeling poorly these days. Beau's share rightly goes to her but until she feels better, I do not think she should be bothered with minor operating problems."

"Fair enough."

"While you're at it, see if you can hunt down Old Bert and remind him not to harass the newcomers at the docks. I caught him accosting Madam Molly's sister and niece upon their arrival. He should be kept away from the upstanding citizens of our city."

"Begging again?" Earl fitted his derby hat over his thick hair and patted the top.

"Possibly." Fred leaned back, banged his boots onto the desk and put his hands behind his head. "He tells people he can see ghosts. Most of them consider him a crazy old miner but we cannot afford to have him making up stories and causing problems around town."

"He's harmless. No one pays attention to his ramblings." Earl placed his hand on the doorknob.

"Let's keep it that way. I run a clean game around this town and I don't want my reputation coming under scrutiny because of one old man."

"Gotcha." Earl touched his finger to the tip of his hat and left, slamming the door.

Fred took his feet off the desk and stared at the ledger with his mouth set in a thin line.

ELEVEN

Tess clasped her hands in her lap and listened as her mother and aunt talked quietly. She inhaled deeply, holding her breath and tapping two fingers together as she counted in her head. Her second day in Dawson and she was stuck in the parlor expected to sit and act like a young lady. Her cheeks puffed as she fought to hold in the air but at twenty seconds it escaped in an audible sigh. Both women stopped talking and turned to stare at Tess.

"Honestly, Tess, must you fidget?" Anna frowned.

"I'm trying, but there is nothing to do."

"That is the whole point." Anna raised an eyebrow as she smiled at Molly. "A young lady must learn to sit graciously, patiently, and with the utmost dignity."

"You are growing up so quickly. Grand things are sure to come your way, like they did for me," said Molly as she struggled to stand. "Tess, darling, would you like to see your room? I must apologize for the lack of space. The hotel is busy in the summer. Every room is spoken for. You and your mother will share a room for now if you don't mind."

Tess's mouth dropped open.

"Not at all," said Anna, holding Molly's arm and raising a finger to her lips as she glowered at Tess. "Shall we escort you to your bedroom so you can lie down before dinner?"

Molly held out her other arm to Tess for support, and together they made their way through the doorway beside the piano into Molly's bed chamber.

Tess gasped at the luxurious room filled with ornate furniture, heavy velvet drapes and brass lamps.

They settled Molly into a chair where she sat as Anna fluffed pillows and drew back the thick comforter.

Tess and Anna helped her into bed, both kissing Molly's cheek before leaving the room.

"My health is sure to improve now that you are here. I am truly grateful to you," said Molly as she closed her eyes. "Your room is on the left at the top of the stairs."

Periwinkle blue quilts covered two single beds. Heavy brocade drapes blocked out the sun but slivers of light peeked through the middle where they didn't completely close.

Tess pulled them open to let in the light. Muffled noise traveled into the room reminding her of their house in Vancouver. If she didn't look outside she could pretend they were home where they belonged.

Anna opened one of the trunks at the end of the bed and pulled out a skirt, shook it then hung it in the large wardrobe. She picked up a wrinkled white shirt and threw it on the bed.

"I have a mountain of washing to do tomorrow. Change out of your traveling clothes and place them on the chair."

Tess stayed at the window as Anna changed into an ankle length navy skirt and white blouse with a high collar.

"Come here," said Anna, opening the other trunk and pulling out a slightly rumpled dress. "We must look presentable for dinner."

Tess grabbed her father's sweater from the bottom of the trunk and held it to her nose. She sniffed, searching for the familiar scent of her father, a cozy fragrance of tobacco and peppermint.

"Why did you bring that old thing?"

"It's all I have left of Father." Tess tucked it under her pillow.

Anna's eyes glistened. She abruptly turned her head and began fussing with her hair.

Tess put on a beige linen dress with a white sash. As she laced up her boots, she asked, "What is the matter with Aunt Molly? She looked like she would blow away in a strong wind."

"Beau's disappearance created a tremendous strain on her. The doctor cautioned her to limit her activities and to rest."

TWELVE

Lou mixed the shaving foam as Fred took a seat in the leather barber chair.

"How's business?" Lou asked.

"Which one?" Fred rested his head against the back of the chair and closed his eyes. "All is well but could be better."

Lou snorted as he picked up a fine boar's hair foam brush and dabbed lather onto Fred's cheeks and chin, whistling under his breath. He set the brush and shaving cup on a shelf under the mirror. Lou ran a long razor against a leather strop before leaning in to scrape it along Fred's skin with precision, cleaning the blade after each stroke. He trimmed Fred's mustache then placed a hot, steaming towel on his face.

Fred shook his head then spoke, his words muffled by the damp towel as he struggled to sit up.

"Say what?" Lou pulled the towel away from Fred's face.

"What're you trying to do, burn off the roots, too?" Fred sputtered.

"Sorry, Fred, don't know what I was thinking."

"Thinking is overrated." Fred smirked.

A man entered the barber shop, removed his black felt hat and hung it on the rack next to Fred's.

"I'll be with you in a minute. Have a seat." Lou motioned to the empty barber chair.

The man sat next to Fred. "Evening, Fred. How's business?"

"Which one?" Fred replied as Lou settled the hot towel onto his face.

"Good one, Fred." The man chuckled, then leaned his head back against the chair.

Lou laughed as he removed the towel, wiped Fred's face, and applied a brisk minty aftershave. He whipped off the cape. "How many you got?"

"Always looking for more." Fred stood, paid Lou, then donned his bowler hat. "Evening, boys." He left the shop avoiding questions he preferred to leave unanswered.

THIRTEEN

Tess stared at her plate. Meatloaf and mashed potatoes, with suspicious-looking green flecks speckled throughout. She and Anna sat at a table near the back of the crowded room.

Molly had been asleep when they stopped by to ask if she felt well enough for dinner.

Voices murmured throughout the dining room. Utensils clinked against porcelain, and an intermittent burst of laughter broke the polite hush. Men and women dressed in elegant clothing filled every table in the room.

"What are those green things in my food?" Tess asked Anna who sat across from her.

"Eat your dinner." Anna glanced around the room then down at her own plate. "I believe those green flecks are special herbs, maybe parsley. Molly told me the chef is from France."

"It tastes funny." Tess set her fork on her plate and crossed her arms. "I'm not hungry. May I go to our room?"

Anna frowned. "Most certainly not. You will stay and present yourself as a dutiful young lady. Are you afraid of a few green specks? Where is your sense of adventure?"

Tess sighed and speared a mound of potatoes onto her fork. She sniffed before taking a small amount into her mouth. She lifted her brow in surprise at the creamy, buttery substance, ignoring the green bits that ruined the smooth texture. "Not bad." Tess cut her meatloaf and tried a bite. She was used to her mother's meatloaf, bland and simple. "I would never have imagined meatloaf could be improved upon."

"Come now, it cannot be better than mine. It's one of your favorites."

"Father and I adore your fine meatloaf."

At the mention of her husband, Anna sniffled and pulled out her handkerchief to dab her eyes. "We will be alright, dear. I promise."

"I know." Tess lowered her head. "It is for the summer, right?"

Anna blinked her eyes. "Oh, Tess. No. Molly will never leave. There is nothing in Vancouver for us." Anna sat straight and smiled broadly. "How exciting to become Sourdoughs once we have lived through a northern winter."

Tess frowned in confusion. "But, you said…"

"I never said we would be returning to Vancouver. You filled in the blanks, as usual, and made an assumption. This is your new home. Molly is family, and we are together again. Isn't it wonderful?"

"But, what of Father?"

"He will find his way back to us."

"He will want to return to Vancouver."

Anna lowered her head and speared her meatloaf with the fork, refusing to meet Tess's gaze.

FOURTEEN

After his shave, Fred returned to the Eagle Saloon and wove his way through the tables. He wanted to go over the ledgers again. There had to be a way to finance the dredge operation without having to include investors. He wanted full control of the operation, and with Beau out of the picture, it was possible, if he could convince Madame Molly to sell her share. Cents on the dollar is what Fred usually paid for what he wanted. He made a pretty penny on prospectors who had been desperate to liquidate so they could chase the next great gold rush in Alaska.

A flamboyant woman dressed in purple velvet and waving a crimson fan hurried toward him. "Freddy baby, have dinner with me."

"My apologies young miss but I have a previous engagement." Fred glanced around the saloon, careful to maintain his image.

"Freddy, it's me, Florrie." The young woman pouted.

"I know." Fred smiled, as he made his way through the early drinking crowd to his office.

People were leaving Dawson in droves, taking the steamships south. Life was not easy no matter where you were, he knew from experience. He would make a life here in Dawson, maybe make it into the upper class if he played his cards right, and stayed on the straight and narrow.

He picked up the voice piece of the oak wall telephone and turned the crank. "Golden Grizzly."

Theo answered.

"How is Mrs Bruin? Have you heard anything?" Fred asked.

"No, Sir. She has not appeared at dinner with her sister and niece. They are eating alone in the dining room."

"I see. Thank you, Theo. Keep up the good work."

"Yes, Sir."

FIFTEEN

After dinner, Tess and Anna knocked gently on Molly's door. No answer.

"Molly must be asleep. It has been a long day. I will go in and check on her."

Tess nodded then ascended the staircase to their room. Each wooden step brought her closer to the realization that this was her new home. A room, shared with her mother, without her father, in a hotel filled with strangers who stayed a night or two before carrying on with their lives. A new group of strangers would fill their place. Tess would never again have a space of her own. Unfamiliar voices carried up the stairs as patrons entered the hotel in search of fine French cuisine. She opened the door to their room and entered, dragging her feet. Her head and shoulders felt heavy with fatigue and despair.

White cotton towels and lavender soap lay next to a porcelain washbasin on a chest of drawers.

Tess washed her face and dried it with the soft towel. She opened her trunk and pulled out a white cotton nightdress.

"Hang your things over the chair and I will see to the laundry tomorrow," said Anna, entering the room and removing the hairpins to loosen her long chestnut brown tresses. She pulled a brush through her glossy hair and plaited it into a loose braid. She motioned to Tess to sit on the bed next to her.

Tess sat with her hands clutching the edge of the comforter while Anna worked the brush through the knots in her hair.

"Ouch.".

"Goodness' sake, Tess, how does your hair get so tangled? It might be best to keep your hair braided. I will have no time to deal with it. Beginning tomorrow I will be helping Molly with the hotel and restaurant."

"Yes, Mother." Tess gritted her teeth as Anna pulled the brush through her hair yanking her head back. A flash of memory struck as she remembered the teasing she endured at school. How was this life any better than the one they left behind in Vancouver?

"Off to bed with you."

Tess pulled back the covers and laid back, sinking her head into the soft pillow, grateful for the luxuries her aunt and uncle had gathered to create the finest hotel in Dawson City. She turned toward her mother.

Anna changed into her nightdress and crawled beneath the quilt on her bed and closed her eyes.

Tess lay listening to her mother who inhaled deeply and sighed, her breathing slowed as she fell asleep.

Tess rolled onto her back and stared at the stamped tin ceiling. Her heavy eyelids refused to stay closed. Despite the late hour, the sun shone as if it was afternoon. Tess picked up her book and read until the sun dipped below the horizon, and the light became a dim twilight.

SIXTEEN

Fred lay awake, staring at the ceiling. He slept in a room next to his office. The rooms in his hotel were for paying guests. The dance hall and saloon kept the guests happy.

He couldn't sleep. When he closed his eyes, the same scene played in his mind, over and over. Each day he expected the North West Mounted Police to knock on his door and arrest him. He told them his version of the events leading up to Beau's drowning. They did not need to know the entire story.

SEVENTEEN

Tess woke from a fitful sleep. Her mother was already downstairs. Tess rubbed her eyes. Her recurring dream felt real, and she regretted waking from a lazy afternoon at the beach with her mother and father. She blinked, her eyelids scraping as if a shovelful of sand had been deposited into her eyes by a mischievous breeze. Maybe the idyllic scene had always been a dream. There was no difference between memories and dreams when both were hopeless wishes for happier times. She sat on the edge of the bed and yawned.

After debating whether to lie down and attempt to re-enter her dream she remembered her aunt, wondering if she had slept well.

Tess pulled on a white cotton dress and beige pinafore, brushed her hair and braided it into two plaits, relieved no one would be pulling her hair anymore.

She opened the door and a faint smell of bacon wafted up the staircase. She dragged her feet down the steps.

"Good morning, Theo."

Theo glanced at her and nodded his head before going back to his ledger.

Tess headed down the hall to her aunt's parlor, peeked in then entered. She tip-toed toward the bedroom door then knocked.

"Who is it?" her aunt's soft voice carried through the keyhole.

"It's me, Aunt Molly."

"My dear Tess, come in."

Tess opened the door and slipped through pulling it closed behind her.

"Did you sleep well, my love?" Molly struggled to pull herself up against two pillows piled behind her.

Tess hurried to help her get comfortable. "Is there anything I can do for you, Aunt Molly?"

"You are a lovely young lady to offer your assistance. Thank you. Your mother has kindly gone to fetch me a cup of tea." Molly smoothed the covers and patted the bed. "But, first, sit with me for a spell."

Tess sat and turned to face her aunt. "Thank you. Your hotel is splendid. But, why do you want to live here?"

Molly's eyes crinkled at the corners as she smiled and took Tess's hand in hers. "Thank you my dear sweet girl. My heart has taken root in the permafrost of this magnificent country. Your uncle and I were truly blessed to discover a wealth of gold on our claim by the creek. However, we paid dearly for what others may perceive as luck. We struggled the first year after we arrived, buried our souls in the earth. Our love saw us through the good and the hard times."

"Mother used to read your letters to me. Did you live in a tiny cabin all winter? Did Uncle Beau actually fight off a bear?"

"So many questions." Molly brought Tess's hand to her dry lips. "Yes, my dearest Beau, strong and brave man of mine saved me. I was washing clothes in the creek down from our sluice box, listening to the music of the rushing water. I stood and turned to pick up the washtub and spotted a black bear nibbling wild blueberries not twenty feet from me. Beau saw it, too and motioned for me to stay silent as he picked up his shovel, slowly moving between me and the bear. It perked up its ears and sniffed the air with a grunt then turned towards me. I backed toward the cabin but the bear followed. I should have kept still, but thoughts of clarity and reasoning were not forthcoming in that moment. The bear was young and curious, and I was struck with a dilemma. Do I continue to the cabin where I had a lovely pie cooling on the table? Could I throw the pie far from the cabin and hope the bear went after it and let us be?"

"My heavens, what did you do?" Tess clasped her hands to her heart.

"My sweet Beau saved the day by hitting a large boulder with the shovel, diverting the bear's attention long enough for me to run inside and grab the rifle. With shaking hands I readied the aim and shot, missing my husband's head by a hair."

"Poor Uncle," Tess gasped.

"The bear was angry and swatted Beau's hand with its claws tearing through the skin. I aimed again, taking care to steady my hands, and pulled the trigger." Molly dabbed her forehead with a lace handkerchief.

"And?" Tess sat on the edge of the bed, her eyes wide with fear and anticipation.

"Boom. Right past the bear's ear. Thank heavens it decided my pie was not worth it and ambled off into the bush." Molly lifted her chin and grinned.

Tess brought her hands to her mouth and gasped. She paused and wrinkled her brow. "You saved the day. You saved Uncle Beau."

"On the contrary. Beau and I worked together to save each other but we each had different versions of the incident. Beau showed the angry scar on his hand to our friends and declared his darling wife saved his life. It was an odd memento of that fateful day."

"Odd?"

"As his injury healed, the scar took on the ragged shape of an 'M.' Beau said it was the mark of his beloved and that fate sent the bear to test our commitment then forever bind us together."

"Is that true?"

"It was he who saved my life that day, my true hero. I regard his scar as a symbol of our love as well as a reminder of the fragility of life."

Tess wrinkled her brow and was silent for a moment, puzzled. "Why would you live in a place where you knew bears were a danger?"

"The lure of gold, my dear, will make any sane person risk their life. We endured hardship, but it made us stronger and I do not regret a single moment." Molly was silent for a moment as she leaned her head against the pillows and closed her eyes. "He has the scar to remind us. My Beau, where are you?"

Tess swallowed a lump in her throat then took her aunt's hand. It was limp and cool to the touch. "Don't cry, Aunt Molly, we are here. I will help in any way I can."

A knock interrupted the silence as the door swung open and Anna entered carrying a silver tray. She kissed Tess on the forehead. "Good morning sleepyhead. Did you sleep well?" She smiled at Tess.

"As well as can be expected when the sun decides to stay up all night." Tess rubbed her eyes. "It feels strange."

"You'll get used to it," said Anna. She set the tray on a table next to the bed and held the back of her hand to Molly's forehead. "Tess, wet a cloth and bring it to me."

"Yes, Mother," said Tess as she ran to the washbasin, bringing back a wet cloth to Anna.

Anna lightly dabbed the cloth on Molly's skin, brushing a limp curl off her cheek. "You are burning up."

"Will she get better?"

"Hush. She needs her rest. Take yourself to the dining room for breakfast. I will join you shortly." Anna motioned toward the door as she laid the cloth on Molly's forehead.

Tess backed away from the bed where her beloved aunt sobbed between ragged breaths. A tear rolled down Tess's cheek as she hurried from the room. She missed her Uncle Beau, and her heart ached. She could not imagine what her aunt must be enduring. What cruel apocalypse had been thrust upon her family? First, her father, then her uncle Beau, and now her aunt. There was no safe haven.

Tess leaned against the wall for a moment and wiped her cheek. She climbed the stairs to the second floor instead of going to the dining room.

As she reached the landing, a floorboard creaked and Tess looked in the direction of the sound. She was alone. The doors to the other rooms were closed. Someone was watching her, she could feel it. Tess hurried into their room and lay down on her bed. She would find escape in her book and leave reality behind.

EIGHTEEN

Eventually sleep overtook Fred, and he awoke the next morning eager to build his empire after a cup of strong hot coffee.

He hummed a tune as he dressed, selecting a snowy white shirt from his vast selection. The laundry service was instructed to use his mother's secret soap recipe on the hotel linens as well.

His bedroom and office were decorated with rich wood paneling and imported oriental carpets. His expensive tastes threatened to surpass his income, adding a sense of urgency to his plan.

Nothing was too good for him, but he continued to live in his saloon, at the heart of his operations. His favorite sounds were raucous dance music, drunken laughter and clinking glasses, the satisfying hum of money filling his coffers.

The saloon was connected to the dance hall and his hotel, occupying half a block across from the Palace Grand. His choice of business had everything to do with money and how to make it quickly. He found it gruelling to be a perfect host and pretend he liked the people who frequented his establishments.

Fred's quest to become a member of upper society exhausted him but it was the price he had to pay.

He drank his coffee at the bar before venturing outdoors.

His horse and buggy stood waiting.

"How is my girl on this fantastic morning?" Fred stroked Daisy's head before hopping into his buggy.

His first errand of the day was picking up cinnamon rolls. A habit he had recently started as an excuse to call on Madame Molly each morning. He was biding his time, waiting for the right moment to discuss business.

Minutes later he was at the Dufour Bakery, a white clapboard building with elaborate gingerbread woodwork. A large window displayed delectable cakes and cookies enticing passersby to enter through the cherry red door.

After hitching Daisy to a post, he entered the warm, welcoming bakery.

Two women stood in line and turned their heads as he removed his hat.

"Ladies." He gave a slight bow in greeting. "Lovely day isn't it?" He picked up a basket covered with a white linen cloth and turned to leave.

"Mr Barrett, will you be coming to choir practice this evening?" asked one of the women wearing a white high-collared blouse and beige silk skirt. A tiny brown bird peeked out from a mass of white feathers atop her hat.

An image of an overstuffed cream puff popped into Fred's head as he smiled broadly. "Good morning, Mrs Wright. I will try my best to attend."

"Either you will be there or you won't, Mr Barrett. The church choir is a prestigious group and requires commitment. I do not believe in the word *try*. I believe in the word *commitment*. Do you?"

Fred's smile faltered, but he held it fast, maintaining a cheerful appearance. "Of course, Mrs Wright. Please accept my apologies. I will be there." He bowed before hurrying from the store clutching his hat and the basket.

Fred patted his horse before jumping into the buggy.

"I daresay, Daisy, most days I prefer your silent presence to the company of humans." He rode past the new construction at the end of the block, making a mental note to drop in and introduce himself to the foreman.

Minutes later he pulled up alongside the Golden Grizzly, secured Daisy to a post before scaling the steps two at a time to the verandah. His heart beat a little faster as he anticipated seeing the woman who had caught his eye the first moment they had met.

He threw open the door and strode into the lobby. "Theo, my boy, how's business?"

Theo looked up, startled. "As brisk as can be expected, Sir. Mrs Bruin is not feeling well this morning."

Fred glanced toward the hall then peered at Theo. "What a shame. I have cinnamon rolls for Madam." He plopped the basket on the desk.

"I will see that she gets them." Theo blinked. "Shall I inquire as to the possibility of a future visit?"

Fred leaned his arm on the polished walnut surface. "That would be mighty kind of you. Surely there is something I can assist her with while she convalesces."

Theo picked up the telephone, waited a moment then spoke softly into the speaker. "Hello. This is Theo, I am inquiring on behalf of Mr Barrett as to your plans for the day. He has brought a gift."

Theo listened and nodded. "I see." He glanced at Fred. "Of course, I will let Mr Barrett know." He put down the receiver. "Mrs Bruin thanks you for coming and will keep you in mind when she is feeling up to having visitors."

"I understand. A wilting flower needs sustenance, something to raise her spirits. Please give her these with my deepest wishes for her well-being. I will call on her again tomorrow."

"I will, Sir." Theo took hold of the basket.

Fred held onto it and said, "Might I request a favor of you? Let me know when Madam Molly goes for dinner. Today, tomorrow, every day. Can I count on you to keep me informed?"

Theo tugged at the basket. "I will contact you if I see her."

Fred let go of the basket and Theo fell back in his chair as the pressure loosened.

Fred tipped his hat. "You're a fine upstanding young man. You will go places." He strode into the dining room, removing his hat as he found a seat at a table next to a window.

Anna approached his table carrying a notebook and pencil.

"Good morning, Mr Barrett."

"Good morning, Mrs Douglas. I trust you are well."

"Very well, thank you." Anna replied. "What will you have?"

"A coffee, please, and the breakfast special with one egg."

"Thank you." Anna left to give the order to the chef, returning with a cup of coffee.

"I must commend you on your excellent care of Mrs Bruin. How is she feeling? It must be difficult for her unable to help."

"She tires easily, but remains in good spirits, considering."

"Ah, yes. Time cannot begin soon enough to heal the catastrophe that has befallen my dear friends."

"My sister is strong. In time, she will recover. We have faith."

"Please, give her my warmest regards. I might stop in for a few minutes this evening to call upon her." He paused, as a dark look passed across Anna's eyes. "A short visit, I won't tire her. I have choir practice tonight and won't stay long."

Anna raised an eyebrow. "That is commendable, Mr Barrett. I would not have guessed you were a singer."

Fred sat straight in his chair and grabbed his lapels. "I believe a person has a duty to share their gift with others. Singing has been a passion of mine since childhood."

"Glad to hear that." Anna smiled and walked away, shaking her head.

Fred grinned, certain she had been impressed.

Moments later she returned with his breakfast and placed it on the table in front of him.

Fred ate quickly, glancing about the room as he chewed. He nodded at a few society people who nodded back. How civil it was to dine in a fine establishment surrounded by the rich and cultured of Dawson City.

He patted his mouth with a white damask napkin, folded it with care then set it on the plate. He paid his bill and left the hotel with barely a nod at Theo.

Fred stood at the railing and lit a cigarette. A thin line of smoke escaped the tip as he held it between his fingers surveying the crowded boardwalks. Other communities had become ghost towns after the Klondike Gold Rush but Dawson was thriving.

Moments later he popped a mint into his mouth, and with a grin on his face he guided Daisy through the streets of Dawson. Someday he would own this town.

NINETEEN

The door creaked open and Tess sat up rubbing her eyes.

"It is well past Noon. You must be famished. I brought you a bowl of mushroom soup and a ham sandwich." Anna set a tray on the nightstand between the two beds. "

"I fell asleep reading." Tess picked up the sandwich and bit into the soft bread. She wrinkled her nose. "This bread tastes odd."

"It is sourdough bread. I never made it at home."

"Sourdough? You said those were people who lived here year-round."

"The bread was named after prospectors who carried their own starter dough and baked their own bread. It was a vital part of their supplies. The chef bakes many varieties of bread but insists on ordering sourdough bread from the Dufour Bakery, Molly's friend."

"I'm not sure I will get used to the food. It is strange." Tess scooped up a spoonful of the mushroom soup, eyeing the frilly pieces of dark mushroom floating in the milky liquid.

"You will do well to remember we are beholding to Molly for taking us in." Anna clasped her hands together and looked at Tess.

Tess dropped the spoon into the bowl of soup. "Was it not she who asked us to come to her aid? Is Aunt Molly not beholding to us?"

"Don't argue." Anna turned, exasperated, and headed to the door. "Bring the tray down when you have finished."

The door clicked shut and Tess fell back onto her bed. "Why does nothing make sense?"

She picked up her book and nibbled the sandwich between spoonfuls of soup as she read. No one would notice if she stayed in her room all summer. Tess tried to read but could not concentrate.

She skipped down the steps and hurried to her aunt's room.

Molly was sitting against the pillows and smiled as Tess entered, patting the bed gesturing for her to sit.

Tess sunk into the soft mattress. "How are you feeling?"

"Better today. Your presence is soothing."

"I will do my best not to upset you."

"Never fear, my darling. Nothing can upset me. I am sorry there is little for you to do."

"I brought my favorite books to read, and I like visiting with you."

"You miss Vancouver don't you? It was courageous of you and your mother to travel so far to be by my side."

"She called it an adventure. I love adventures but the safe ones in stories. I miss Vancouver, especially **Stanley Park**. Father and I would build sand castles and watch the ocean waves wash them away."

"Why didn't you build it further up the beach where the waves could not touch it?"

"Father used to tell me that, but it was easier to fill the moat."

"Easy is not necessarily better, but it was your castle. Sometimes our castles must fall so we can rebuild them bigger and more durable somewhere else." Molly sighed.

"What's the use?"

Molly laid her head against the pillow. "Some days I feel the same."

Tess left Molly's room and ran upstairs to retrieve the forgotten lunch tray.

She sat on the bed then fell against her pillow. What was to become of them? What if her father never returned? Her statement to Molly was true. What was the use of building sandcastles? Her happy reminiscences with her father were fading, washed away by the tides of change, turning joyful moments into painful memories.

TWENTY

After leaving the Golden Grizzly, Fred returned to his own establishment, entering the saloon with a broad smile.

"Afternoon, Boss," The bartender called as he poured a shot of whiskey for a customer.

The customer waved drunkenly and slurred his words. "Fternoon, Bosh."

An obnoxious chorus of voices added to the greetings.

"Hey Fred, come have a drink with us." A voice rose from the back of the room.

Fred smiled and shook his head gesturing toward the office door. "Sorry, some of us have to work."

Laughter rolled through the saloon.

Another voice punctured the cheerful atmosphere. "Save any lives today?"

Fred bristled at the mention of the unfortunate event. He turned toward the voice. He clenched and unclenched his fists, took a deep breath before responding. "Nope. If there's no money in it, I'm out."

He ducked out of the room into the safety of his office and shut the door. Loud piano music overpowered the laughter and conversation as Fred sunk into his chair.

Weeks had passed since Beau's death and Fred was tired of the comments. He preferred to think of it as good-natured teasing but knew they had their doubts about Fred's story.

"Should've had two entrances built." He knocked on the wall between the hotel lobby and his office.

Fred didn't like being noticed, preferring to go about his business with as little interference as possible. He made a mental note to hire a carpenter.

TWENTY-ONE

Hours later, Tess carried the tray downstairs. Her mother looked up as Tess entered the dining room. Mid-afternoon was slow, allowing time to prepare the tables for the dinner crowd.

"Where have you been? I could have used help with the cutlery." Anna placed her hands on her hips. "Take your tray to the kitchen."

Tess walked past the counter that served as the reception, pay and serving station, and entered the kitchen.

Shelves covered one wall, filled with bowls, pans, and bags of flour, sugar and potatoes. A large stove sat against another wall, its black pipe snaking up and through the wall.

A large, beefy man in a chef's white hat and double-breasted jacket hunched over a butcher block with a large knife in his hand. He rocked the knife back and forth, slicing carrots in a blur of efficiency.

A fragrant, meaty smell rose from the pot simmering on the stove.

Tess stood holding the tray, her mouth wide open, until the chef stopped, rose to his full height and glared.

"Oui, may I help you, young miss?" He held the knife, gleaming in his hand.

Tess backed away remembering the tray. "I brought this... my mother told me... I..."

"Out with it, I don't have all day." He glanced at the tray and pointed the tip of the knife toward the sink. "Leave it. Carl will see to it upon his return."

Tess was about to ask who Carl might be but clamped her mouth closed, setting the tray and its contents in the sink. She hurried out of the kitchen without looking at the angry chef.

Her mother was nowhere to be seen so Tess ran upstairs to the safety of their room.

Moments later Anna entered their bedroom.

"For goodness' sake, Tess, you can't spend your life within these four walls. Molly is awake and is asking for you. Do not tire her with your questions."

Tess's face brightened as she rushed downstairs. Her aunt looked better, her face was pale pink and her brown eyes sparkled as she smiled at Tess.

"You look better." Tess sat on the edge of the bed.

"My rest did not refresh my fatigue. The doctor reassured me I will recover fully, if I allow time to be my ally not an enemy." She touched Tess's cheek. "No need to worry, my dear."

"I'm glad you are feeling better. I can't stop thinking about what happened to Uncle Beau."

"Dear child. It is best not to think about it. My mind entertains me with joyful memories to keep me going."

"Your wedding day was one of my favorite memories. I was five but remember dancing with Grandpapa," sighed Tess. "I miss Grandmama and Grandpapa."

"Me, too."

"Do you think they are missing us?" Tess asked.

"I am sure of it. Grandmama writes regularly to tell me of their life back in England."

"Mother said you and Uncle Beau made it possible."

"Yes, I was elated to fulfill the dream of retiring to their beloved village outside London."

"Someday we will travel to see them."

"It is an extensive and dangerous journey across the Atlantic Ocean."

"It couldn't be worse than our trip to see you. Mother would love to go. It would be a fabulous adventure." Tess realized that a few days earlier she had told her mother she preferred to experience adventure through books in the safety of her own home. She was surprised at her sudden change of heart.

Molly stared at the window. "Beau and I had been planning a trip in a few years." A curtain of melancholy fell across her eyes.

"How did you hear about the gold rush?" Tess changed the subject anxious to keep Molly's mood elevated.

"Beau's friend sent word the Yukon was the place to go to get a new start. Beau heard news of a vast discovery of gold. A month after we married we left to make our fortune!"

"And, you did."

"We did indeed. I will never forget the day Beau ran into the cabin with the first of many gold nuggets."

"You and Uncle Beau were incredibly brave."

"I must be brave for both of us. The future frightens me, Tess. How will I navigate the unknown without the love of my life?" Molly took Tess's hand in hers.

Tess put her other hand on top and leaned over to kiss her aunt on the cheek. "Mother and I will be by your side."

"Thank you, Tess. This has been the most wonderful afternoon I have spent in a long time."

"Me, too," said Tess, thinking how refreshing it was to be treated as a young adult instead of a child.

A loud crash resounded throughout the main floor of the hotel.

"Oh dear, run and find out what happened."

TWENTY-TWO

Fred emerged from his bedroom, rubbing his eyes and yawning. An afternoon nap had eased the tension of his earlier encounter with the patrons of his saloon. He went to the window and leaned his hands against the frame, watching the afternoon activity.

Across the street, Judge Wright made his way toward the post office, pausing to exchange greetings with men and women who recognized him.

Never one to let an opportunity pass by, Fred grabbed his hat and hurried out of the saloon.

He crossed the intersection at Third and King Street and entered the post office following the short, stocky man who was breathing heavily.

"Afternoon, Judge Wright." Fred tipped his hat.

"What? Oh, it's you. Good afternoon Mr Barrett. Fine day today."

"It is indeed, Sir."

Judge Wright stood in line, Fred behind. "The wife's got me running errands when I should be preparing for court." He let out a rolling belly laugh then coughed.

Fred nodded and smiled. "Mrs Wright is a fine woman. We both sing in the church choir."

"Ah, yes, the choir. As long as she sings outside the home I am a happy man. Her voice is an acquired taste."

"That it is, Judge." Fred controlled a slight shiver. Mrs Wright was a terrible singer, but no one had the heart, or the courage, to tell her.

Judge Wright took his mail from the postmaster and headed to the door. Fred retrieved his mail and left the post office. They walked together for a bit.

The sun shone brightly, and the boardwalks clattered with people strolling along or hurrying into stores and businesses.

The whole of Dawson City was taking advantage of the favorable weather.

Fred avoided eye contact with the dance hall girls enjoying the sunshine outside his dance hall. He kept his eyes forward and slightly nodded his head as he passed, careful to maintain appearances in front of the judge.

As they passed Fred's saloon he paused. "Fancy a quick drink before you head home, Judge?"

Judge Wright squinted his eyes as he peered into the dark interior and licked his lips. "A shot of whiskey would do the trick."

Fred gestured for him to enter, but Judge Wright shook his head and his shoulders slumped. "I best be getting home. If the wife smells whiskey on my breath, she will tan my hide. Another time?"

"It would be my honor. You are welcome in my humble establishment anytime."

"Excellent. Good afternoon, young man."

Fred watched the judge wander down the boardwalk and turn the corner. "Now, that was a good day's work."

TWENTY-THREE

Tess ran along the corridor and met Theo standing at the dining room entrance.

"What happened?" Tess asked.

"No idea. I was at my desk when I heard the crash." Theo moved past her and headed toward the kitchen.

Tess followed.

They stood inside the doorway, unwilling to venture further into the chaos.

"I cannot work in these conditions," said Chef Pierre, with wild eyes and angry red blotches on his face.

"It was an accident," said Anna, brandishing a broom and shaking it in his direction. She lowered the straw end to the floor and jabbed at the mess, sweeping glass and oozing bloody puddles of goop into a corner. "You did not have to be so dramatic and drop the mixing bowl."

Theo rolled his eyes. "Not again." He left the kitchen.

"What happened, Mother?" Tess stood with one hand against the doorframe, her stomach lurched. "Ew, what is that?"

Anna blinked. "Tess? Stay back, there is glass everywhere."

"Is that blood?" Tess gulped, willing the contents of her stomach to remain calm.

"That, mademoiselle is the last two jars of my blood, sweat and tears, hand-picked from a secret location, where the largest most succulent berries in the Yukon thrive. I prepared a batch of sauce last fall, preserved for all to enjoy. My decadent dessert, wild low-bush cranberry meringue was meant to confirm my status as premier chef of Dawson, creator of culinary masterpieces."

Tess glanced at the gory mess on the floor, wishing she could erase the image Chef Pierre's description had implanted in her mind of blood and sweat. Tiny round berries floated in the muck. "Cranberries?"

"Oui. Gone, smashed into oblivion by your evil mother and her wicked broom."

"How dare you?" Anna clutched the broom handle as she glared at the chef. "You set them teetering on the edge of the counter. It was most likely the wind current created by you storming around here like a rhinoceros that blew them onto the floor."

"Madam, meal preparation is a masterful choreography of dance in my kitchen, and if you cannot tread lightly you have no business in here."

"Well, I never," huffed Anna. "You are a beast, not a chef, and I demand an apology."

"Apology? I am sorry it has come to this. I refuse to be treated like a lowly camp cook, churning out slop for the workers."

Anna stood tall, her mouth set in a grim thin line. "May I remind you I am Mrs Bruin's sister, and confidante?" She held his gaze with a slight twitch in her eyebrow. "You and I both know you have risen to the top like rich cream through her gracious support. It would be wise to show your appreciation by avoiding the development of an inflated ego and ugly arrogance." She leaned the broom against the wall and approached him with her arm outstretched.

Chef Pierre bristled, his eyes sharp, but a grin emerged and he grasped Anna's hand, and instead of a handshake he turned it and brushed his lips against her skin with a kiss. "Ah, Madame, your wisdom and insight once again leave me speechless. Your love and loyalty toward Mrs Bruin is admirable, and you have my deepest apologies. I promise you shall never again witness the volcanic anger of Chef Pierre."

Anna smiled at the chef. "I apologize for attacking the kitchen floor like a mad woman. Tess and I are willing to help you pick cranberries when the time comes." She winked at Tess. "If you are willing to divulge your secret cranberry patch to outsiders, that is."

Chef Pierre turned toward Tess. "Ah, the meek little girl with the tray. We had an unfortunate beginning to our acquaintance." He approached and offered his hand. "May I officially introduce myself?"

Tess gingerly raised her hand, wrinkling her nose as he held it to his dry lips.

Anna placed her hand on Tess's shoulder. "This is my daughter, Tess."

"I am Chef Pierre, at your service. Not the vegetable chopping ogre you previously met."

Anna chuckled. "Despite appearances, Chef Pierre is a toothless bear without claws."

Chef Pierre threw back his head and laughed. "I might have described myself a bit more regal but your mother is correct."

Tess stood, frozen to the floor, as she gazed with wonder at her mother and the chef who moments before had been yelling at each other with anger and animosity. "What about the broken bowl and jars?"

"I am sorry you had to see that. Tensions run high in a busy atmosphere," said Anna.

At that moment, the back door opened and a scruffy young man entered. He stopped, staring at the crowd in the kitchen. "What's going on?"

"You have two less jars to wash," said Chef Pierre. "Have you met Tess?"

Tess took a step back. "Hello."

Carl nodded, brushing dusty blond hair back from his face.

"Another smoke break? Those dishes won't wash themselves," said Chef Pierre.

Carl scowled and headed to the sink.

"I better get the tables ready for dinner," said Anna as she finished sweeping up the cranberry sauce and glass.

"You have not been taking care of yourself properly, doing too many things at once." Chef Pierre crossed his arms, giving Anna a stern look. "You should take a break."

"This situation is temporary until Molly recovers and is well enough to return." Anna brushed away a tendril that had escaped her upswept hair.

"This hotel was too much for her to run on her own, probably the cause of her illness."

"Other factors are in play, besides her debilitating grief. We mustn't judge or presume to know all the facts. Time will tell," said Anna.

"Maybe Aunt Molly might like to join us for dinner?" Tess asked, hoping to change the subject.

"Grand idea. We will let her rest awhile longer before inquiring. We can eat at the earlier sitting to avoid the late hour, and the crowded dining room." Anna walked Tess out of the kitchen. "Find something to do until then, unless you want to help me fold tablecloths."

Tess glanced toward the lobby, eager to go upstairs and read for a while, but hesitated. "The task will go quicker with two people."

They folded tablecloths, then set napkins and cutlery on the tables before the first customers arrived.

Once Anna was satisfied everything was in place she said, "Thank you for your help. We should check on Molly."

Anna peeked into Molly's room then opened the door, motioning Tess to follow.

She and Tess approached the bed. "Molly, do you feel up to joining us in the dining room?"

Molly turned her head toward them. "I believe I shall. It is silly of me to spend all day in bed. Although, it has been most enjoyable having Tess around to keep me company." She winked at Tess.

Anna helped her dress in a loose gown of green muslin and brushed her long hair, twisting it into a bun.

"I feel better already."

Anna's arm felt thin and brittle within Tess's hands as they guided her along the corridor to the dining room.

Anna gripped her arm and held her around the waist. "I'm not sure about this, Molly, you are still too weak."

"Nonsense, I need fresh air and wholesome food to keep my strength, as well as the company of my two favorite people."

As they entered the lobby, Theo glanced up from his desk and jumped to his feet. "Mrs Bruin, how good to see you up and around. May I offer assistance?"

"Thank you, we are managing quite well." Molly smiled and straightened her back, taking a deep breath before continuing.

The three of them made their way into the dining room settling at the table nearest to the door.

Anna pulled out a chair and Tess helped Molly settle in.

The murmur of voices stopped. Soon men and women approached to speak with Molly in hushed tones.

"You are looking in good health, Madam." A distinguished gentleman bowed.

"Molly, my darling, it is wonderful to see you up and about," said a woman dressed in the latest fashion, a forest green gown with gold birds embroidered on the skirt. She touched her blonde upswept hair. Her other hand held a white handkerchief close to her rose-colored lips.

"How gracious of you. I trust you are enjoying Chef Pierre's fine cuisine?" Molly smiled as she spoke cordially.

"His creations are divine. Be well." The woman waved her handkerchief as she and her husband returned to their table.

Heads turned to nod at Molly, who smiled and waved. Curious eyes regarded Anna and Tess.

"I should stand and introduce you to my guests, Anna."

"No need. The regulars will know me soon enough." Anna took a white napkin and opened it with a flourish then settled it in her lap.

"I do appreciate your help. As soon as I am able, I will return to my duties." Molly lifted a glass of water with two hands and took a sip.

A young woman hurried to their table, carrying three plates balanced on her arms. She set each plate down then wiped her hands on her apron. Wisps of light brown hair framed her face softening the sharp lines of her high cheekbones and slender nose.

"Madam Molly, lovely to see you. Hello Anna." She looked at Tess and smiled. "And, this must be Tess."

"Nellie, your presence never fails to warm my heart. Yes, this is my favorite niece." Molly grasped Tess's hand.

"I am your only niece, Aunt Molly." Tess giggled.

"And that is why you will always be my favorite." Molly tapped Tess's nose with her finger.

"Tonight's special is moose bourguignon with pearl onions, Yukon potatoes and garden fresh carrots. Dessert is chocolate mousse. Enjoy." She set the plates in front of them.

Tess stared at her plate. "Moose?"

"It is delicious. Eat your dinner." Anna whispered.

"But, chocolate moose? Chef Pierre may be a good chef but even I know it is impossible to make a dessert from meat."

"Tess, how rude." Anna raised her finger to her lips. "Hush or I will send you to your room."

Molly laughed. "Don't be hard on her. I never thought of it that way, Tess. When dessert arrives, we will both taste the chocolate mousse and I await your reaction with unbridled anticipation. You will be pleasantly surprised."

Tess sighed and took a bite of stew, wrinkling her nose at the bits of green and orange floating in the red wine sauce. New and unusual flavors burst in her mouth and she didn't know whether to keep chewing or discreetly spit into her napkin. She took a drink of water. "Delicious," she said as she slathered butter on her biscuit.

Men and women stopped to give their regards and express condolences. A woman clasped Molly's hands in hers and said, "You must come to tea at your earliest convenience, my dearest friend."

"In time, thank you. Allow me to introduce you to my sister, Anna and my niece, Tess." Molly pulled her hands back and gestured toward them. "They are staying with me."

Tess waited for her to elaborate on her comment, waiting for Aunt Molly to include a time limit in her comment, like 'for the foreseeable future' or 'until I regain my health.' She did not say 'forever' either. If Tess could successfully convince her to give up life in Dawson City, there might be a chance to return to Vancouver.

"Lovely to meet you, Anna and Tess. It will be my pleasure if you would join Molly as my guests as well." The stout woman threw her head back and shook the ebony curls gathered upon her head with a ruby encrusted gold hairpin.

Tess wanted to reach up and pull one, whispering 'sproing' as it bounced into place.

Anna nodded. "We would be delighted."

With a swish of her cream satin gown, the woman left the dining room followed by a weary older man who tipped his dusty miner's hat to Molly.

"Don't let the tattered hat fool you. He struck it rich the first week he arrived. She had her hooks in him before he could spend a particle of gold dust." Molly chuckled as she speared a potato with her fork. "Some people dig for gold without resorting to a pick and shovel."

Anna laughed. "I wonder which is tougher, living with a gold miner or with a gold digger?"

"They seem happy." Tess murmured, wondering what they were talking about.

Nellie appeared and took their plates. "Everyone ready for chocolate mousse?"

"Yes, please." Molly clapped her hands together and winked at Tess who grimaced.

Nellie returned with three crystal goblets filled with brown foam.

Tess dipped her spoon into the fluffy brown cloud and prepared for the worst. At least the moose meat was smooth. She opened her mouth and licked the spoon as a whiff of delicate chocolate tantalized her nose. Her taste buds swooned as velvety chocolate cream melted into delectable heavenly sweetness on her tongue. Tess finished the confection at a pace one might have considered uncouth, then scraped the insides of the goblet to get every last bite.

"I am at a loss for words, Aunt Molly. Chef Pierre is a genius. I could not taste a hint of moose whatsoever." Tess licked her spoon.

Molly and Anna laughed until tears ran down their cheeks.

"Oh my, Tess, you are a gem. I must tell Chef Pierre."

"I'd rather you didn't." Tess remembered her encounter with him this afternoon.

Anna rose from her chair. "Speaking of Chef Pierre I best go see if I can help Nellie with serving and clean-up. Tess, help Molly to her room and go straight to bed. I will be up later." She hugged Tess, picked up their dessert goblets and hurried into the kitchen.

Molly pulled herself up to stand, her hands on the table for support.

Tess put her arm through her aunt's and they walked toward the corridor.

"See me into the parlor. I wish to sit awhile. I almost feel normal again after that wonderful laughing fit," said Molly.

Tess guided her aunt into the parlor, settled her in a chair and placed a lap blanket over her legs. "Is there anything else?"

"No, my child. Give me a kiss and have a restful sleep."

"Good night, Aunt Molly," said Tess as she leaned closer to kiss her aunt's cheek.

As Tess climbed the staircase, she heard a deep voice talking to Theo at the front desk. She turned her head to place the familiar voice. Mr Barrett. What was he doing here?

She hesitated on the landing. It was not polite to eavesdrop but children her age were curious. If adults decided to keep certain things from them, it was up to the children to fill in the blanks if it might affect their lives in any way.

She listened. Of course, he was here to visit Aunt Molly. Mr Barrett seemed like a nice man. It will do her good to see an old friend.

TWENTY-FOUR

Fred strolled down the hallway to the parlor and knocked. Earlier, Theo had informed him of Madam Molly's appearance in the dining room and Fred had hurried through his own dinner.

"Who is it?"

"Mr Fred Barrett."

"Come in."

Fred removed his hat and stepped into the parlor.

"Leave the door open, please." Molly sat in her chair with a quilt over her legs. "Good evening, Mr Barrett. What brings you here at this hour? Have you had dinner?"

"I had to see you. I spoke with your sister this afternoon and she said you have been feeling poorly with no relief in sight. If I can help make you comfortable, please let me know."

Molly laughed. "Your daily supply of cinnamon rolls has been a welcome treat but please do not feel obligated to see to my well-being. You are a busy man. How is Clara these days? I miss our afternoon teas with her delectable scones."

"She is well and happy in her new kitchen. The Dufour Bakery is popular."

"I knew it. Give her my best next time you see her."

"She would rather be the one delivering cinnamon rolls each morning but business has been booming and she cannot get away."

"When I feel better, I will visit." Anna smoothed the quilt and smiled at him.

Fred held his hat in his hand. "I cannot stay long. I am expected at choir practice in a few minutes."

"What a lovely pastime. You must sing for me, sometime."

"It will be my greatest pleasure to serenade you."

Molly lowered her head avoiding his gaze and folded her hands in her lap.

"I mean, I will entertain you with a few songs one day."

"That would be lovely."

Fred bowed. "I must be going. Mrs Wright will have my head if I am one minute late." He laughed, hoping to lighten the atmosphere that had grown awkward. He must remember not to rush Molly.

"Good evening, Mr Barrett."

"Madam." Fred gave a deep bow. "I remain your humble servant." He left the parlor and strolled down the hallway.

TWENTY-FIVE

Tess pulled out her book and settled into bed to read. The northern sky continued to play tricks on her making it feel like a sunny afternoon. She felt wide awake thanks to the nap she had taken earlier.

The floor creaked right outside her door. She jumped from her bed and ran to the door, placing her ear against the wood. Creak. There it was again. She pulled open the door and peered out.

The corridor was empty.

She shuddered. Those hotel guests were quick on their feet, disappearing into their rooms before she could see them. She peeked through the crack as she closed the door then went to the window pushing aside the heavy curtains to welcome the late night sunshine.

Creak.

Tess pulled the pillow over her head and held her breath. Her books of mystery and suspense were familiar and safe. She preferred not to think of the harrowing tales of the Yukon.

Eventually she slept.

TWENTY-SIX

Fred pulled up to the St. Andrew's Church on Fourth Avenue and Church Street. He tied Daisy to the hitching post and entered the building, removing his hat and smoothing his mustache before approaching the group.

Fred cleared his throat and popped a mint into his mouth before approaching the other choir members.

"Evening, Fred," said a tall, slender man who reminded Fred of a cricket. He played piano for the group.

"Evening, Floyd. What great adventures have you been up to this past week? Any excitement at the bank?"

"Things have been quiet since the stampede of prospectors headed to Alaska. Business, as usual. How about you?"

"My establishments have remained busy despite the exodus, I am happy to say."

"Excellent. What business did you say you were in?"

"Mr Barrett. Mr Gardall. Gentlemen, this is neither the time nor the place. Such talk is vulgar and unwelcome." Mrs Wright clapped her hands together. "Places, people. We have oodles of work ahead of us. The annual summer dance is not far off. Mr Percy?"

A man sporting a handlebar mustache curled at the tips raised his baton and silenced the chatter. He glared at Floyd.

Fred nodded to the banker who settled onto the piano bench and flexed his fingers.

The group of twelve men and woman took their places, women in front and men in back.

Fred stood on the end. He caught the mint between his teeth and pulverized the candy before Mrs Wright noticed.

Piano music soon turned the atmosphere into a dance hall. Fred half-expected the women to turn and smile coquettishly at the men then choose partners.

As Mr Percy raised his baton, Mrs Wright clasped her hands, took a deep breath then let loose with a high note.

Fred snickered, as did the man beside him. They glanced at each other and grinned.

Soon, the other women added their voices, and the men joined in, their deeper voices filling in the gaps.

Fred placed a hand on his chest and his voice joined the others in a cacophony of sound, until each voice faltered and competed for air time on its own.

Mr Percy sliced his baton horizontally through the air, and Floyd, the banker stopped playing.

"What a racket. Who was out of tune?" Mrs Wright called to the choirmaster.

The man with the baton avoided Mrs Wright and pointed to the back row, stopping at Fred.

Fred frowned and shook his head. "It could not have been me. My voice has always been a crisp clear tenor."

"I beg to differ, Mr Barrett." The choirmaster crossed his arms. "You are a common baritone and should be situated in the middle."

Fred bristled at the word. "I am not a common anything."

Mrs Wright pursed her lips as she glared at him.

Fred clenched his fists but maintained an air of calm. "Forgive me. I apologize for my outburst. Perhaps my voice has changed over the years."

"Perhaps your tobacco use has also played a factor." Mrs Wright raised an eyebrow. "We expect the highest moral character in our church choir members." She glanced at each of the people around her.

The five women met her gaze and nodded.

The six men studied the ceiling, shrugged then nodded.

Fred moved to the middle of the line, coughing to clear his throat. He and the others knew whose voice was to blame, but no one was willing to confront Judge Wright's wife.

"We have a lot of work to do," said Mrs Wright, nodding to Floyd to begin playing.

Fred sang with the others and wondered what other activities might allow him access to the upper level of society. He might have to take up tennis or croquet.

TWENTY-SEVEN

Tess awoke refreshed and cheerful with no idea of the time. It was as light out as the hour she went to bed. Her mother was already downstairs. She hadn't heard her come in last night.

Tess dressed and went downstairs to Molly's room. Voices floated through the key hole, but she could not place the deeper of the two.

"Bed rest is imperative at this stage. Your grief is debilitating and could be harmful if your emotions were to get the better of you. I suggest a strict regimen of rest and quiet, no strenuous activity or stressful situations."

"But, doctor, ever since dinner last night I have been feeling much better. I truly believe laughter is the best tonic. My niece has been a restorative influence on me."

"Your niece is welcome to visit but for short intervals. Too much stress on your nervous system is detrimental to your health," said the doctor.

"Very well, I will follow your advice. Thank you."

Tess jumped back as the door opened and a short, bespectacled young man strode out of the room carrying a leather satchel.

"Pardon me, young lady," he said, as he strode past her and down the hall without a pause.

Tess opened her mouth to answer but peeked into her aunt's room instead.

"Good morning, Aunt Molly. Was that the doctor?"

Molly lifted her head slightly and wiped a tear from the corner of her eye. "Sadly, yes. The messenger of bad news and sound advice, I'm afraid. I must heed his words if I am to be well again."

"Would you like me to read to you this morning?" Tess approached the bed.

"Maybe after lunch. Go enjoy your breakfast and do not worry about me. I am a fighter." Molly raised her arm with clenched fist then let it drop heavily to the bed surface.

"You most certainly are, Aunt Molly." Tess kissed her soft papery cheek. Her aunt was the bravest person she knew but losing a loved one was a massive devastation to the heart.

Tess missed her father with every piece of her heart. Her father meant the world to her, and she refused to believe he was gone, but how long before reality set in. She was quite comfortable allowing denial to keep her company.

Her mother coped in her own way, telling Tess not to give up hope but be prepared for the worst. Tess refused to prepare herself for the worst. How does one prepare for that outcome?

She let herself out of the room and dragged her feet along the carpeted hallway and down the stairs. She spotted Theo at the front desk.

"Good morning, Theo."

Theo glanced up, nodded his head then went back to his ledger.

She stopped in front of the reception desk. "

"Yes, Miss Tess. Is there something you need?" He wrote numbers and notes, his pen vigorously scratching the paper.

"No," said Tess, standing on her toes to peer over the reception desk. "Do you live behind that desk?"

Theo raised his head and stared at Tess. He frowned, paused, then laughed. "Of course not, but it would certainly save money."

"You are here all the time."

"I work long hours but I rent a room in the boarding house down the road. Your mother fills in when I'm not here."

"When do you arrive?"

"Usually by nine a.m. until nine p.m."

"That is a long time to sit at a desk."

"It's a job. I enjoy the comings and goings."

"You are a people watcher."

"You might say that, yes." Theo chuckled. "Go on with you, I best be getting back to work."

"There's nothing to do around here."

"You should find children your own age."

"I am not a child. I'm almost twelve." Tess clenched her teeth. "How old are you?"

"Me? I'm almost twenty."

"You're a teenager."

"Am not. I'm a working man." Theo crossed his arms and leaned back in his chair. "I've been on my own since I was fifteen. Followed the stampede and tried my luck on the creek but discovered nothing of value so I moved to town. Met Mr and Mrs Bruin and worked for them ever since. Decent folks." Theo lowered his head and sighed. "Sorry about your uncle."

"Thanks." Tess fought back the tears. "I'll let you get to work."

"Have a good day, Miss Tess." Theo smiled.

TWENTY-EIGHT

Fred opened the drapes and leaned his palms against the window frame. The roads were busy at the early morning hour and Fred grinned. The Midnight Sun played tricks on people's brains, urging them to play all night. Good for business at his dance hall and saloon.

He stared at the bank down the street. Floyd Gardall was the manager. A good man to know in a crisis. He chuckled as he thought about choir practice last night. It was amazing how many high society people thought they could sing. Fred smiled. His natural singing talent was an excellent way in the door. With his charm and good looks he planned to befriend Mrs Wright, the judge's wife. In good time, he expected to be invited to dinner, and introduced to the heads of the largest companies in Dawson. He vowed to make them his peers, and merging his businesses with Beau and Molly Bruin's empire would see to that.

He dressed carefully, trimmed his mustache, and attached his gold watch before stepping into his office.

He inhaled. "Coffee." He headed into the saloon.

The bartender grabbed the coffee pot, poured the steaming black liquid into a cup then slid it down the bar.

Fred held out his hand and caught it splashing a drop onto his sleeve.

"Your aim needs improvement." Fred shook his arm.

"Your catch needs work." The bartender pulled the towel off his shoulder and threw it to Fred.

Fred ignored it and stormed into his suite to change his shirt.

TWENTY-NINE

Tess entered the dining room and her mother waved from the back of the room.

"Am I late for breakfast?"

"Go see if Chef Pierre has any leftover French toast." Anna returned to a pile of receipts, lowering her head in concentration.

"Any more French food and I will begin speaking with an accent." Tess sighed as she peeked into the kitchen.

Chef Pierre was hunched over the counter.

"Good morning," said Tess, entering the kitchen with caution, noticing a large knife in his hand. "Mother said you might have a piece of French toast left over from breakfast?"

Chef Pierre stood, placing both hands on his hips as he arched his back, the knife in his grasp. "Good morning, ma petite. There is a plate on the counter near the ice box unless Carl has gotten there first."

Carl grunted from his position at the sink, his arms deep in soapy water.

"Good morning, Carl." Tess picked up the plate and left the kitchen. She sat on a tall stool at the serving counter and ate the cold toast. She preferred a bit of powdered sugar or syrup but was afraid to ask. Any sign of weakness in the kitchen seemed to invite a barrage of questions or scowls.

What was their problem? Tess thought chefs loved their jobs but Chef Pierre stayed in a perpetually gloomy mood. Carl never met her eyes, which was fine with her, but he made her nervous.

Anna had often told her to stop being suspicious of people so Tess probed her imagination and came up with a story for Carl to explain his shifty behavior. He had wanted to become a chef but his lack of smell became the major obstacle to his dream. Tess figured he must not know he lost his sense of smell because a waft of cigar smoke and sweat followed him wherever he went. Maybe that was why Chef Pierre was forever in a bad mood.

Tess giggled.

THIRTY

Fred shook the reins and guided Daisy toward the Dufour Bakery.

Pedestrians and traffic congested Front Street. Fred avoided crowds when possible and tensed as he searched for an empty space to hitch up Daisy. Eventually finding one, he stopped the carriage and jumped down, narrowly missing a brown pile of steaming residue from the previous horse.

By the time Fred stepped onto the boardwalk and strolled toward the bakery he was not in the mood to talk to anyone.

A woman turned her head. She reminded Fred of a cream puff, and who sung like a shrill ocean bird.

Her eyes brightened when she saw him. "Good morning, Mr Barrett."

"A fine morning, indeed."

"I declare, last evening's choir practice was a rare success, don't you agree?"

"And a rare occurrence to have the entire group present, thanks to your persistence, Mrs Wright. I appreciated the reminder. My life can get hectic at times and choir practice is a welcome diversion."

"It is my duty to ensure the choir is successful. Mind you, I cannot take all the credit. We have mighty fine voices in the group."

Fred brought his hand to his mouth and coughed.

"I do hope you are not coming down with something." Mrs Wright stepped back. "We need your strong, clear voice."

Fred shook his head. "My apologies. It may have been sawdust from the new construction. The air quality is poor in this area."

"Rather." Mrs Wright sniffed. "I cannot abide the clumsy people in this town. I declare."

"I agree. The majority of residents rely on oil lanterns and candles for light, but with the eternal light of day there should be no threat of fire for a while."

"Let us hope not. These buildings are fragile, built in haste as cheaply as possible." Mrs Wright adjusted her basket. "I must be off. The bread is cooling quickly. Mr Wright prefers a nice warm slice slathered in butter first thing in the morning."

Fred tipped his hat in her direction. "Please give my regards to the judge." He peered through the bakery window, breathing a sigh of relief at the empty store as he entered. He approached the counter. "Good morning, anyone here?"

"Coming," said a voice from the back room. A woman appeared, brushing flour off her hands onto her apron. She stopped inside the doorframe. "What a shock. You decided to stop and say hello for once instead of popping in and grabbing the prepared cinnamon roll basket like a common robber bird."

"Yes, indeed. How are you, Clara?" Fred pointed to her nose then pretended to brush his.

Clara wrinkled her nose and touched it, leaving flour on the tip.

Fred laughed.

"You fiend. I did not have flour on my nose, did I?" She smiled. "Your basket is ready to go. Was there something else you needed this morning?"

"Now, Miss Dufour, I take a moment in my day to say hello to a dear friend and you immediately assume I want something."

Clara crossed her arms and nodded. "Is there any other explanation?"

"You know me too well."

"Have your deliveries been successful?" Clara asked, her eyes twinkling with amusement.

"I saw her for a few minutes last night. But, alas, there has been a wrinkle in my plan."

"Let me guess. Mrs Bruin's sister has arrived."

"Correct. I fear it is worse than that. Mrs Bruin has not been responding to her doctor's care and is bedridden most of the day. I will not give up. A few moments of her time would give me hope that she has forgiven me."

"Of course she has. You tried to save Beau. You said so yourself. The Yukon River is treacherous, and you should not be hard on yourself. Beau is in a better place, and Molly will carry on. It will take time."

"You are wise, Clara, but time is not on my side. I am in business with people who believe their time is more valuable than mine."

"Don't worry, Fred, things will work out for you. Deep inside that highly polished exterior lies a kind heart." Clara moved toward Fred, closer than social norms allowed. She looked into his eyes then at his mouth before abruptly stepping back, grabbing the basket and pressing it to his chest. "I'd love to chat but I have a batch of cookies in the oven."

Fred took the basket. "Thank you, Clara. Send the bill to my office. I'll throw a little extra in for your sage advice."

"You scoundrel," said Clara, laughing as she went into the kitchen.

Fred tipped his hat and left the bakery. He first met Clara Dufour when she was a dancer at the Palace Grand follies. Her golden hair fell to her waist, and Fred was immediately enamoured with her talent. He hired her on the spot to work for him at his dance hall and toyed with her heart. He felt awful about his selfishness but business was business. Manipulation was a gift, and when Clara's looks faded he convinced her it was time to step aside. She was a good sport. He helped her set up the bakery, and she paid him back as quickly as possible. Clara was a tough cookie but Fred knew she still had a soft spot for him. He couldn't help it if he was the most eligible bachelor in town.

THIRTY-ONE

Mornings came early and Tess was already bored. She missed not being able to spend time with her aunt, and she read every book she could find. Writing in her notebook had proven fruitless with nothing exciting to document. Her stomach growled urging her to head to the kitchen for breakfast.

The floorboards creaked at the opposite end of the hall and Tess felt the hair rise on the back of her neck. She debated returning to her room.

"Hello?" She took one step toward the noise.

A door slammed shut and Tess jumped. She rushed down the stairs into the lobby, her heart racing.

"Tess, please walk." Anna stood at the front desk. "There are guests who are still asleep."

"I heard something upstairs. Maybe one of the guests is a ghost?"

"Absolutely not. Why would you say such a thing?" Anna strolled into the restaurant and took her place behind the service counter.

"Something is making noise but I never see anyone."

"It was probably a hotel guest. It is disrespectful to speak of ghosts. Your Aunt Molly is in mourning and your talk will put her over the edge."

"I'm sorry. I won't speak of it again."

"What are your plans for today?" Anna asked, as she greeted a customer and motioned for him to take a seat at a nearby table.

"I finished my books and even read the newspaper."

"Nellie could use help, I'm sure. Go find her and offer your assistance."

Tess began to protest but Anna's stern look stopped her in mid breath. "Yes, Mother."

Tess turned on her heel and went in search of Nellie.

THIRTY-TWO

Fred carried the basket of cinnamon rolls and as he set them on the seat of his buggy, Old Bert approached him from the direction of the new construction.

"What have we here?" Old Bert sniffed the air. "Are those for me?"

Fred scowled. "Why are you talking to me?"

"I have a right to talk to whoever I want in this town, and you can't stop me."

"Is that a threat?"

"Of all people, you should recognize a threat when you hear one, seeing as you sent your henchman to deliver one to me personally. And it was not delicately wrapped in a sweet-smelling basket. It stank to high heaven of something rotten and despicable."

A couple of people passed by the two men and raised their eyebrows in curiosity but kept walking.

"How dare you approach me in public with your false accusations? I should have you thrown in jail." Fred glanced around as he raised his voice. "I am a fine, upstanding citizen in this town and I resent your tone of voice. Have you been drinking again? You smell of whiskey, old man. Be off with you before I call for a policeman."

Old Bert raised his finger and held it close to Fred's face. "We will talk later. I have information of which you may find interesting enough to compensate me." He staggered off the boardwalk into the street.

A man on a horse veered to avoid hitting him.

Old Bert stepped onto the boardwalk across the busy road and turned to face Fred and nodded toward the river.

Fred shivered. What did Earl mess up this time?

THIRTY-THREE

Tess fluffed pillows and emptied washbasins in the room across the hall from their own.

"Nellie, do you believe in ghosts?"

"What a strange question. This hotel is three years old. The Bruins had this built shortly after they moved into town. Ghosts reside in old buildings where they have met their demise and do not know they are dead."

"What happens to people who die outside?"

Nellie gasped. "Don't ask such a horrible question. Your uncle is not a ghost."

"I wasn't thinking of Uncle Beau. Is there a ghostly presence making the floor boards creak on this floor? I keep hearing them and yet there is no one there."

"This town is built on a bog. Maybe the ground is settling from the winter thaw."

Tess bit her lip. "Have you heard creaking when you're up here?"

"Not personally."

Tess gulped as she smoothed out the pillow she had crushed against her and set it on the bed. "What do think about while you clean rooms?"

Nellie shook the comforter then raised it in the air allowing it to settle onto the bed. "I dream of faraway places," she said, smoothing the wrinkles.

"Maybe someday a prince will stay at the hotel, fall madly in love with you and whisk you away with him."

"What a silly girl you are." Nellie tucked an escaped tendril of dark hair into her bun before picking up the pile of bedding. "I have no need for princes. Go tidy Mrs Bruin's parlor. I will finish in here."

A squeak escaped Tess's lips. She hopped down the stairs and hurried along the hall to her aunt's parlor.

Molly was asleep in her room.

Tess moved about the parlor like a church mouse. She ran a cloth along the piano surface, startling herself as faint music notes broke the silence as she dusted the keys.

When the parlor was tidy Tess collected a few pillows and piled them onto the settee to form a cozy nest. With a book in hand, she sank into the soft pile, moving pillows around to cradle her head. Adventure beckoned through the pages of the book and she allowed the words to pull her into a different life.

Within moments of complete immersion, she was yanked back into reality by her mother's voice traveling along the corridor. She was arguing with someone at the front desk.

"Mrs Bruin is grateful for your help over the past few weeks, but I will oversee the businesses while she is unwell. Whatever document you are trying to get her to sign, this is not the time."

"That was not agreed upon. Beau distinctly told me if anything happened to him I was to step in and manage his affairs."

"Molly is his wife. She has final say. Have you anything in writing that outlines Beau's request?"

"I have the word of my friend and partner, told to me in confidence."

"That is not good enough. I appreciate your well-meaning intentions, as does my sister, but she has put me in charge."

"Very well. It is understandable Madam Molly should want to carry on after Beau's death, but I question how well she can handle the crews without some kind of male authority. I need her signature in order to improve the dredge operation."

"She will want to read over the document before signing. If you leave it with me, I will make sure she gets it. And, as for your comment about our ability to handle the crew, we will deal with that preposterous notion if and when it arises. Good day to you, Mr Barrett."

THIRTY-FOUR

Fred frowned as Anna marched down the hallway toward the parlor. He tucked the papers into his pocket and turned to see Theo smirking. Fred stared at him for a moment then slapped the desk with the palm of his hand, grinning as Theo jumped.

"A fine woman, Mrs Douglas." Fred removed a small bag from his pocket, took out a mint and popped it in mouth. "Mint?"

Theo shook his head and then nodded. "Yes, Sir, she is indeed. Is there anything I can help you with today?" Theo squirmed in his chair, glancing toward the parlor.

"You're doing great. Keep up the good work, lad, eyes and ears open." Fred flipped his hat onto his head, sauntered out of the building onto the verandah. He touched the brim of his hat as he approached a man at the railing who had turned his head in his direction.

"Fine day to you, Sir."

"Good day, Fred. How is Mrs Bruin?"

Fred opened his gold cigarette case and held it out to the man who shook his head at the offer.

"Poorly, I suspect. Her sister has taken it upon herself to keep me apprised of her condition." Fred spit the mint from his mouth as he took a cigarette from the case. He lit the end with a gold-plated lighter, inhaled and exhaled, his gaze following the curl of smoke.

"Not allowing a gentleman caller to see for himself, is she? What a shame." The man chuckled.

"I have managed one short visit since that woman arrived. She is rather protective of her sister." Fred leaned his arms on the railing and watched the passersby. "I assure you the dredge operations are not affected by this setback. Your investment is safe with me."

The investor shook his head. "Odd choice of words. His death was a tragedy not a setback. I liked Beau. I trusted him."

"We all did." Fred turned to face the investor, tensing his jaw. "My choice of words was meant to reassure you. My men are capable of upholding the integrity and hard work Beau instilled in them. I did not intend to insinuate his death was an inconvenience to you and our venture. He was my friend."

"I am glad to hear it."

Fred extinguished his cigarette with his fingers, replaced it in his case and snapped it closed. He put the case in his pocket and then removed the bag of mints. He offered one to the investor who declined. Fred popped one in his mouth.

The two men leaned against the railing and watched the people, tipping their hats to many who acknowledged the two businessmen.

THIRTY-FIVE

After hearing her mother speak to Mr Barrett, Tess sunk lower into her reading nest and tried to concentrate on the story, hoping her mother would head to the dining room.

Anna peered into the parlor from the doorway.

"Tess, what in heaven's name are you doing in here?" She hissed. "We must not upset Molly, do you understand? I insist you clean up this mess immediately. This is a first-class hotel, not our house. You cannot do whatever you want, whenever you please."

Tess glared at her mother from her comfortable haven and slammed her book shut. "You told me this was our new home. Now you tell me it is not, and that hotel guests take priority over your own daughter."

"Do not speak to me in that manner. We must make the best of our situation. Please, think of your Aunt Molly and try to understand the heartache and loss she has endured."

"How am I supposed to help her? I am a child as you continue to remind me."

"She appreciates your help with the rooms. I am sure Nellie does, too. You can help by being happy. It pains me to see you miserable. I am sorry we had to leave our home in Vancouver but there was nothing left for us."

"That is not true. Father will return. We should have stayed where he could find us."

"I left word. He will find us. Go outside and get some fresh air. Have you been outdoors since we arrived?" Anna headed toward the dining room. "Clean up this room before I bring Molly in for tea."

Tess tossed pillows onto the settee, not bothering to arrange them in a presentable fashion, grabbed her book and headed up to the room she shared with her mother.

Tess grabbed her coat, checking the pocket for her pencil and notebook then went into the hall, closing the door with a soft click. She took each stair with a heavy foot fall as she slid her hand down the polished railing. When she reached the main floor, she wandered down the hall to greet her aunt before venturing outside.

Voices traveled through the keyhole of the closed parlor door.

"Do not worry about Fred. He was a good friend to Beau. He wants to help."

"It is obvious he is attempting to build on his friendship with you, inappropriate under the circumstances, as far as I am concerned. He seems to have an unhealthy interest in your business affairs, a vulture going after easy pickings."

"You are the suspicious one. We will manage." Molly laughed. "He is a good man, Anna."

"On that note, I am worried."

"You worry too much, dear sister." Molly spoke with a tremor in her voice.

"Another problem has been causing me sleepless nights. There has been no sign of activity in the account I set up at the bank."

"There is no need for money while you are living here. The hotel and restaurant are busy. The saw mill and dredge company are doing well. I am sure James's soldier pay will be assigned to your account once it is sorted out," said Molly.

Tess stopped in her tracks, frozen to the spot. She should not eavesdrop but this was a chance to fill in the blanks. She was never told anything, so despite the guilt, she listened to her mother's reply.

"If it had not been for support from the **Canadian Patriotic Fund**, we would have starved. The income from my job at the chocolate shop should have been enough but prices rose with no end in sight. I tried to plant a garden but, you know me, I was never good with plants. We barely survived, until that nasty woman set her sights on me."

"What happened?"

"Do not misunderstand me, the government has helped many families affected by the Boer war, but it was humiliating to be at their mercy. It would have been easier if I had not been forced to face inquisitions each time I picked up our payment."

"Inquisitions?"

"Yes, I was confronted with questions about how the money would be spent. That nasty woman, high and mighty Blanche had it in for me the first day I appeared at her desk. I don't know where she got the idea she was in charge of behavior and morals, but I assume the power went to her head. She accused me of spending the money frivolously and cut off my support."

"What a horrible woman. How could she? You are the thriftiest of housewives. You had to be. Making ends meet on the salary of a teacher was hard enough before James went off to war."

"We made it work. He was a fine teacher."

"He will be again, Anna. Do not give up hope. That woman had no right to do that to you."

"I do not know how she found out I had been purchasing a weekly magazine for Tess. Blanche called it frivolous and a misuse of funds. They were worth every penny because Tess loved the serial stories. It was my way of helping her get through uncertain times."

Tess fell against the wall and brought her hand to her mouth to stifle the gasp threatening to betray her eavesdropping. Clutching her coat she hurried down the hall, anxious to put as much distance as possible between her and her mother's words.

She went out the front doors without greeting Theo and sat down on the bench near the door, on the verandah spanning the length of the building.

Tess knew exactly who her mother had been talking about.

Her heart beat furiously inside her chest making her ears ring. The horrible incident came to mind. Unresolved memories had a way of resurfacing when least expected. The nasty woman had to be Agatha's mother.

Sitting on the bench outside her aunt's hotel thousands of miles from Vancouver Tess felt the searing burn of that horrible girl's self-satisfied smile. She should have stood up to her and taken back what was hers.

"Aren't you the sourpuss?"

Tess jumped as a childish voice pulled her out of her thoughts.

Two scuffed and dirty black boots stood on the wood slats of the porch in front of her.

As Tess raised her head, a shadowy figure appeared in front of her with hands on hips. A grubby boy grinned, the stub of an unlit cigar hung from his lips.

"You are too young to smoke," Tess said, rattled from the rude interruption.

"Am not. I can do what I want, I am already dead."

"Pardon me? What a horrible thing to say. You are not dead. You are standing right in front me."

"I am a ghost."

"Some days I feel like a ghost, too, when adults look right through me as if I am not there." Tess rolled her eyes.

"No, you do not understand. I am a real ghost."

"I do not believe you. You are as real as I am. Go away."

"Maybe you are a ghost, too. Who says you are real?"

"Don't be silly, of course we are real." Tess reached out and touched his patched jacket. "Why would you say such a thing?"

"If you don't believe me, I will show you." He took her hand and pulled her off the bench.

"I am not supposed to go anywhere without telling my mother."

"Who's gonna know?"

He was right. Who would know? Her mother and aunt were having tea. Besides, she had been told to go outside.

"I am staying right here. I do not know you but something tells me you will get me in trouble." Mischief most likely filled his days, and Tess certainly did not want to go anywhere with him.

"You are a sourpuss. I knew it."

Tess scowled at him. "Go away. Let me be."

The boy laughed. "I will have you know there are a lot of us floating around."

"That's nice. Why don't you go play with your ghostly friends and leave me alone."

He intrigued Tess, this boy who had appeared in front of her without warning but she was not about to give him the satisfaction of piquing her curiosity. He felt real, but she had read stories in which ghosts materialized in front of the hero and they had seemed quite real, too.

Two men stood at the railing near the other end of the building, focused on the passersby. Maybe this boy was a ghost. Tess was beginning to think anything could happen in this strange town. This felt like an adventure too good to pass up.

The boy stood with his arms crossed, chewing on the unlit stub of the cigar and tapping his foot.

Tess glanced over at the two men then replied, "I can't be gone too long, or Mother will be angry." She turned her head, but the boy was gone.

One of the men looked at her with a quizzical expression before returning to the conversation with his friend. It was Mr Barrett. She remembered her mother's comments. Was he being nice to her aunt in order to gain control of her businesses?

Tess leaned over the railing searching the road then hurried down the steps to check the side of the hotel. Men and women strolled along the boardwalk. Parasols twirled, and skirts swayed around women's ankles as they walked. No strange boys.

THIRTY-SIX

Fred pushed away from the railing. "I best be getting back to work. Drop by my establishment later and have a drink, on the house. The Eagle Saloon."

Fred shook the investor's hand and headed down the steps. He jumped into his carriage and flicked the reins. His preferred method of travel around town kept his boots clean, a sure sign of a genteel and prosperous businessman.

Traveling by horse and carriage also aided in keeping the possibility of running into concerned investors to a minimum, but the man had obviously been waiting for him. Fred wondered how long he had been followed. Investors were a necessary evil in his business plan, their thick wallets of cash useful in his quest to enter high society and access larger wallets and vaults.

Molly's niece had been sitting at the far end of the porch. She was a strange girl, talking to herself. He knew someone else who did that, narrowing his eyes as he thought of Old Bert.

He plastered a smile on his face which did not change the steely look in his eyes, flicked the reins and headed toward Front Street.

THIRTY-SEVEN

Tess ran into the hotel, ignoring Theo, and hurried to Molly's room.

"Where is Mother?"

"She is giving Chef Pierre a hand with the lunch crowd. Is there anything I can help you with?" Molly lay back on the pillows that had been propped up so she could look out the window. Her pale face had an unnatural rosy glow from the bright pink quilt that covered her listless body up to her chin, beads of perspiration glistened on her forehead.

Tess shook her head. "No, I wanted to ask her a question." Tess picked up a cloth, wet it, then dabbed her aunt's forehead. "You don't look well."

Molly raised her arm, placing her hand on Tess's.

"You are such a dear. Would you be so kind and bring my special drink? Chef Pierre prepares it for me every day but he seems to have forgotten. I believe it is a good sign, however. He must be busy in the kitchen which means we have a big crowd for lunch. It frustrates me to be in this condition." Molly closed her eyes and sighed. "I should be helping."

"Of course, right away." Tess hurried along the corridor to the dining room, slowing her walk to a civilized pace to avoid the inevitable scolding.

Well-dressed men and women occupied every table in the room.

Tess admired the beautiful dresses, the long flowing skirts and fitted bodices. If she were required to grow up, she supposed she wouldn't mind wearing stylish dresses like those instead of her muslin dress and lace-up boots.

Anna stood near a table talking to a man and writing on a small notebook.

Tess went into the kitchen to find Chef Pierre.

Steam rose from a kettle on the woodstove and a large pot of soup bubbled next to it.

Chef Pierre stood in the center of the kitchen placing final touches on plates, curling thin lengths of carrot with a knife.

Carl washed dishes in the sink, puffing at a lock of hair that kept falling across his eyes.

Nellie stood on the other side of the table peeling potatoes.

Tess held back, unsure if she should interrupt them.

"Nellie, mon amour, this is craziness. If I ran this hotel, there would be changes made. These barbarians descend upon us without notice. They do not appreciate the time it takes to create my masterpieces of culinary delight."

"Elmer… I mean… Pierre, you are the finest chef in the city, remember that. People flock to this restaurant because they love your food. Please calm down and stick with the plan. You will have your restaurant soon."

"You are right. We must have patience." Chef Pierre tapped Nellie's knife with his as they smiled at each other. A secretive look passed between them.

"Carl. You are not washing quickly enough. We need those plates. Now."

Tess took a step back. What were Chef Pierre and Nellie planning? Why did she call him Elmer? How were they going to get their own restaurant? She backed out of the kitchen to avoid being seen, but it was too late.

"Young Tess. How is my petite fleur? You are hungry, no?" Chef Pierre stopped chopping and held his knife in mid-air. "The soup is a delicate bouquet of flavors that will sing sweet melodies to your taste buds."

"It smells delicious. I am here for my aunt's special drink."

"But, of course. Please give her my sincere apologies. I have not been able to keep a clear thought in my head these days," said Chef Pierre, taking a small porcelain cup and saucer from a shelf. He placed them on a silver tray. Pouring hot water from the kettle on the back of the stove into a jug, he added milk and cinnamon. He went to the back of the kitchen, unlocked a cupboard and took a jar from a shelf. Chef Pierre pinched a few dried yellow threads between his thumb and forefinger and dropped them into a stone bowl, crushing them with a pestle. He stirred them into the milk and with a flourish grated nutmeg on top.

"Voila. This will help Madam Molly feel better."

Tess moved forward but Chef Pierre put his hand up.

"Wait, I almost forgot." He grabbed a sliver of ginger, quickly crushed it under the blade of a knife and dropped it into the jug. "You may take this to your aunt. My special recipe will take good care of her."

Tess held the tray and walked slowly, careful not to trip as she headed to Molly's room. She took shallow breaths to avoid smelling the concoction in the jug. Chef Pierre had used unusual ingredients and Tess wondered what kind of spice he had added. She sniffed the rising steam and gagged at the bitter smell of tin.

Molly snored softly.

The heavy floral curtains kept the room dark despite the efforts of the pretty glass lamps to throw cheerful light into each corner.

The tray rattled as Tess placed it on the side table, but Molly did not wake up.

Instead of returning to the restaurant to help, Tess went upstairs, entered her room and lay down on the soft bed. She stared at the designs in the stamped tin ceiling, deep in thought about her earlier encounter with the strange boy who had left her flustered. It was probably best she had not run to her mother with her question. She would have thought Tess was mad. Ghosts existed in their imagination, in stories. That boy was alive and healthy, Tess was certain of it. How had she let him make a fool of her?

Tess worried about her aunt's health. If someone did not do something soon, her aunt would become a ghost all too quickly. Why didn't the doctor know what was wrong with her? Maybe she was ill from the awful drink Chef Pierre kept preparing for her each day.

Tess sat on the edge of the bed, her heart pounded and her ears roared. Did the doctor know about the drink? Could it be causing her aunt's illness? Chef Pierre and Nellie certainly seemed like they were up to no good. Did they think they could take over the hotel and restaurant if her aunt died? That would never work because Tess's mother was next-of-kin. Unless, Mother was next on the list of obstacles to their devious plan.

Tess knew who might have an answer. She unbraided her hair, brushed it into waves and tied a pink ribbon into place. She checked her appearance in the ornate mirror and forced her mouth into a smile. Best look presentable so the doctor would take her seriously.

THIRTY-EIGHT

Fred slowed his carriage in front of the building that housed the office for his lumberyard on the river's edge. The hastily built shack leaned slightly to the left, showing signs of poor workmanship using low quality materials, an unfortunate advertisement for their product.

A wooden fence surrounded a large yard stacked with piles of wood. Men worked the sawmill producing building materials for the constant construction around the city.

Fred jumped down from the carriage and secured his horse. He stepped onto the boardwalk and surveyed the office, inhaling the earthy fragrance of sawdust. He owned this shabby enterprise through an elaborate maze of names, rarely showing his face at the lumberyard. Deals were made, money changed hands, and progress continued constructing flimsy buildings susceptible to fire, but his hands stayed clean. He had a reputation to maintain.

Fred pulled his hat low over his eyes, lifted the latch and strolled into the shabby office.

A walrus of a man sat at a makeshift desk, the tips of his mustache grazing the paper on which he focused his attention. His head bounced up and his eyes widened as Fred walked in, and he shoved the paper under a messy pile.

"Can I help you, Sir?" The man growled, irritated at the interruption.

"Did I catch you at a bad time?" Fred held out his hand in greeting as he continued to walk up to the desk then leaned over and before the man could slap his hand on the pile Fred pulled out the paper. "What have we here?" He turned his back and glanced at the numbers on the page.

"Hey, you can't walk in here and do what you want."

"As a matter of fact, I can." Fred glanced around the dingy room, popping a mint into his mouth. "Do you know who might be your boss?"

"Never met him."

Fred held out his hand. "Pleased to make your acquaintance. You are?" He clicked the mint against his teeth.

"Walter. I was working on the balance sheet, like Earl asked." Walter pushed his chair back and stood, clasping his hands together.

"These are sad numbers. What's going on?" Fred snapped his fingers against the paper with a loud slap.

Walter held his hands in front as he backed up, bumping into the wall. "Sadness makes for fickle customers. We are losing money because people are buying from the Bruin Lumberyard in support of the widow."

Fred casually approached him, enjoying his effect on the man who quivered in his boots as he raised his chin to meet Fred's ice blue eyes. "Interesting."

"You know we can't compete with that."

Fred stared at a lock of Walter's hair standing straight up. It bounced back and forth as the man's shoulders shook.

Fred turned and walked to the door. "There is always a way even when there's no will. I'll get back to you. Is Earl in the yard?"

Walter exhaled then pulled out a soiled handkerchief to blot his forehead. "Sure, boss. Yep, in the yard."

Fred walked through the gate, finding dry spots to step onto as he searched for Earl.

Earl piled lumber onto a wagon and waved as Fred approached.

"Hey Boss, are you sure you wanna be seen with us low-class working stiffs?" Earl curled his lip and glanced at the scruffy thin man helping him load the wagon.

The man rubbed the back of his hand across his nose and snickered.

Fred laughed. "Nothing could be further from the truth. You men are important cogs in the golden wheel of progress. You keep this enterprise moving onward and upward. Soon this will be the most successful business in town."

The employee slapped his hands together. "I like the sound of that."

Fred snapped his fingers and winked. "Back to work."

"Will do, Boss."

Fred caught Earl's eye and jerked his head to the front of the yard. The two men strolled in silence between stacks of lumber, and groups of men operating saws and hauling logs.

Fred acknowledged the men with a nod, controlling his facial expression as muck pulled at his boots while he walked toward the street. He scraped the soles of his boots on the edge of the boardwalk before moving closer to the office, out of sight of the street.

Earl followed.

"Walter tells me we're losing business to the widow," said Fred, opening his gold case. He spit out his mint as he took out a cigarette and held out the case for Earl to take one.

Earl shook his head then opened a tin of chewing tobacco.

Fred took out his lighter with his initials etched into the gold enamel and flicked it until a flame appeared.

Earl rubbed his forehead, pushing his hat further up on his head before pinching tobacco between his stained fingers and tucking it between his teeth and lips. "Not sure how we can compete at the moment. Beau had no enemies."

"I'll stop by the Front Street construction site and have a word with the foreman about switching suppliers. Every man has his price." Fred glanced up and down the street before speaking. "With regard to the competition, I'm working on a couple of ideas."

"We will have to watch our backs. The new police sergeant has been poking around. Why do the new ones have to be so eager to make their mark in a new town?" Earl kicked his boot against the fence.

"Maybe we should give him a distraction. Stir up trouble as far away from us as possible." Fred pulled smoke through his cigarette then exhaled, watching it curl upward to float along an invisible current before disappearing completely. "Do whatever it takes, Earl, and I'll make it worth your while."

"Still waiting on that promise." Earl spit a brown gob onto the dirt.

Fred pinched the end of his cigarette, extinguishing the embers before placing it back in his case. He popped a mint into his mouth and turned away from Earl. "See you at dinner." He hopped into the buggy and clicked his tongue at Daisy as he shook the reins. With a jerk, the buggy rolled away from the shabby construction shack toward the civilized part of town.

THIRTY-NINE

Tess hurried outside onto the boardwalk in front of the hotel, pausing to tie the ribbon in her hair as she looked up and down the road. Where might a doctor live?

She considered going back inside to ask Theo. He should know, but he would also tell her not to bother the doctor if she was not sick. Tess decided to make inquiries at one of the stores instead of attracting attention.

Across from the Golden Grizzly was an abandoned log building. Next to the hotel was a hardware store. Men entered, and others left with large sacks and tools over their shoulders. A barbershop faced the hardware store across the road. No one took children seriously in those businesses.

The Dufour Bakery. A fitting place for a child. Tess had been meaning to visit, so she turned away from the noise and commotion and walked one block to Front Street. The bakery was three blocks down, and Tess had to step around the construction of new buildings. Blackened posts remained amidst the new construction.

The scent of yeast soon replaced the smell of newly cut lumber as Tess approached the bakery. A fragrance of fresh bread overpowered her as she stepped inside. She was in heaven. Chef

Pierre's baking was nothing like this. She stared longingly at the bright strawberry tarts.

"May I help you, young lady?"

Startled, Tess stuttered as she tried to find the appropriate words. It was a continuous frustration to her as a reader who loved words that she did not know exactly what to say at all times.

"Oh, um, I… was wondering… lovely store, Madam."

The woman stood with her arms folded across her chest, holding a rolling pin in one hand as she tapped her black boot on the floury pine floor.

"I don't have all day. If you are here to buy something, make up your mind. If you are not, you are taking up precious amounts of my time. You will be to blame if my rolls burn."

"Yes. I mean, no. I have no money." Tess lowered her chin and stared at her boots. Her stomach rumbled and gurgled. She thought she saw the baker chuckle. Tess had forgotten to ask her mother for money. This was not turning out how she had expected.

"Why are you here?" The foot tapping increased and became louder.

"I was wondering if you could tell me where I might find the doctor."

The woman snorted. "You realize you are in a bakery, child? I declare. Which one are you looking for? We have four in town, all quacks, if you ask me."

"I do not know his name." The conversation worsened each time Tess opened her mouth. "I should go. I apologize for taking up your precious time." She stepped back, inching her way to the door.

"I should say so. Bring your parents with you next time. Slow-witted children should not be allowed to run around town harassing businesses."

Tess shook her head. "I am not a child. I am almost twelve. You won't see me here again."

"I am the finest baker in town." The baker turned abruptly and walked into the back of the store. "You will be back, mark my words."

Tess stood on the boardwalk with tears streaming down her face. What a horrible woman. She assumed bakers were kind and friendly, round and jolly from all the delicious treats they made. Tess could never step foot in there again. The baker would spot Tess at the threshold, throw her head back and laugh her out of the store. Tess dabbed her handkerchief to stop the flow of tears but a few escaped down her cheeks and darkened her coat with wet spots. The comforting smells of her childhood were lost forever as the humiliating experience replaced them, and from this moment on she would choke on strawberry tarts that reminded her of the rude baker.

Tess stomped on each wooden slat of the boardwalk until she reached the construction. She clenched her fists. The baker's impatience at being interrupted had turned her into a sniveling child. How could she ever gain confidence if she allowed people to intimidate her? She planned to stay in her room for the rest of the summer.

"Hello there little lady. What are you doing wandering alone? Tess, isn't it?"

Mr Barrett stood in her path, arms crossed. A benevolent, amused smile flickered at the corners of his mouth.

"I was visiting the Dufour Bakery." Tess wrinkled her nose, trying not to breathe in the scent of mint and onions with an aftertaste of tobacco. She turned her head away and pretended to look at the goings on at the river.

He glanced at her damp handkerchief. "Is there anything I can do for you? Was Miss Clara out of cinnamon rolls? They are the first to sell out."

"No. I am fine, thank you. I was heading back to the hotel."

"Give my finest regards to your mother and aunt. I will bring extra cinnamon rolls tomorrow." Mr Barrett winked and touched the brim of his hat. "Good day to you, Miss Tess."

Tess nodded and hurried past, pushing away the uneasy feeling that surfaced when she had to speak to the man. Nice as he was, it did not seem genuine, and she imagined him as a frog, sitting silent on a lily pad waiting and watching for an innocent fly to venture close, then Zap! Tess did not want Aunt Molly to be his fly. Tess glanced back and spied Mr Barrett entering the building under construction.

Tess stopped and bent over to retie the lace on her boot that came undone in her haste to make herself presentable. After her confrontation with the baker, she could not imagine a visit with the doctor would have been wise.

FORTY

Fred regarded the construction site before entering. A man stood at a makeshift workbench measuring a wooden plank.

"Hello, good sir. A fine example of quality workmanship is evident in your work. Where, may I ask, do you purchase your wood?"

"The Bruin lumberyard. Best quality wood in town."

"What a shame about Mr Bruin. It is unfortunate there is no longer a guarantee they will have enough wood on hand, considering the circumstances." Fred removed his hat and lowered his head.

The man lowered his head in respect. "Such a tragedy." He lifted his head, his eyes filled with concern. "What do you mean? How has their supply dwindled so quickly?"

"Kind souls have purchased out of a sense of charity with condolences to the widow. There has been uncertainty regarding future supplies due to Mrs Bruin's delicate constitution and questionable business sense."

"Understandable but not sustainable. We need a reliable source of lumber."

"I agree. Have you considered the option of using thinner planks in the construction of your building, sir?"

The man stood and considered Fred with suspicion. "Why would I use thinner planks? Have you any idea how cold it gets in the winter around these parts?"

"That is the reason we have efficient wood stoves, and an insufficient wood supply. Great for business. The reason I mention this idea is that I know for a fact on a project of this size you would be in a position to save a considerable amount of money."

The man's eyes lit up. "Now you mention it, I could use a considerable amount of money." He snickered. "Do you have reliable information on how I might make it work in my favor?"

Fred removed a thin gold case from his pocket and withdrew a card. "Here is the contact information for a lumberyard I've had dealings with. Tell them Fred talked to you." Fred put his hat back on and shook the man's hand. "They look forward to doing business with you in the future."

"Absolutely." The man nodded his head then turned back to measuring the plank.

Fred exited the wooden skeleton, rising from the ashes of a fire that destroyed half the block. Fire was a constant hazard with the use of candles and wood stoves, and a great source of business for Fred.

FORTY-ONE

Tess hurried back to the hotel and sat on the verandah to write in her notebook.

Mr Barrett was a convincing salesman, but she was confused. He sounded sneaky when talking to the builder. She tapped her pencil on the paper. She was glad her aunt's hotel was built soundly. Tess frowned as she thought about her new home.

Soon she found herself jotting down her frustrations instead. Home meant love and attention from family, not loneliness. Her mother was too busy to notice her anymore.

Tess enjoyed her freedom, but it came with a cost, a sad feeling of abandonment. Her mother didn't care where she went or who she spent time with.

"Hey, sourpuss, whatch'ya doing?"

Tess jumped up, dropping her journal. "You, again? Where did you go? I looked away for one second and you were gone. How'd you do that?"

"Like I said, I am a ghost."

"You are not."

"I can show you proof."

"I should let Mother know where I'm going."

"But, you don't know where you're going. It is best if you leave, and once you are back you will be able to tell her where you went."

"Strangely it makes sense. Mother won't miss me. She is so busy I feel forgotten. She will probably yell at me."

"I know how you feel. We won't be gone long. You can remind her she has a daughter later."

"What if she gets worried and comes looking for me?" As soon as Tess spoke, she rolled her eyes. No one knew she was gone. It might teach her mother a lesson and make her realize her daughter was more important than her aunt's hotel.

"Not likely," the boy said as he jumped the full four steps onto the boardwalk.

Tess crouched, preparing to leap after the boy, but at the last moment decided to take one step at a time. She made a mental note to practice later.

They turned the corner and headed down the boardwalk at the side of the hotel towards the mountain that overshadowed Dawson.

"What is your name?"

"Henry. Are you staying at the hotel?"

"Yes. My name is Tess. It is my Aunt Molly's hotel. It used to be my uncle's, too, but he drowned in the river."

Henry jumped off the boardwalk and picked up a stick, clacking it along the slats of the boardwalk as they walked.

"I know. I helped them search the riverbank. It was creepy."

"Thanks." Tess shuddered, imagining her uncle's body caught under a submerged log, bobbing in the current as curious fish nibbled.

Rusting equipment and broken furniture nestled in tall grass beside the boardwalk as they walked further from the river. A cool breeze whispered among the abandoned buildings, calling to Tess and Henry, urging them to stay awhile.

"Where are we going?"

"You will see." Henry searched the grass, grabbed a stick and handed it to Tess.

They clacked until they arrived at the end of the boardwalk, and the street.

A breeze moved through the aspen trees and the noise of the downtown streets faded. Log cabins hid among the trees along the base of the mountain.

The two children walked along the base until Henry headed toward a thick stand of aspen and willow. He pushed through the foliage and disappeared as branches fell into place across the hidden entrance.

"Wait for me." Tess quickened her step before she lost her nerve.

The birds stopped chirping and silence pressed down on her as she pulled branches aside to follow Henry. Her stick became a hiking stick, and she stumbled and struggled to climb the rocky path. Her boots were no match for the damp earth, and she slipped, tripping over an exposed root. She regained her balance and narrowly avoided falling headlong into a wild rose bush.

The temperature cooled as the sun disappeared behind the canopy of trees.

Tess's ears rang as she searched for the comforting sound of a bird that would reassure her they were not alone as they headed further from civilization.

Henry navigated the steep path with ease. His patched and dusty trousers quickly disappeared around each bend.

"Slow down. I can't climb as quickly as you." A branch caught on the bow in Tess's hair and pulled it loose as she walked past. After a few minutes she reached Henry, and a level section of the trail.

Henry waited as Tess bent over to catch her breath, one hand on a knee to keep from falling over.

"How far is it?" Tess asked, hoping they had arrived.

Dawson City, with its wide grid of roads, sprawled along the river, barely visible through the leaves of the trees.

Henry put a finger to his lips and motioned with his other hand for Tess to follow.

Sharp cracks pierced the silence like gun shots as they stepped on dry brittle sticks.

It was dim for early afternoon, and Tess barely made out the figure moving silently ahead of her. She shivered uncontrollably, realizing it was not because she was cold.

As the trees closed in on Tess and Henry, the leaves brushed against their arms and faces, depositing droplets of dew on their clothes.

Tess felt a rush of icy air as they emerged into a clearing surrounded by a short white picket fence. A small mound of dirt was marked by a cross.

Tess gasped.

"You brought me to a graveyard? Why? Fine way to treat your friends." She crossed her arms and kicked a spruce tree.

"You wanted proof, didn't you?" Henry walked toward the wooden cross.

Tess moved slowly, careful not to step on the mound. As she approached Henry, he seemed to flicker in the dimness as the leaves played with a finger of sun that shone through to the ground. Tess kneeled in front of the cross and read the inscription. She shrieked then fell back into the grass beside the freshly dug grave.

"See?"

Tess read the grave marker. *Henry Smith, Beloved Son, our angel in heaven. Taken from us too soon."*

"It cannot be." Tess struggled to comprehend what she was seeing.

"Look at the dates."

Born 1895. Died 1905.

"It's 1905 and I'm ten. It's me. My name is Henry Smith."

The soulful sound of crying came from above and when Tess looked up, a black bird glared at her, as if warning her to stay away. She would gladly do so but felt compelled to get to the bottom of the surreal situation.

"That is a common name." Tess sat on the ground. "You probably set this up to fool people. I am not falling for it."

A pine needle poked through her stocking but she welcomed the tiny prick of pain, a reassuring sign she was not dreaming. "You shouldn't make fun of the dead. Unless they find his body, my uncle will never have a cross marking his grave. I miss him."

"I know. We all do." Henry picked up a pinecone and threw it at a tree. "He was a good man, kind to the men he employed. He always had a lemon drop in his pocket for me."

"You knew him?"

"My Pa worked for him. Pa says he might be alive."

"He has no business saying that." Tess pulled the pine needle from her stocking and broke it in pieces.

"Pa says if there is no body where is the proof he is dead?" Henry picked up another pine cone and pulled off the scales one by one.

"He drowned. There is no surviving the Yukon River. I know. I came here on a boat that struggled on those waters. What if Aunt Molly heard your nonsense? It might give her false hope."

"Hope is better than nothing, false or not." Henry tossed the pine cone aside.

"You sure picked a fine place to talk about hope. I don't like it. Take me back right now." Tess stood, brushing twigs and pine needles off her skirt.

She hurried back along the path, pushing branches out of her way as she ran from the reality of her father's absence, the horror of her uncle's death, and the ghostly silence of the strange clearing.

Henry stayed close behind.

"If someone is buried in that grave, Henry, you have no right to claim it. That little boy was someone's son, someone who was loved and cherished. Why would you say it was you? It is impossible." Tess called back to him. The ribbon that had been neatly tied in her hair hung from a branch on the path ahead of her. She grabbed it as she passed.

"Think about it. You saw the name. I am ten years old. What if I died at the age of ten then came back to life? Maybe my parents loved me so much they wished me alive again."

"You have a creepy imagination, Henry. It is a coincidence. Stop scaring me."

Tess burst through the trees and onto the dirt road. The sun touched her face, and she stood until it warmed her through. She raised her shaking arms to tie the ribbon in her hair, but gave up and put it in her coat pocket. She grabbed Henry's arm.

"Who are your parents? I should ask them what's going on. Or I could visit the newspaper office and search the obituaries for the recent death of a ten-year-old boy. That grave was fresh. It must have happened not too long ago."

"Naw, that's dumb." Henry pulled back. "Wanna see something?"

"Why are you changing the subject?"

Henry bounced around me. "Do you want to see something amazing?"

Tess rolled her eyes. "Isn't a visit to a grave enough for one day?"

"This is different. It's not far. Just down this road." Henry jogged backwards waving his hand. "Come on."

Tess shaded her eyes as she looked at the position of the sun but could not tell how late in the day it was. It could be midnight for all she knew. It seemed like they had been on the mountain for hours. Tess headed down the road after Henry. Soon they were below the giant scar in the hillside, an ancient landslide above the river.

A deserted log cabin slouched among the trees, forlorn in its emptiness, the sod roof caved in on one side. Tess felt a sense of melancholy. The cabin missed its family, or the men who called it home while they worked and searched for gold. It might be interesting to live in a cabin during the summer. She had to come up with a plan to convince Mother and Aunt Molly to move back to Vancouver or she would be experiencing a Yukon winter firsthand. If she did, maybe Henry could call her a Sourdough instead of Sourpuss.

Tess passed another log cabin, in slightly better shape, and an old man sat on a low stool shaking a gold pan side to side, bringing it close to his nose. He jotted something in a tattered notebook, looked up, smiled and waved.

It was Old Bert, the man who accosted Tess and her mother the day they arrived.

Tess waved but quickened her pace toward the empty lot where Henry picked his way through a pile of rusting metal objects.

"You're new in town." Bert called as Tess hastened past.

Her young lady manners forced her to stop. "Yes, sir. Mother and I are staying with my aunt."

"What is your name?"

"Tess."

The old man was silent for a moment, closing his eyes and nodding before opening them to squint at Tess.

"Why are you doing that?" She asked, pointing to the pan in his hands.

"I am panning for gold, young lady. What does it look like I'm doing?"

"I thought you needed water. That's what my aunt told me."

"I don't." He waved a grubby hand towards the trees at the base of the mountain. "I can tell if there's gold in this here pan from the smell of the dirt."

Tess tilted her head to one side and wrinkled her forehead. "I'm confused. What does gold smell like?"

"Have you ever eaten a fried egg?"

"Of course."

"Freshly churned butter melted in a cast iron pan sears the edge of the egg. If the yolk is punctured a distinct aroma occurs, a fusion of metal and organic, a melding of the sun and moon, and the reward is a champagne bubble bath while I puff on a ten dollar cigar." Bert chuckled.

Tess wrinkled her nose, picturing the dull and boring eggs she had eaten in her life. "Are you sure?"

"Been panning for gold my entire life, from California to the Yukon, and I ain't been wrong yet."

"You don't look rich." How rude of me, Tess thought. She should not be talking to this strange man. She edged away from his yard, if it could be called a yard. Spindly tufts of tall grass and weeds jutted out of mounds of gravel and dirt. A trail dotted with stones led from the road to the weary porch that sagged in the middle.

"There's not a lot here, but I found my share back in the day. When thirty thousand people descend upon a chunk of land there doesn't tend to be much left after they turn over every stone and dig up every tree. I'm too old to trek through the hills but I am content with the little I find in town. Folks think I am crazy, but I've got more nuggets up here than the lot of them." He tapped his head, knocking his hat askew.

Tess stepped back with her hands up. "I believe you."

Old Bert hung his head for a moment before staring at Tess with a blank look on his face.

"What are you doing here? This here's my claim, my gold. Get outta here."

Startled, she opened her mouth to remind him they had just met but instead turned and ran until she reached the junkyard.

Henry held up a mangled harmonica, wiped off the dirt then put it to his lips and puffed.

A ghastly sound emerged through the muck and rust, screeching like a ghost caught in an old coffee pot fading to a strangled whimper.

Tess covered her ears and motioned for Henry to stop.

Henry dropped it, spitting dirt and saliva onto the ground.

"That is disgusting," said Tess as she leaned over to catch her breath. "You could catch germs poking around in there."

"Can't if I'm already dead."

"You are as crazy as that old man."

Henry kept his head down as he searched the ground, tossing a broken chair aside. "He can see me. Did he tell you he sees ghosts?"

"No. He did not." Tess stayed near the edge of the yard, amazed at the piles of broken furniture and rusted old woodstoves. "Why are we here?" She dared not risk falling and getting cut by a rusty piece of metal. That was not the way she wanted to meet the doctor. She spied a delicate blue and white bone china cup buried in the mud and ran over to investigate.

Tess bent down to rescue it from its muddy grave. "Yuck." She peered at a bug clinging to half a broken cup in her hand and threw it on the ground. She stepped over a battered old photo, the image faded and torn. "Who throws out things like these?"

Henry climbed a precarious pile of wood and canvas, appearing to know his way around the junkyard. He also seemed to have completely forgotten their earlier conversation.

The innocence of childhood, Tess thought with longing. Or was it? What was Henry hiding?

"Probably miners who left town for Alaska, to the next great gold rush. They did not want to carry more than they needed."

"They threw away everything they owned?"

"Uh huh. Think about it. If you had to walk hundreds of miles what would you be willing to carry?"

"But how could they mine for gold in Alaska without equipment?"

"My Pa says they got paid in exchange for their claims and any old equipment still good enough to work. He says the men probably didn't get much money, seeing as how those money guys are thieves and interested in getting as many claims as they can."

"That is terrible. Those men should be put in jail."

"They did not do anything wrong. They were helping the miners, making it easier for them to get to Alaska and try their luck."

Tess sat down on an upturned bucket and leaned her elbows on her knees. "It doesn't sound fair to me. I hate this world. It used to be fun when I was a kid."

"You are a kid. How old are you?" Henry twirled a tattered pink parasol.

"I am almost twelve."

"That makes you eleven. You are still a kid." He threw the parasol into the heap like a spear and picked up a rusted pot.

"No, I am almost twelve, and when I turn twelve, I will have to become responsible and forget about playing or pretending."

"That's dumb. When is your birthday?"

"May."

Henry threw down the pot with a clunk and laughed.

"May? You just had your birthday two months ago. You are barely eleven, you crazy girl."

"I might as well accept the fact now and prepare myself for what is coming, no sense pretending it won't happen." Tess's twelfth birthday loomed in her near future, and she had ten months to worry about it, no time to think about being eleven. She did not want to grow up, but she had to be ready to accept her role in the world without question, without fear. She was not doing too well in that department, struggling with numerous fears and questions, and adults who had no patience to offer answers.

"Shouldn't you enjoy being eleven instead of ignoring it? If this is your last chance to be a real kid why waste it?"

"Never mind. You would not understand." Tess stood, kicked over the bucket and made her way through the junk onto the dirt road. "I should go home."

When Tess's mother told her of her uncle's death, the door to childhood had swung shut and crushed her spirit. If Uncle Beau was dead, what were the chances her father was alive? If she clung to the hope Uncle Beau was alive, maybe that would keep her father alive, too. Henry's dad said without a body there was hope.

But who would believe her and Henry? Unless they found a body, or a live person, no one would take them seriously.

Tess hurried to the hotel, lost in thought, formulating a plan to investigate her uncle's death. Before she rounded the corner to go up the steps of the hotel, she turned to wave to Henry but he was gone. Tess had no idea where he had come from or where he lived, but something told her she would see him again. She hoped it would not be in a nightmare.

FORTY-TWO

Fred leaned his forearms on the white damask tablecloth in the back corner of his hotel dining room.

Brass lamps hung from the stamped tin ceiling, and low conversation hummed throughout the room, accompanied by soft music from the piano.

Earl sat opposite, picking his teeth with a sliver of wood. "Wasn't my fault. The guy hadn't slept in days. One minute he was manning the bucket line then he keeled over onto the trommel. The guys found him buried in the tailings."

"Then it's not our problem."

The waiter brought their plates, and both men waited in silence as he placed their meals in front of them. "Enjoy your meals," he said. "May I offer you anything else?"

Fred and Earl shook their heads and waited until he was back in the kitchen.

"Depends on what you consider a problem, Fred." Earl picked up his knife and fork to cut into his rare steak, bloody juice staining his plate.

Fred leaned forward and inhaled the aroma arising from his plate of liver and onions with a rash of bacon. He waved his hand to fan the delectable smell towards Earl.

Earl wrinkled his nose. "You're disgusting." He chewed for a moment then spoke. "Turns out it was the same guy who came to see you the other day."

Fred cut a piece of fried liver, stabbed it with his fork and brought it to his mouth, along with a scoop of onions. "Refresh my memory, would you please?"

"The guy who confronted you in the bar, the one who hadn't gotten paid?"

"Ah, yes." Fred smiled. "What did you do with the body?"

"Nothing, yet. I'm working on it. The real problem is we are having difficulty finding guys to run the dredge. Word has gotten out it is dangerous and employees are treated badly. The noise on the dredge is deafening and men can only work for short times. No one wants to be paid low wages for a few hours work each day then be overcharged for room and board at camp."

"Why was the guy exhausted?"

"He had been working shifts after other men quit. I went over the payroll, like you asked." Earl speared a forkful of mashed potatoes, moving them around the plate to soak up the steak juice.

"Good man. We wouldn't want any more men appearing at my saloon with complaints about not getting paid then dying horrible deaths. It's bad for business."

"I'm doing what you told me, Fred, but there is no money to pay the guys. I keep telling you, the guys want cash not credit slips. The guys don't want to spend their wages in your saloons, no offense. Many have families and they gotta send money home now and then."

"Are you going soft on me, Earl? If they're hurting, by all means suggest they seek out charity. It is available for everyone who is in need. A lot of people have seen me donate to the poor. I have also helped numerous poor miners by purchasing their claims for a fair dollar value so they can move on. Don't tell me the men have no options."

"Sure, we all have options." Earl scowled at Fred and speared a piece of bacon from Fred's plate.

Fred raised his knife then brought it down close to Earl's hand. "Leave the bacon, if you know what's good for you."

"Ma loved you best," Earl muttered, bringing the piece of bacon to his mouth.

"She would have given you bacon, too, if you ate the liver. She was smart, I'll give her that." Fred chuckled.

Earl laughed. "Pa never liked that meal, says he hated the smell of onions."

Fred frowned, using his knife to point at Earl. "I wondered why he didn't like me. It was the onions."

"Nobody liked you. Had nothing to do with onions." Earl snickered.

"You were Pa's favorite. You're a lot like him. Ma gave me extra bits of bacon to make up for being the youngest."

"Sniveling brat. Ma made us take you with us wherever we went."

"Smart, wasn't I? Don't you realize you should charm your way into the good books of the one in charge? You and the others picked on me but I used it against you to get Ma on my side. Brains beat brawn."

Earl snorted as he stabbed at his steak with the knife and fork, tearing it into pieces.

"If the authorities hear about the accident, they'll come snooping around, wondering why my guys are working long hours for zero pay." Fred snarled. "Take care of the dredge problem. Don't tell me how, just do it. I can't afford to have blood on my hands."

"You gotta do your share," Earl objected.

"I will deal with the paper trail. You deal with the clean-up. Remember, you and I are not partners. I am the boss, and you are my hired hand. You'd be wise to keep that in mind." Fred used a chunk of bread to clean his plate, downed his whiskey then popped a mint into his mouth, clicking it against his teeth as he grinned. His eyes remained slivers of ice.

"You insinuating I might end up like the dredge guy?" Earl raised his voice slightly, but lowered it as other diners glanced their way.

"Not at all." Fred smiled, leaning back. "Your demise would not be accidental."

FORTY-THREE

Tess entered through the hotel doors and waved to Theo at the front desk as she headed toward the dining room.

Theo lifted his hand briefly but kept his attention on the hotel guest in front of him.

The gentleman shifted his head slightly but continued writing in the guest book without acknowledging Tess.

Clinking dishes and cutlery signalled the restaurant was busy. Tess peeked into the kitchen.

Chef Pierre emerged from the kitchen with a plate of steaming beef and potatoes, muttering to himself. "This is ridiculous. No one appreciates my genius. All these idiots want are steak and potatoes. What is this world coming to?"

Tess shrank against the wall and held her breath until he passed without noticing her. She ducked into the kitchen, spotted a thick piece of bread, grabbed it and ran into the corridor. As she ate the soft brown bread sweetened with molasses, she giggled. What had happened to Chef Pierre's accent?

She frowned and ran a finger along the wall pondering his deception on the way to her aunt's suite.

Who was Chef Pierre? Was he a real chef or a con man trying to steal her aunt's restaurant?

The parlor was empty, so she crept up to the door of Molly's bedroom and pushed it open slightly.

Molly's eyes were closed and her breaths came in short, shallow puffs. As Tess approached the bed, Molly opened her eyes. Her lips curled into a thin smile.

The empty jug and stained cup sat on the tray beside the bed.

"Darling, thank for you bringing my drink. How sweet of you to visit. Sit." She patted the bed and moved over to make room for Tess. "How was your day? Dear me, what happened to your hair?"

"It was fine." Tess smoothed her wild hair. "I wish you were feeling better. I hate seeing you like this. Why isn't the doctor helping you? Maybe there is something you should not be eating or drinking?" Tess glanced at the empty cup.

"I am feeling better. I was able to eat a few bites of the cinnamon roll Mr Barrett brought this morning."

"Why does he bring you cinnamon rolls? Chef Pierre could bake for you."

"Dear Tess, I have forgotten to let you in on the best kept secret in Dawson City."

Tess leaned closer, her hands held tight to each other. "What secret? I love secrets."

"My friend, Clara Dufour owns the bakery on Front Street. She makes the best cinnamon rolls in the country. We are lucky indeed."

Tess gulped. Of course, her aunt was friends with the baker. Dawson was a small, isolated community. Her mouth quivered as she smiled, pretending to be pleased, secretly relieved she had not been given the chance to give her name to the baker, or admit where she lived. However, it was inevitable Miss Dufour would soon discover the identity of the rude little girl who had wasted her time. Tess did not look forward to that day.

"You are blessed to have kind-hearted friends, Aunt Molly." Tess took her frail hand in mine. "I love cinnamon rolls, too."

"I will send word for Fred to bring more tomorrow."

Tess let Molly's hand drop back onto the quilt.

"That would be lovely, but I do not understand why Mr Barrett brings them every day. What are his intentions?" Tess frowned.

"You are a suspicious one, like your mother. Fred is a dear friend. He was your Uncle Beauregard's partner in the dredging company they started a year ago. He owns many properties in town and is a highly respected businessman."

"But Uncle Beau has passed. Why does Mr Barrett continue to pay you visits? Should he not leave you to your business and concentrate on his? It does not feel right. I do not trust him."

"Please, for my sake, be nice to the man. He is trying to make up for his failure to save his friend."

Tess tensed. "What do you mean?"

"Poor Fred was one of two witnesses to my dear husband's accident. They were together when Beau tripped and fell off the dock. Beau hit his head on a submerged log and before Fred could dive in to rescue him it was too late. He had to watch helplessly as Beau floated downriver and out of sight. He found Beau's bloodstained hat and brought it to me."

"Who was the other witness? Why didn't he help?"

"A man saw the incident but was too far away to help." Molly leaned back against the pillows and sighed. "There was a thorough investigation, and it was deemed an accident."

"Did you force them to extend the search for his, um… for him?" Tess avoided saying the word that sounded permanent.

"I questioned everything, and every person involved. They did what they could." Tears ran down Molly's cheeks and onto the comforter, pink cotton deepened to scarlet as tears saturated the material.

Tess handed her a handkerchief then pulled out her own and dabbed at the tears welling up in her own eyes as she witnessed

Molly's grief. Tess held her aunt's frail hand and waited until her sobs subsided.

Molly laid her head back against the pillow and closed her eyes.

"Forgive me for upsetting you. I will let you rest." Tess wiped her eyes. "Mother must be wondering where I have been."

"Your concern is endearing. I am grateful to you and Anna for coming to my rescue. My grief is debilitating and I cannot seem to move forward, but there is strength in family. Go. You must be hungry. Chef Pierre will take care of you."

Tess kissed her soft cheek dusted with lavender powder. Chef Pierre certainly would take care of her, especially if she told him she knew his secret. "Aunt Molly, when will your doctor be back to see you?"

"Tomorrow, dear. Why?"

"No reason," said Tess, plastering a bright smile on her face. She hurried out of the room and headed upstairs.

She pulled a brush through her tangled hair, wincing as she tugged on it.

As she entered the dining room, Chef Pierre stood by a table near the back of the room. An idea came to her at that moment. She needed evidence he was up to something. Tess had to acquire a few of those strange yellow threads Chef Pierre had crushed and added to her aunt's drink.

She flattened her back against the wall then peeked into the kitchen. As luck would have it, no one was there. Carl, the dish washer was gone, probably on a break as usual.

Watching the kitchen entrance out of the corner of one eye Tess searched the shelf where Chef Pierre had grabbed the jar, silently thankful it was not locked. Jars of all sizes held unrecognizable contents, brown, green, and yellow, all unappealing and unappetizing in their dried state. Tess spotted the jar of yellow dried threads just in time.

"Carl, we need clean cups." Chef Pierre's voice grew louder as he approached. "Are you on a break again, you no-good slacker?"

Tess grabbed the jar and ran out the back door as he and Nellie entered the empty kitchen.

Tess froze as she stood on the stoop. In the yard below, Carl stood by the storage shed, talking to someone behind the building. It was light out despite the late hour. Tess hurried down the steps, hoping he had not seen her. She tucked the jar into her pocket and prepared to pass Carl as if she was out for a walk.

"Stop messing around and get the job done." A man spoke, low and threatening.

Tess froze then backed away from the two men, searching for cover.

"I have to wait for the right moment," Carl whined.

"Any time will suffice. I am tired of your incompetence."

"Fine, I will do it. Get off my back." Carl snarled and threw down his lit cigar, crushing it under his boot before heading into the kitchen.

Tess ran to the front of the hotel before she was discovered. Who had Carl been talking to? What was he up to? Her mind reeled. She must stay close to Carl and discover his plan, certain that, if it required secret meetings behind hotels it was not respectable.

She walked through the lobby hoping her shaking hands were not noticeable.

Anna appeared at the door to the dining room. "Young lady, where have you been? Have you eaten anything today? Come in here and sit yourself down. Chef Pierre has prepared a special meal for you."

As Tess sat on one of the wooden chairs at a table in the corner, Anna pulled out the other chair and sat beside her.

"I am sorry I have not been able to spend time with you. The hotel and restaurant are busy. Molly and Beau created a wonderful place and everyone who stays here has nothing but great things to say about it.

"I made a new friend. He is ten and a bit strange, but he has been showing me around." Tess was not sure she should mention his insistence he was a ghost. She wanted to investigate further on her own.

"How lovely, dear. Here comes your meal. Eat and then go up to bed. It is getting late." She stood and smoothed her apron. "I must get back to work."

"But it is light outside. I am not tired."

"Do as I say. Or you will be confined to your room tomorrow, without books. Do I make myself clear? I will check on you later."

"Yes, Mother."

Chef Pierre set the plate in front of Tess and smiled, exposing a missing bottom tooth she had not noticed earlier. It gave him a sinister look that sent chills through her body. "Bon appetite."

"Thank you. It smells delicious." Tess picked up the fork and speared a roasted golden potato sprinkled with brown and green flakes. Tess held her fork above the plate, hesitating, but her stomach rumbled in protest. Who cared if Chef Pierre added crushed poison to the spicy crust on the chicken? She would die happy with a full stomach.

She hoped whatever Carl was up to, he would not have time tonight.

FORTY-FOUR

After dinner, Fred and Earl attended a performance at the Palace Grand Theatre.

Fred retained a private box in the balcony, useful when impressing prospective investors. Upper boxes were occupied by Dawson's finest, respectable and rich citizens.

"Is there a reason we have to sit through another boring performance?" Earl lounged in his seat, draining his glass of whiskey.

Fred ignored him. "Have you noticed a change in the atmosphere around town now that the majority of prospectors have moved on to Alaska?"

"We should've gone. I heard there's a lot of gold to be found."

"A lot more violence, too. Dawson is becoming a place where people want to live and raise their families."

"You thinking about raising a family, Fred?" Earl smirked.

"Maybe." Fred watched the actors move about the stage speaking loudly and flailing their arms.

"Got your eye on the prize already." Earl tipped his empty glass to his lips to catch the final drip.

"I could make a fine living in this town, once I have a monopoly on lumber, first-class hotels, and drinking establishments."

"You're not interested in making money by respectable means. You're too impatient." Earl set his glass on the table. "Let's get out of here. I prefer an exciting performance at the Eagle." He stood, lurched down the narrow staircase and staggered toward the exit.

Fred rolled his eyes as he put on his derby hat and grabbed Earl's hat, following him out of the building, while an actor onstage raised his hand in the air and questioned his character's existence.

The Eagle Saloon allowed wild behavior behind closed doors other establishments did not, which meant greater profit for Fred.

Performances at his dance hall included women dressed in black lace corsets and voluminous red and black skirts who kicked their legs in the air and twirled around the stage to raucous piano music. They flirted with the audience of drunken men who were not as successful as their counterparts in the upper balconies of the Palace Grand but knew how to have a good time.

The piano player moved his fingers back and forth on the keyboard, swaying with the energetic music, as drunk as the audience.

Earl staggered to a table and plopped into a chair, striking up a conversation with a heavily made up woman who leaned forward instantly enamoured with her new prospect.

Fred stood at the back of his establishment watching Earl make a fool of himself, then he smiled and assumed the role of host as he mingled with the patrons.

A pretty young woman sidled up to Fred, leaning into him as she batted her eyelashes. "Freddy, I'm ready for that drink you promised me." She adjusted her blue velvet corset and brushed a blond curl away from her face.

"Don't you have a song to sing to me first, Florrie?"

Florrie pouted, but brought her fingers to her merlot lips and blew a kiss before heading up to the stage. She stood with her hands clasped in front, her lips flickered with a slight smile as she waited for the noise to dwindle. The house lights dimmed leaving one soft light on her.

The piano player began to play and Florrie's voice carried throughout the room, clear and delicate. As the music flowed, her voice floated on the melody, gradually drawing emotion from each person in the room.

Fred watched her perform, meeting her gaze. He touched his fingers to his lips and blew a kiss. Fred knew he was handsome. He had used his strikingly good looks to charm and con his way through life to get what he wanted. He was confident he could win over Molly Bruin and use his charm to get her to sign over the dredge company.

FORTY-FIVE

The next morning, Tess helped Nellie with the housekeeping chores, listening for the doctor's arrival. She held two corners of the sheet while Nellie held the other two and they lifted it in the air, allowing it to settle onto the mattress. "What do you think is wrong with my aunt?"

"Goodness, child, if I had recently lost my husband I would bury myself in bed, too, never to emerge again. Grief takes time to run its course but never completely goes away. It changes a person by removing a piece of their heart and soul."

"I believe something else is wrong with Aunt Molly. When does her doctor usually visit?"

"Don't go bothering the doctor with your childishness. He is an important man with a busy schedule. He arrives at the crack of dawn to check on Madam Molly. You missed him by a few hours, silly girl."

"But I have evidence." That was a mistake and Tess instantly regretted having voiced her suspicions. Nellie and Chef Pierre were suspects. "Never mind. You're right, he is a busy man and I am a child who doesn't know better."

"Good girl. Your stories are going to your head, filling your mind with unsettling ideas."

Tess finished her chores in silence, fluffing pillows and nodding.

Nellie glanced at her strangely a few times but Tess merely smiled.

After chores, Tess drifted into the dining room for lunch. The jar was safe in her trunk, and Tess vowed to rise early tomorrow morning to catch the doctor. She trusted the doctor to know what was in the jar. If it was poison, he would thank Tess for her help and contact the authorities. Her aunt would get better and they could return to Vancouver, and to her father.

She sat at a table near the door, staring at the polished wood surface of the table, nibbling the thick sandwich filled with smooth, creamy egg salad.

Her mind traveled back in time.

◇◇◇

Tess dug her fingers through the coarse sand, humming as she created a deep moat around her castle. She lifted her face toward the sun and licked her lips tasting the salty air.

Waves rolled in from the Pacific Ocean and filled the miniature trench with foaming water and tiny seaweed snakes.

Gulls hovered above the beach, shrieking as they lazily rode the air current.

Tess pushed sand in place to trap the water then sat back on her heels to admire her handiwork.

"Look Papa. My tiny royal family are sitting at their fancy driftwood table. The regal king and queen are laughing at a joke told to them by their little princess."

Her father placed tiny shells on the piece of driftwood.

"Here are their golden goblets filled with nectar of the gods."

"I built this castle really strong so they can be happy forever."

A tiny leaf impaled on a stick flapped in the breeze from the highest turret.

"A castle fit for my little princess." Tess's father knelt and put his arm around her shoulder and kissed the top of her head.

Tess sighed and leaned against her father, feeling protected and loved.

Waves crawled up the beach closing in on the sandcastle. Rivulets of water attacked the moat, eroding its walls.

"Oh, no, my castle."

She watched with disappointment as the walls of her castle collapsed and the ocean dragged the little leaf flag and driftwood table out to sea.

"It will be alright. We can build another one, bigger and stronger, further away from the waves. I'll help you."

Together they dug into the sand and built a new home for Tess's little family.

Tess swallowed, forcing the lump in her throat to loosen its grip, holding back tears as reality crashed in around her. She glanced at the other diners to see if they had noticed.

Her mind had whisked her away on a trip through time. Another escape into the past, to a joyful, carefree moment before her life changed forever. It merely served to make the present worse.

After lunch she headed outdoors to the verandah to read.

Moments later Henry appeared in front of her, chewing on his unlit cigar. "Hi Sourpuss."

"I am getting tired of that name. Why can't you call me Tess?"

"Naw, that's boring."

Henry seemed to know the second she turned her head or blinked. Tess did not know where he lived, but it must be nearby.

"Do you live under the verandah? Where do you come from and where do you go?"

"Around. Don't you remember? I am a ghost. I am not alive so I don't live anywhere."

"You do so. Maybe that should be my first case as a sleuth. I will look for clues that prove you are a live person."

"That's no fun."

"I guess it is more fun being friends with a ghost. Besides, I know a better mystery we can investigate."

"Tell me." Henry bounced in place.

"We should investigate my uncle's death."

"Why? He fell off the dock and drowned. Where is the mystery?"

"You told me the other day. They never found his body. In the stories I read, there is always a body. If we could find Uncle Beau's body maybe Aunt Molly would get well again if she knew for sure."

"Wouldn't it be better if we could find him alive? She would be happier if we could make that happen."

"That is true, but no one could have survived for long in freezing water." Tess stood.

"We can search the riverbank again. I will show you where we figured he ended up, but there was no sign of him. If he made it to the other side of the river we're out of luck in searching for him over there. No one on that side saw any sign of him."

"Unless you know someone with a boat."

"Nope."

"What do you think would be left of him at this point?" Tess shivered as her mind conjured an image of murky black water swallowing her uncle, chewing him up then depositing him onto the riverbank. "Let's go." She said, jumping down the four steps in one leap.

They grabbed their sticks from beneath the verandah, stashed for safekeeping, and clacked along the boardwalks to the river west of the city beneath the ancient landslide. The ravens called to one another from the trees.

Tess and Henry headed downstream as far as they could go before the rocky cliff touched the water. They pushed through the trees to the river's edge. A log floated past, swept up in the swift river current, bobbing up and down. They searched under logs and poked their walking sticks between rocks along the shore.

"This is useless. We would have to go further downriver," said Henry. "Your uncle would have floated a long ways down."

"What if he made his way to shore?"

"Maybe. Then what? He would have been too cold to pull himself to safety."

Tess's head tingled. The river hid many secrets beneath its silent surface, swallowing trees and bodies out of sight. She was used to ocean waves rolling onto shore with a soothing rhythm. A lump caught in her throat and she wanted to give in to her sadness but Henry would laugh at her. What if she never saw the ocean again?

They turned back toward town, and a dense thicket of birch blocked the path along the edge of the water so they climbed the bank, moved past the trees then crept through smaller bushes down to the river's edge. Neither felt like going for a swim.

A piece of leather flapped in an eddy of water, stuck between two branches.

"What is that?" Tess's heart jumped as she made her way towards it, poking it with her stick before pulling it free. An old leather boot dangled from her fingers. "Maybe it was Uncle Beau's boot." She held it between two fingers and examined the sodden object, dripping with icy water. How does one's shoe come off in the water? Uncle Beau would have tied his laces securely unless that's why he tripped. Maybe his foot got caught between rocks and his shoe was yanked off. Tess shuddered. It looked too small to be her uncle's.

"Naw. A lot of junk was left by the prospectors."

"That must have been an exciting time to live in Dawson City. A lot more exciting than it is lately." Tess threw the boot into the water and watched it float downstream.

They made their way along the bank until the trees thinned. Through the leaves Tess saw a long stretch of black sand. She gasped and pushed through the branches until she stood on the beach. "I didn't know there was a beach."

"There are beaches in some spots, mostly outside of town. The docks hog the river in town. We don't swim much, it's too cold, but I like to look for frogs."

Tess pushed her toe into the sand. "We should make a sandcastle." She chose a spot next to the water, and laying her stick beside her, crouched to move it into a pile. As she scooped sand into piles and formed walls and turrets, her eyes filled with tears blurring her vision. She blinked, then wiped her eyes with her sleeve. It wasn't the same without her father.

"Naw, let's look for frogs."

Tess stared at her sandcastle for a moment then jumped to her feet. She trudged along behind Henry. "Sandcastles are for babies anyway."

Further along, Henry crouched then sprang forward cupping his hands. "Got you." He stood with his hands closed and turned toward Tess opening them slightly. "See?"

Tess peered through his fingers at the tiny frog blinking at her. "Ew, he's kind of cute, in a slimy sort of way. Can I hold him?"

Henry held his hands over hers and let the frog drop.

It immediately took advantage of Tess's inexpert frog-handling skills and launched itself into the air, landing in the water.

Tess groaned. "Sorry. I'll find another one."

An hour passed as the two children searched the bank, each catching and releasing frogs. Tess's skirt was soaked, but she didn't care. "It finally feels like summer."

"What do you mean? It's been summer for a couple weeks already."

Tess shook her head, grabbing her walking stick. "Never mind."

Branches cracked behind them, and the two children jumped. They froze as branches rustled and broke.

"What if it's a bear?" Tess whispered as she scrambled up the bank and tripped, falling to the ground. Her muscles tensed as she stared at the mass of green leaves and branches where they had emerged.

Henry was close behind, falling onto the dirt beside her. "I don't hear anything."

They sat on the bank breathing heavily.

"It wasn't a bear," Henry whispered.

"What is that?"

Before Henry could answer, a large figure appeared from behind a bush and they scrambled backward, pushing at the ground with their feet.

"You rotten kids, why are you spying on me?"

Henry struggled to his feet then grabbed Tess's hand to help her stand. "It's Old Bert. He's crazy," he whispered.

"I know." Tess clutched her walking stick with clenched fingers and glared at the old man. "We were not spying on you. You frightened us. Why were you spying on us?"

"This is my claim, and you are trespassing." Bert shook his finger in their direction, glaring at them from under scruffy grey eyebrows.

"We are on official business, investigating a case, a missing body, my Uncle Beau."

"I haven't seen a body. I only see ghosts." Old Bert narrowed his eyes as he stared at her, tapping the side of his nose with a gnarled, tobacco-stained finger. "Tough egg, soft shell."

"See? I told you he's crazy. We should go." Henry inched backward with his hands in front of him as if to calm an unpredictable wild animal.

Crazy Bert took one step closer to Tess speaking slowly. "Your name is Tess. I remember you." He pulled at his beard then pointed to the docks. "What are you investigating? All I saw was two men arguing that day. Jeepers, I can't remember ten minutes ago but I sure remember that day."

Tess looked at Henry and both raised an eyebrow.

"What were they arguing about?" Tess pulled out her notebook, licked the tip of the pencil as she gazed at him expectantly. Men argued all the time but maybe that argument had involved her Uncle Beau.

"You expect me to remember something someone said weeks ago?" He pulled off his battered leather hat and ran his arm across his forehead.

"Of course, you just finished saying so. I promise I won't ask you what happened ten minutes ago."

"Naw. Can't remember." He sniffed, avoiding her stare. "Besides, I was too far away."

Tess groaned. He may have witnessed an important clue but they would never know the true story.

"You kids skedaddle. I don't like being spied on." He jabbed his thumb toward town then disappeared through the branches, muttering to himself. "Silence. Everyone stop talking at once, you'll get your turn. Now, who shall we say is the murderer?"

They ran towards town as fast as they could, not stopping until they reached Front Street.

In front of a lumber yard, Tess bent forward with her hands on her knees to catch a breath. "What do you figure Crazy Bert was doing down by the river? Did you hear what he said? He knows something." She stood and glanced up and down the boardwalk. "The other day I saw him outside his cabin panning for gold and he wasn't using water. He said he knows if there is gold in his pan by smelling the dirt."

Henry pinched his chin with his thumb and forefinger, mocking her curiosity. "Bert's just a crazy old man. Is that against the law? Should we alert the authorities?"

"Not funny. I think Old Bert is smarter than he lets on." Tess crossed her arms. "He remembered my name." She paused. Her mouth fell open. "Hey, he saw you. You are officially not a ghost."

"I told you, he sees ghosts. Didn't you hear him? We should stay away from him." Henry jumped off the boardwalk, landing in a muddy rut then ran down the center of the road.

Tess ran after him, careful to stay out of the mud.

Henry slowed so she could catch up and they wandered along the edge of town past log cabins and tiny houses with tin siding.

Flowers and vegetable plants filled the front yards, taking full advantage of the constant sunlight.

Henry stopped and surveyed a garden. He dropped to his knees, rummaged among the plants and pulled out two carrots by their feathery tops. He stood and handed one to Tess.

She took a step back, glancing around and shaking her head. "I do not steal."

"Come on Tess, don't be a sour puss." He held the carrot under her nose, waving the leafy tail.

"Stop that." Tess scrunched up her face and turned away, but the earthy young carrot transported her to their beloved backyard, and she reluctantly took it. Tess rubbed off the dirt and savored the nostalgic fragrance before biting off a piece and chewing it into sweet, juicy mulch. She reveled in the familiar crunch of garden soil between her teeth. She wished she was back in Vancouver playing on the beach with Sally. Her lips quivered and her world blurred through tears.

"Hey, get outta there." A woman waved her broom from the porch then marched down the steps toward them.

Tess dropped her carrot and ran.

Henry, with his heightened sense of alertness was far ahead of Tess, almost slipping off the boardwalk as he turned the corner at a gallop.

Tess turned the corner moments later and bumped into Henry who had his ear firmly caught within the fingers of the tallest man she had ever seen, taller than her Uncle Beau, but she had been five at the time.

The man in uniform, a North West Mounted Police officer, raised his eyebrow as Tess skidded into Henry.

"I see you acquired an accomplice, Master Henry." The corners of his mouth lifted in a fleeting smile, creasing the outer edges of his eyes.

The officer's eyes were the same chocolate brown as her father's. To Tess, they represented trust and protection.

"I've never seen her before." Henry wrinkled his nose at Tess. "I don't play with girls." Henry waved his hand. "Run along, little girl." He mouthed the word, *Go*.

Tess froze. Before she could control her reaction and run away, she gasped and shook her head, crossing her arms in front. "He told me he was a ghost. I didn't know what to believe, but you can see him as clearly I can."

"Absolutely, Miss. He is clear as mud, and twice as slippery." The officer let go of Henry's ear and laughed. "Maybe you can steer him in the right direction, keep him on the straight and narrow so his parents won't have to worry about him. The other townspeople would appreciate it."

Tess lowered her eyes to avoid his gaze. "Yes, Sir."

"Sergeant Roberts, at your service." He touched his hat and his eyes twinkled as he straightened the jacket of his uniform but his face grew stern as he glared at Henry. "I mean it. No more antics."

Tess glared at Henry who grinned at her as if it was a joke. Her cheeks grew warm as she raised her chin to meet Sergeant Robert's gaze, and her mouth quivered. "We won't cause trouble, I promise. Right, Henry?" She scowled. How mortifying to be noticed by an officer of the law and associated with a known lawbreaker.

Henry stuck out his chin and snickered, kicking a loose board.

Tess kicked his shin.

"Yeah," he mumbled.

"Glad to hear it." Sergeant Roberts clasped his hands behind his back and inhaled, expanding his chest then letting out a loud sigh. "First order of business is making amends to Mrs Peters."

Henry shook his head, taking a step back, wildly searching for an escape route.

Tess grabbed his arm, pulling him along as they followed Sergeant Roberts back to the garden, and the woman with the broom.

FORTY-SIX

Fred arrived at his usual time to purchase cinnamon rolls for his daily attempt to visit Molly.

"Morning, Fred."

"How are you this fine morning?" Fred removed his hat and surveyed the baked goods on display.

"Better than yesterday but there is room for improvement." Clara dusted her hands and placed two cinnamon rolls into the basket.

"I need three, today. I promised Tess."

"Tess?"

"Mrs Bruin's niece. I believe you met her the other day."

Clara wrinkled her brow. "I did? Oh yes, the little girl who was too shy to speak."

"Did you scare her off, Clara?"

Clara laughed. "Not intentionally. I should work on my customer service skills." She laid a red and white checkered cloth over the basket and handed it to Fred.

Fred chuckled. "Why change now?"

"Give my best to Molly. Is she feeling better?"

"As far as I know. Her sister keeps a tight rein on Madam Molly's visiting hours. These cinnamon rolls are my access ticket." He raised the basket. "Thank you, Clara. Have a successful day. See you tomorrow."

Clara nodded as she set the rest of the rolls on a tray before serving two ladies who had entered the bakery.

FORTY-SEVEN

Tess lay in bed staring at the ceiling. Her mother rose early, helping serve the breakfast crowd. Tess was dressed, lying on her bed, waiting for her aunt's doctor. Her clenched stomach grumbled as she turned on her side and stared at the suspicious jar clutched in her fist. With her heart skipping a beat she realized she should wait downstairs and leapt off the bed, skipping down the steps two at a time.

Muffled voices floated through the closed door, and moments later the doctor rushed past Tess.

"Sir," She called, running to catch up with him before he left the hotel.

The doctor stopped in the lobby and turned slowly. "May I help you young lady?"

"Is my aunt going to be well again?"

Theo raised his head from behind the desk.

"In time, yes. Are you doing your part to make her comfortable? Not too much noise. Don't stomp around like you kids do."

Tess's fingers tightened around the jar as she lifted it toward the doctor. "Can you tell me if this is poison?" She quickly glanced at Theo then at the doctor. She would explain to Theo later.

The doctor raised his eyebrow as he took the jar and examined it closely. Chuckling, he handed it back to her. "Do you enjoy wasting my time with your jokes? What are you up to?"

"It's not a joke. I think the chef is poisoning my aunt. He wants to take over her restaurant."

"What a preposterous notion. Does your mother know you are making up stories and accusing people? I have a good mind to talk to her before I leave."

"No, please don't. I wasn't making it up. Chef Pierre mixes a special drink for her every day. It smells terrible. I put the clues together and wanted to ask a trustworthy expert. If it is not poisonous, what is it?"

"Saffron is an expensive spice. You best get it back to Chef Pierre's kitchen as soon as possible before he takes the meat cleaver to you."

Tess brought her hand to her mouth and gasped.

The doctor's lips curled into a smile and he winked. "I'm joking. Maybe you should leave the medical advice to me and go play with your dolls. Don't worry your pretty little head about matters that do not concern you." He patted his medical bag, adjusted his hat then left.

Embarrassment simmered and flowed through the veins in her cheeks, breaking through the surface to announce to the world how stupid she felt. She glanced at Theo, who had lowered his head and was scribbling furiously in the ledger.

She raised her hands to cool her skin to no avail. How dare he treat her like a child? She pounded her fists against her legs. She hated being in limbo, no longer a child but not quite an adult.

"Everything alright, Miss Tess?" asked Theo. The corners of his mouth quivered and his eyes twinkled.

"Don't you wonder why my aunt doesn't seem to be getting better?"

"It is not my place. I just work here." Theo raked his fingers through his hair. "Trust me. The chef is not trying to poison your aunt."

"How would you know?" Tess crossed her arms and ran down the hall. She froze at the parlor door. Molly and her mother entered from the bedroom.

Tess didn't feel like talking to them and moved toward the end of the hall to hide in an alcove past the door. She would be mortified if they saw her burning cheeks. She would die if they questioned Theo.

"You are a dear sister, Anna. I don't know what I would do without you."

"You will have to manage without me this morning. I have a few errands to run. Will you be alright when Fred arrives?"

"I told Tess to meet me in the parlor. Fred is bringing her a cinnamon roll, too."

"Of course, you mentioned that. I apologize for my failing memory these days."

"Understandable, Anna, don't be hard on yourself. One person alone cannot do everything to run a hotel and restaurant. I have staff to help wherever needed."

Anna lowered her voice. "I have my doubts about a few of them."

Tess held her hand over her mouth to stifle a gasp.

"What are you saying? I have the greatest trust in all of my staff."

"You may be right. I don't know them well."

"I won't be gone long."

"Thank you, dear sister."

Tess waited for her mother to disappear into the dining room. Mr Barrett's voice traveled down the corridor.

Theo spoke.

Trapped for the moment, Tess waited while Mr Barrett strode past into the parlor.

Tess was anxious to return the jar to the kitchen before her theft was discovered. Chef Pierre may not be a murderer but he had a bad temper. She would have to wait until after the parlor visit, unable to sneak into the kitchen without her aunt and Mr Barrett noticing.

FORTY-EIGHT

Fred smoothed his hair, running his fingers along his mustache to the tips, and brushed an invisible fluff off his lapel. He cleared his throat then smiled as he carried his morning offering into the parlor.

Molly sat with her eyes closed but opened them upon his presence, subtly touching her handkerchief to her nose.

"Tess will be arriving soon."

Molly motioned to a black-leather wingback chair across from her.

"Good morning, Madam. I trust you slept well?" He set the basket on a table next to a stack of three plates.

Molly lifted the red and white checked cloth, inhaling deeply.

"I never get tired of the smell of cinnamon, the familiar scent of a loving home."

Fred placed a cinnamon roll on a plate and handed it to Molly.

"I feel better but my doctor recommends two weeks of rest before I return to work. Thank goodness for Anna."

"You take as much time as possible. No sense wearing yourself out. Mrs Douglas has been a godsend. Where is your sister today?" Fred asked, inwardly pleased.

"Theo had a request from the lumberyard to check out a problem with a bill but Anna offered to take care of it. We have a large group checking in this morning."

"You should have asked me. The lumberyard is no place for a woman."

Molly frowned. "Fred, you know full well she is more than capable of handling the men."

Fred lowered his head. "My apologies. You are right as usual. And, may I say, you are looking lovely this morning." He took her delicate hand in his.

Molly smiled and pulled her hand away. "Thank you, Fred. Please don't."

"I am delighted we have time to ourselves this fine morning."

"Tess will be along shortly. She told me you promised to bring her a cinnamon roll."

Fred frowned slightly then softened his gaze. "Of course, dear Tess. How is she finding things in a foreign place such as Dawson City?"

"She manages to keep busy. Nellie has her helping with the housekeeping."

"She is a great help, I am sure." Fred nodded. "This is a difficult time for you, and it must be a struggle to oversee Beau's businesses."

"They are my responsibility, as well. Anna has been invaluable in helping while I am unwell."

"I am concerned your doctor has not been successful in remedying what ails you, dear Madam."

"What ails me has no known remedy." Molly lowered her head. A tear dropped onto her hand resting in her lap.

"Allow me to present an offer to take the burden from your shoulders." Fred pulled the papers from his pocket and spread them on the side table. "Your signature is all that is needed to alleviate your stress and worry."

"What do you mean?"

"I am prepared to take on full ownership of the dredge operation and am willing to pay you a handsome dollar amount in exchange. The offer stands for your other businesses, too. Think of the possibilities. You could travel to Vancouver with your sister and niece and take up residence in the city, away from the solemn reminders of a once happier time."

"Thank you, Fred, but I cannot leave. My life is here, with Beau."

Fred nodded slightly. "I understand your attachment and will continue to look out for you. It is my duty as a friend. If I may be so bold, consider it a token of my feelings toward you which have grown stronger by the day."

"Unthinkable at this moment. Beau has been gone but a few weeks."

"Forgive me, Madam, I lost my head for a moment as my heart took control. I will rein it in for both our sakes." He picked up the papers and put them back in his pocket, a thin smile wavered on his lips.

FORTY-NINE

Tess stopped outside the open door of the parlor in disbelief. Mr Barrett had expressed his feelings for her aunt. Why did she turn down his offer to buy her companies? That would have been a perfect solution. The sooner they left Dawson for Vancouver, the better, as far as she was concerned.

She put the jar in her pocket, then coughed loudly before entering the parlor. She was anxious to return the expensive spice before it was missed.

Tess kissed Molly's cheek. "How are you this morning? Has the doctor given you good news?"

"Not particularly. Mr Barrett brought us the most delicious cinnamon rolls. Help yourself." Aunt Molly gestured to the basket on the table.

Tess curtsied. "How thoughtful of you, Mr Barrett." She lifted a heavy, sticky roll onto her plate, inhaling cinnamon and caramel as she sat next to her aunt.

Molly and Fred looked at one another then focussed on Tess, watching her as she ate.

Molly spoke. "What are you up to today?"

"When lunch is finished, I will help set tables for dinner and hopefully spend the afternoon reading."

"What are you reading these days? Maybe I can rustle up reading material for you." Fred set his plate on a lace-covered table.

"That would be lovely," Tess said, between bites. Her fingers stuck together from the glorious sweet syrup. "I love mysteries, and I want to be a detective when I grow up."

"Tess, goodness, what nonsense. Why not become a teacher like your father?"

Fred chuckled. "Interesting choice. I will find compelling stories for you."

Tess stood, touching her sticky fingers together then pulling them apart. She stood, turned away from her aunt and wiped her hands on her skirt. "I should go. Thank you for your thoughtfulness, Mr Barrett."

Mr Barrett stood and bowed.

Tess curtsied then turned to Molly. "I hope you feel better soon."

Tess snuck into the kitchen. Fortune was in her favor. Chef Pierre and Carl stood on the landing outside smoking. She replaced the jar on the shelf then washed her hands.

In the dining room she joined her mother in setting tables for dinner. The back door slammed as Chef Pierre and Carl returned to the kitchen. Soon, the air was filled with the fragrant aroma of garlic and beef roasting in the oven.

Tess placed the last napkin and headed toward the kitchen, in time to see Carl pull off his apron. He grabbed his cap and hurried out the back door.

Chef Pierre reached into the cabinet and pulled out the jar of saffron. "What on earth?" He carried it to the sink and wiped the sticky jar.

Tess gulped, backing out of the kitchen. She ran through the lobby and out the door, hurrying toward the back of the hotel. She caught sight of Carl and followed him down the alley.

He glanced back and quickened his pace.

Tess stopped and shrunk against a wall, ducking behind an open door before he spotted her. She wrinkled her nose at the acrid tobacco smoke, and horrid, unidentifiable smells. Her eyes watered and she peeked around the door, squinting in Carl's direction. She wiped her eyes with her handkerchief then held it to her mouth.

Carl had disappeared.

Tess leaned against the building. She had failed her first chase. She looked down at the ground, muddy and covered in garbage, and wiped her boots on the edge of the step.

"Hey little girl, you shouldn't be hanging around here unless you're looking for trouble." A lanky young man with a red handlebar mustache and bushy beard leaned out the door with a spittoon in one hand ready to toss the contents into the alley.

Tess shook her head and stepped back. "I… I apologize. I was looking for…" She glanced past him into the saloon catching a glimpse of a beautiful woman dressed in a tight red corset and velvet skirt, laughing with a smartly dressed man smoking a cigar. Her mouth opened in amazement and wonder. She thought saloons were awful places, frequented by horrible people. The woman glanced at Tess, her eyes widened then she lowered her head and looked away, moving out of the line of sight.

"I'm sorry. I shouldn't be here."

"You got that right, kid." The man gave her a one-second head start then dumped the contents of the spittoon on the spot where Tess had stood.

She caught a disgusting whiff of tobacco and alcohol soup as she took off down the alley toward her hotel. She made her way around to the front and fell onto the little bench on the verandah and stared at her boots caked with mud. A tear splashed onto the mud. What was she thinking? She had no business poking her nose into things she did not understand. Tess had put herself in grave danger, and without thinking of the consequences followed a suspicious man into perilous surroundings. Maybe not grave danger, but terrible, horrible, smelly surroundings, not too perilous but certainly not meant for little girls.

Tess looked up, half expecting Henry to be standing in front of her ready to say I told you so but she was alone. *Face it, Tess, you will always be alone. Mother is too busy to spend time with you. Aunt Molly is ill and might die, or worse, marry Mr Barrett. Father is not coming back, and neither is Uncle Beau. Face reality and grow up. Find presentable friends who won't get you in trouble. Give up your ridiculous plans to be a detective and leave the danger to people who can handle it, like Sergeant Roberts.*

The verandah floor was wet with tears and mud beneath her feet. She moved her foot and smeared mud onto the floor boards, feeling the grit and smiling at the mess. Exhilaration flowed through her as she remembered the thrill of chasing a suspect down a seedy alley before losing him in a moment of panic at being seen. Next time she wouldn't be so careless.

Next time.

Tess wiped her face with the back of her hand and pulled out her notebook.

FIFTY

Fred rode down Front Street, nodding to men and women as he passed. He spotted Old Bert near the end of the docks. He dismounted, tied his horse to the post, and walked toward him.

Bert, startled, turned to walk away, but Fred quickened his pace and caught up to him.

"Going somewhere?" Fred said under his breath as he smiled at the people nearby. "I'll walk with you." He held his hands behind his back and walked beside the old prospector until they were away from the crowds, at the river's edge below the ancient landslide called Moosehide.

"You had pertinent information for me?"

Old Bert stopped. He wrinkled his brow as he stared at Fred.

"I did?"

"Just the other day, you accosted me on my way to my buggy. You said you had information I would pay to hear."

"Can't say I remember seeing you."

Fred's shoulders relaxed as he realized Old Bert was not a threat. He was an old man with more than his share of problems.

"What's this I hear about you bothering the new visitors to our quiet town?" Fred pulled his hat lower over his eyes as he stared at the flowing river.

"You know me better than anyone, Fred. Just greeting the newcomers."

"Not your job, old man." Fred clicked a mint against his teeth as he talked. He pulled a bag from his coat pocket and offered one to Bert who shook his head. "Your job is to avoid talking to anyone, do we have an understanding?"

"Like I told you, I won't tell anyone about that day. I don't know what you and Beau Bruin were arguing about. It was none of my concern."

"We were not arguing. We were discussing business." Fred stiffened, closing his hands into fists at his sides. Old Bert was a threat after all.

"Strange way to discuss business."

Fred turned to glare at the old man beside him. "Beau's death was an accident. I should know. I was there."

"Whatever you say. But let me remind you, it is in your best interests to stop harassing me. People will begin to notice you enjoy spending time with a crazy old man."

"What would you have me do? Allow you to go around town spouting off your mouth whenever you feel like it, or whenever the whiskey loosens your tongue?"

"No one listens to me. They think I'm mad."

"We both know that's not true. It's all an act so people stay away from you. All that writing you're doing is useless. Trust me no one wants to read your ramblings."

"Maybe they do. I can make up whatever stories I want and someone will be interested. Maybe even Sergeant Roberts."

"Do not threaten me."

"Why not? It's an entertaining game."

"You say one word and you'll never know what hit you."

"Kind of like what happened to Beau?" Bert snickered.

"Get out of my sight." Fred turned away from him and stared at the river.

Bert staggered down the road toward his cabin.

Fred's shoulders sagged. "It was an accident," he whispered. His legs shook as he moved to a nearby boulder and sat for a moment. "I miss you Beau, but your idea of conducting business would have run us into the ground. Give me a year and I'll have both our businesses built into the biggest empire in the Yukon. In your honor. Rest in peace, friend." He stood, tipped his hat toward the river then turned and walked along the beach, oblivious to the sandcastle that stood in his way, crushing it with his boots.

FIFTY-ONE

After Tess's run-in with the saloon keeper she searched for Henry, scanning the boardwalks, peeking under porches and bushes. Her mother and aunt were occupied with the hotel and restaurant so Tess took advantage of her new independence. Growing up was looking better all the time. Henry was nowhere to be found. Tess passed Old Bert as she ran toward the junkyard.

"Tess. How are you today, young lady?"

Tess stopped and turned around. "How do you know my name? I only told you once."

"Tough egg, soft shell." Bert's wild eyes softened and crinkled at the corners as he grinned.

"What are you talking about? Is that why they call you crazy?"

"T. E. S. S." Bert tilted his head, waiting for her to understand. "That's my system for remembering things like names. I guess you could say I sound crazy. People give me funny looks when I come out with my peculiar phrases but I enjoy impressing them with my exceptional memory."

"T. Tough. E. Egg. That is brilliant." Tess brought her hands to her mouth. "What was your phrase for Henry?"

"Henry?" Bert narrowed his eyes, searching. "Is that the little boy who's haunting you?"

"He's not a ghost. Sergeant Roberts already confirmed that, so don't try to pull the wool over my eyes."

Bert chuckled. "Half egg, not ready yet."

Tess laughed. He was right. Henry was a little kid. "Not ready yet? Why?"

"He will tell you when he is ready."

"Have you seen him around lately?"

"At least once a day. He and I write stories together."

"You're a writer?"

"Indeed. There are countless stories in this part of the world. Mystery, intrigue, danger. You name it, the gold rush had it."

"That explains why you babbled on about murder the other day."

"Murders are a handy way of getting rid of problem characters. The ones who refuse to do what I want in the story. They do that, you know, take control of the pen and write themselves a better, more interesting role."

"I try to write every day, but mostly take notes on mysteries I want to solve."

"Daily writing is imperative, but often my writing overlaps reality and that drives me crazy, makes me see ghosts that are not there."

"But, not Henry, right?"

"Nope. Henry is very much alive, but Henry is dead." Bert points toward town. "I believe you will find Henry near your hotel."

Tess was confused. "You are not making sense. I was just there."

Bert stared at her, a blank look in his eyes.

He had already forgotten their conversation.

"I should go." Tess waved.

Bert nodded, stepped onto his porch, and pulled the wooden door open, ducking his head to avoid missing the low doorframe before disappearing into his cabin.

Tess flew down the boardwalk toward the hotel. Thoughts tumbled over each other in her mind as she ran. She had to talk to Henry. The verandah at the hotel was empty, so she carried on to Front Street, breathless and gasping.

Outside the row of stores, Henry sat on a bench, chewing the stub of a cigar and listening to the old miners who had stayed behind, too tired to continue chasing the siren call of gold.

"Henry, there you are. I've been looking all over for you."

"Maybe you should've looked here first."

"Funny. We need to talk. Carl is up to something."

"Who's Carl?"

"He washes dishes at the hotel. I followed him down an alley but I lost him. We have to find out what he's up to."

"Too late. He's probably back at the hotel already." Henry sniffed the air. "Let's see what's cooking."

They crept along the storefronts toward the bakery until they could peek in through the window and spy on the baker.

Henry nudged me. "Look."

Clara carried a tray of dainty cakes to a shelf near the window then placed them on a silver tray before returning to the back of the store.

"Watch this." Henry tiptoed toward the door, inched his way into the store, grabbed two petit fours and ran out again.

Tess hurried toward him as he held out the sweets but tripped and bumped into him. They fell backward onto a wooden table filled with bread and buns.

Tess lay sprawled among the loaves of bread.

Henry took off running.

Clara yelled. "What on earth is going on out here?" She spotted Tess and immediately grabbed her arm. "You, again."

Henry disappeared around the corner.

"You best tell me what happened or I will call the authorities." She shook Tess who was too shocked and frightened to speak. Clara yelled at a man riding past. "Get me Sergeant Roberts."

The man turned and smiled at her, pulling on the reins to slow his horse. "What have we here? Is that young Tess? Allow me to smooth things over. No need to get the authorities involved, is there?"

Tess closed her eyes and groaned. Must he always stick his nose into other people's business?

Fred jumped down from the buggy and strode towards the shop.

Clara's cheeks flushed a vivid flaming red. "Fred Barrett, you can't sweet talk me this time. Look at the loaves of bread, a whole morning's work ruined."

"Now, now, I'm sure it was an accident, was it not, Tess?"

Tess looked down at the pink petit four squashed between her fingers and nodded her head. She was doomed. And Henry let her down, again.

"I dare say, a visit from Sergeant Roberts may push this young lady into a life of crime rather than scaring her into obeying authority. Think of the service to society you would be offering, taking this delicate flower under your wing and teaching her responsibility. Let her help you in your shop to pay off the damages. Keep her out of trouble. I'm sure her mother would be grateful."

Clara narrowed her eyes as she surveyed Tess. Her eyes softened, but she pressed her lips together in a thin line. A tiny smile played on her lips.

Tess felt two inches tall under her scrutiny. She dared not say a word. Words that came out of children's mouths in the heat of the moment were quickly grabbed, twisted into unrecognizable blobs, thrown onto the floor and stomped upon, regardless of their importance.

FIFTY-TWO

Fred patted Tess's shoulder then gestured to Clara. "Shall we discuss it in the back room?"

Tess inched toward the door.

"Have a seat, young lady. We won't be long." Fred spoke firmly before following Clara behind the counter and into the kitchen.

As Fred entered, Clara crossed her arms over her floury apron. "What are you doing, Fred? I don't hire children."

"She is Molly's niece. Think of it as a favor to her. Get the child out of her hair for a few hours."

"Has she been a menace? Molly doesn't need chaos to continue to wreak havoc in her life." Clara threw her hands in the air then dropped them to her sides, launching a cloud of white powder. She turned to Fred. "Fine. If it will help my dear friend, give the child to me for a few hours a day and I'll straighten her out."

Fred chuckled. "Clara, you talk tough but everyone knows you are as sweet as the sugar sprinkled on your cakes."

"You didn't think so." Clara lowered her voice. "Tossing me aside so you could pursue the latest floozy at the dance hall."

"We both know I would have broken your heart."

"You made it stronger, impervious to sweet talk. I'm not the first queen of hearts you discarded, I'm sure." Clara smiled. "If the upstanding citizens of this city knew the real Fred Barrett, they would be scandalized."

Fred froze.

"Don't worry. Your secrets are safe with me." Clara patted his back then pushed him through the doorway into the bakery. She crossed her arms over her apron and towered above Tess as Fred stood behind Clara.

"Young lady, I have agreed to let you assist me a few hours a day until you pay off the damage."

Tess lowered her head, clasping her hands in front. "Yes, Madam." She gritted her teeth, angry at Fred. His actions were too familiar toward the baker and her. He was a stranger, a busybody, and he would never become her uncle, if she had anything to say in the matter.

FIFTY-THREE

Fred held the door as Tess made her way across the floor, dragging her feet.

"I will take you home. Your mother and aunt will be worried about you."

Tess's shoulders dropped. When her mother heard about what happened Tess would lose her freedom for the rest of the summer. This was not the kind of attention Tess wanted. She had to be careful what she wished for next time.

"You certainly are a take-charge kind of guy," said Clara.

"Glad I could help." Fred tipped his hat.

Clara held her palms up. "I'm sure you are." She rolled her eyes.

"I apologize for ruining your day. Thank you for giving me a chance to make amends." Tess turned to Fred. "You don't have to take me home. I don't need your help."

"I'm heading that way. Hop in."

Fred helped Tess onto his buggy and took her to the hotel. She dreaded her mother's reaction, hoping anger at Fred's overstep would overshadow her irresponsible actions. A tiny smile flickered on her lips. Excitement bounced against her rib cage, holding hands with her heart and spinning in circles, jumping up and down. She had a job. In a bakery. How magnificent was that?

Within minutes they were home. Fred helped her down and escorted her into the hotel.

Theo glanced up in surprise but remained silent.

They strode down the hall and into the parlor.

Anna and Molly looked up from their tea in shock.

Tess had pink frosting smeared across her front and mud on her boots from her wild goose chase. Her hair had escaped the braids and was full of bread crumbs.

"Fred, what has happened?" Molly reached for Anna's hand.

Anna stood abruptly. A splash of tea spilled on the carpet. "Are you hurt, Tess?" She looked at Fred. "What is the meaning of this?"

"Don't worry. Fate stepped in and I arrived on the scene in time to deflect a serious misfortune from befalling our young Tess. There was an incident at the Dufour Bakery. Tess inadvertently demolished Miss Clara's display."

"What were you doing?" Anna set her cup on the piano and folded her arms.

Tess opened her mouth to speak but Fred interrupted.

"All is taken care of. I talked to Miss Dufour, and she agreed to allow Tess to pay off the damages by working in the bakery."

"Work?" Anna brought her hand to her heart. "It is not your place to negotiate my daughter's punishment. She is too young."

"I am not. I think it would be fun. Please, Mother? It would be good to have something to keep me occupied."

"What about your chores in the hotel?"

"I will do them before I go to the bakery. Nellie won't mind."

"Mrs Douglas, it would be a few hours a day. Miss Dufour could use the help." Fred held his hat in his hands.

"I am appalled, Tess. Who has been leading you into trouble?" Anna moved toward Tess, her long skirt swishing against her ankles.

"He's nobody important. I promise you won't see me spending time with him."

"I am a wreck waiting to hear if James is alive, and you are running wild in the streets. It is time to grow up, Tess."

"I'm sorry, Mother." Tess truly was. Tomorrow she would start living and working towards becoming a responsible adult, and she couldn't wait.

FIFTY-FOUR

The next morning, Fred placed his hands behind his head and leaned back with his boots on the desk, watching the cigarette smoke float to the ceiling in lazy swirls after each puff. His morning coffee sat, untouched.

A bang at the door startled him, and he instinctively reached toward the top drawer. Weapons were illegal in town but the authorities didn't need to know. Fred required insurance against theft and threats.

The door knob turned.

"Who's there?"

Earl poked his head around the door. "What's got you on edge, little brother?"

"I have a plan that could make or break me." Fred motioned to the empty chair. "Sit."

"I am intrigued." Earl sat in the chair opposite the desk.

"You still got that body on ice?"

"Yep."

"Molly Bruin is stubborn and I am becoming impatient. I gave Beau an offer weeks ago, and he refused to take it. Mrs Bruin has also declined to sell to me. I'm done being nice."

"What offer was that?" Earl asked.

"To buy him out of the dredge operation so he could concentrate on the hotel and lumber business with his wife. I threw in an offer to buy their other assets as well, pennies on the dollar, of course. It's the way I do business."

"And you wonder why they refused." Earl shook his head.

"Beau and I had different ideas on how the dredge business should be run."

"Let me guess. He didn't find it good business sense to let funds go missing, misrepresent gold findings, and abuse the workers?"

"Beau insisted the crews were treated fairly. We would never have made a profit that way. Sometimes life has a funny way of working out."

"What a shame. I was beginning to like Beau."

"Shut up." Fred scowled.

FIFTY-FIVE

After morning chores, Tess walked with Nellie the short distance to the Dufour Bakery.

"Despite what Mother says, I am old enough to help in the bakery, and I am capable of walking there by myself. I wish she would trust me." Tess wished her mother had offered to walk with her, to show she cared, and to protect her daughter from the grumpy baker.

"Trust is earned, Tess. Once it is lost, it takes a lot to regain. You can show your mother by behaving in a manner befitting a responsible young lady."

"I will. Thank you for walking with me. I must admit, the baker scares me."

"Don't worry. She has a heart of gold." Nellie patted Tess's arm with her gloved hand. "I am happy to help. Shall I pick you up when you are done?"

"I can find my way home. I'm not a child anymore."

"Technically you are, Tess, but I understand. Have fun."

Tess stood outside the bakery staring through the window as Nellie walked away, prolonging the moment when she would enter and become a baker's helper, hoping Miss Dufour was a kindly employer not prone to yelling or belittling her helpers.

Tess took a deep breath then exhaled as she turned the latch and entered the warm store. The glorious fragrance of yeast, sugar and cinnamon brought an image of a mysterious candy jungle to mind, wet bark, glistening leaves, and thousands of birds singing in the trees. She stood in the middle of the room and closed her eyes.

"I wasn't sure you would come."

Tess froze, opening her eyes wide as Clara's large voice boomed throughout the bakery from the back room.

"I am." Tess struggled to form a sentence as she spied five different kinds of cookies on a display shelf. "Here." Her mouth watered as she clasped her hands in front and waited for Clara, unsure if she should enter the kitchen area.

"I appreciate your integrity. Most young people lack the moral fiber of dependability and fine social skills these days." Clara brushed her hands together releasing a fine cloud of dusty white powder. "I can help you with those social skills, if you like." She snickered.

Tess licked her lips, tasting a subtle sweetness in the air, and the corners of her mouth curled into a smile. "I look forward to helping you as best I can, Madam."

"Call me Miss Clara, everyone does." Clara turned and headed into the back room.

Tess followed, concentrating on keeping her steps small and demure, setting a serious look on her face that showed she was mature and ready to work.

Clara took an apron from a hook near the back door and handed it to Tess. She smirked. "Why so sour?"

"I'm not a sourpuss. Did Henry tell you that?"

"Who? I was merely commenting on your facial expression. No need to be afraid. I won't fatten you up so I can eat you." She winked.

Tess giggled. She had read the fairy tale many times, knowing she would have used a better trail marker than bread crumbs.

"Have you any experience baking, Tess?"

"I help Mother in the kitchen. She promised she would teach me how to bake when I was old enough."

"Old enough? How old are you?"

"Almost twelve."

"My goodness, your mother didn't do you any favors. I began baking when I was five. My mother fell ill and my cooking healed her. I'm sure you would have done the same if you had been given the chance."

"I want to help my mother, and my aunt, but they don't think I am capable. They think of me as a child."

"What a shame. They underestimate you." Clara looked at Tess, tilting her head to one side. She picked up a bowl and handed it to Tess. "Let's see how you do with cookies first."

"Yes, please." Tess bounced on her toes. "I love cookies."

FIFTY-SIX

Fred was in a bad mood, ignoring the bartender and the saloon patrons as he stormed into his office after his business lunch. The investor was not willing to part with his money without evidence Fred was in control of the dredge company.

His cinnamon roll plan was not working. He knew his charm and good looks would wear her down eventually but time was not on his side. The sister and niece were not helping, either. He had to figure out how to get them out of the way, all the way back to where they had come from if possible.

He pulled the office door closed and hung his hat on the rack beside his door. Spying the crystal decanter he stalked over to the side table, poured an ounce of the finest whiskey money could buy and threw it back, ignoring the burn as the amber liquid flowed down his throat. He stood and stared out the window, then refilled the glass. Deep in thought he carried it with him to his desk and dropped into the soft leather chair.

Earl walked in unannounced.

"Don't you knock?" Fred growled.

"What's eating you today? Every time I see you you're scowling." Earl dragged a wooden chair across the floor and sprawled in it with his long legs in front and arms folded across his chest.

"Tell me how we're going to make sure I get what I want?"

"Say the word. I got guys who will make it happen." Earl chewed on a toothpick.

Fred raised his glass and grinned.

"A little early to be drinking heavily, ain't it?" Earl raised an eyebrow. He jumped to his feet and poured a drink, returning to his chair.

"Time to shake things up."

"You won't believe this. There's a rumor going around town there was a case of food poisoning in the Grizzly Hotel restaurant."

"Excellent, keep it up and we'll empty the place in no time. She'll have no choice but to sell to me."

FIFTY-SEVEN

Tess arrived early the next morning as Clara pulled a batch of bread from the oven.

Clara laughed. "Perfect timing."

Tess inhaled the rich aroma hovering in the air. Sadness overcame her as the smell of yeast and wood fire smoke brought forth a memory of their cozy kitchen in Vancouver.

Clara set the pans on the wooden table. She motioned to Tess. "Grab two plates. The butter is in a dish in the pantry."

Tess pulled the red and white checkered curtain aside and stepped into the tiny closet. She spied the delicate pink ceramic bowl and carefully set it on a stack of two plates then carried her precious cargo to the table.

Clara poured two cups of tea and set one beside each plate. "Sit. Let's get to know each other."

Tess sat at the table, her mouth watering as she watched Clara cut thick slices of the warm bread.

"Help yourself. I don't know about you but I work better on a full stomach." She patted her apron covering her round stomach. "You can help me test the product."

"Thank you. Why would you have to test your baking? You told me you are the best baker in town. But, I am happy to help in any way I can." Tess spread a generous glob of butter on her bread.

Clara pulled a chair back and sat. "Life is short and sweet, like me." She buttered a piece of soft bread then took a bite. "You remind me of myself when I was your age."

"Did you have a horse's mane of brown hair you had to braid every morning and night, too?"

"Your hair is lovely, Tess. Have you ever noticed how the sun brings out the cherry color in your dark chocolate brown locks?"

"My hair sounds delicious." Tess took a big bite of her bread.

"Indeed." Clara smiled. "I believe the more I bake, the whiter my hair gets. And I'm not talking grey. My hair is a permanent shade of confectioner sugar and flour." She winked and touched her hair. A poof of white powder launched and floated in the air.

"You could be a lady-in-waiting in the king's court." Tess munched, talking with her mouth full. She brought her hand to her mouth and swallowed. "Pardon me."

"I wonder if they sneezed a lot back then." Clara laughed.

Tess giggled. "I never thought of that."

Clara set her mouth in a thin line. "How is your aunt holding up?"

"Aunt Molly seems tired but she joined us for dinner and we had a marvelous time. She laughed a lot."

"Your presence must be doing her good."

"Not according to the doctor."

Clara sputtered. "That quack? He has no idea what's wrong with her. He would order chicken soup for a rooster if it complained of a cold."

"She is in mourning. I don't know how I can help her."

"Give her a reason to get better," said Clara as she slathered butter on another piece of bread.

"I was going to convince her to move back to Vancouver with us, but she said she'd never leave the Yukon. Her soul is buried here."

Clara nodded. "The North takes root in a person's heart pretty quickly. I can't explain it but I knew I was home the moment my feet touched the ground."

"Why did you come here?"

"The lure of excitement and untold riches. I used to be a ballerina." She chuckled. "A long time ago."

Tess widened her eyes.

"I worked in dance halls during the gold rush, but it was not the romantic career I dreamed it would be." Clara stared across the table deep in thought, her forehead creased and her eyes darkened.

"What happened?" Tess leaned her elbows on the table, cupping her chin in her hands.

"Nothing catastrophic. It was not a good fit for me. I was lucky to persuade an investor to help me open this bakery, and I have been blissfully dancing in my very own kitchen to the smell of vanilla and rose petals ever since."

"I'd be happy if I owned a bakery, too," said Tess.

Clara laughed. "Before I'm through with you, you will know how to bake bread, decorate cakes, and I might let you in on my secret cinnamon roll recipe someday." She tapped Tess's arm lightly, affectionately, and smiled.

They finished their bread then Clara showed her how to make frosting.

FIFTY-EIGHT

Fred sat at a table in the far corner of his saloon, swirling golden liquid around in the glass.

Earl grabbed a drink at the bar and joined him.

"Are you going to drown your sorrows in whiskey?"

"Shut up."

"Our problem has been solved."

Fred growled. "Which one?"

"The problem that has become rather pressing, in a pungent sort of way. My plan is brilliant. It takes care of two problems, and no one will connect them to you."

"I don't want to know the details. Best to keep my nose clean."

"You should be paying me double for doing your dirty work."

"Ma told me I could get away with anything if I kept my nose clean. No sense getting my hands dirty."

"No wonder her handkerchief smelled. She was forever wiping your snotty nose." Earl snarled.

"Charm and good looks will get you far, but cunning will take you to the finish line. I learned at an early age how to get what I wanted."

"I looked out for you when we were kids, kept the others off your back. The least you can do is share the wealth."

Fred drained his glass. "You have a mighty selective memory, brother. I remember you were the leader of the pack of dogs that dragged me through the mud by my boots. Left me hanging by my coat on the outhouse door."

"I taught you to stand up for yourself. Older and wiser, you know how the world works. These days you gotta pay for protection, and I'm the best, little brother."

"I know how the world works, that's why I am the boss. Don't forget it. No one crosses Fred Barrett."

"Hey, I'm on your side, remember?" Earl held his hands out, palms up. "How's Ma doing?"

"And, that, my brother, is your biggest problem."

"What?"

"Ever wonder why I was the favorite? Did you ever give Ma anything but grief? I made sure Ma knew she was loved. Everyone needs a little acknowledgement and appreciation in life."

"She's Ma, always has been. Her job was to raise kids, make sure we were looked after and well fed. I'd say she did a pretty bad job of raising me and my brothers."

"It's tough to raise ignorant, selfish brats who don't respect anyone. At least I respect the people I take money from, appreciate their hard work to earn it, admire the way they can be easily conned out of it." Fred smirked.

"Get off your high horse, Fred. I work hard for my money. You never had to do physical labor in your life."

"I've done my share. That chain gang in California was no picnic. They had us digging graves for days in the hot sun. I knew I should have listened to my gut before stealing that prospector's grub. Even made it look like the culprit was a wild dog. I learned plenty from that mistake."

Earl lifted his eyebrow and curled his lip. "You got off easy."

Fred ignored him. "I learned to eliminate the obstacles first before approaching the prize."

FIFTY-NINE

Henry peeked through the bakery window, waving his arm. Tess scowled at him.

He stuck out his tongue and ran away.

Irritated, Tess pushed the straw broom across the floor in quick, jerking motions, swatting at the corners of the store, causing crumbs and flour to rise into the air.

"Tess, slow down. We don't need a dust tornado spoiling the food. Please be careful," said Clara as she carried a tray of cakes over to the shelf in the window. "Once you have swept the floor, I guess that's it for today. Where does the time go?"

Tess finished sweeping the floor then removed her apron and hung it on the hook by the kitchen door. "I lost track of the time, too. It's past lunchtime and I'm not hungry."

"Might be all the bread and leftover cake filled you up." Clara winked. "Out with you. Enjoy your afternoon."

"I will." Tess stepped onto the boardwalk and glanced around. Despite her irritation with Henry, she missed him, but would never admit it to him. He was nowhere to be seen, so she walked past the construction and turned the corner onto the road leading to the hotel.

"Hey, Sourpuss, got any cake for me?" Henry jumped out from behind a dusty bush.

Tess stopped and crossed her arms. "You startled me." She narrowed her eyes. "Go away. I have nothing to say to you."

"Why? What did I do?"

Tess snorted. "You abandoned me, left me to take the blame for your mischievous behavior. You are no friend of mine." She moved around him, bumping his arm as she continued toward the hotel.

"Wait." Henry ran after her. "I'm sorry. I got scared."

"Leave me alone. You are nothing but trouble."

"Am not." Henry hopped from one foot to the other. "I gotta show you something."

"I am not going anywhere with you."

"It's important."

"I don't think so."

"Come on, admit it. You have fun when you're with me."

Tess stopped. "You call it fun to drag me to a cemetery, steal carrots and get caught by the police, run into crazy old men, and make me work to pay for damages you caused?"

"You get to help out in a bakery and eat all the cake you want."

"You are impossible." Tess stamped her foot. "I am being punished for your bad behavior."

Henry put his hands on his hips. "I am not bad."

"I didn't say you were, but you must stop getting into trouble."

"Would you rather sit back and do nothing but read all day?"

"Yes."

"I thought you said you wanted to help your aunt."

"I do, but we're just children. We can't do anything."

"Yes, we can. Follow me. I think I found your uncle's body."

Tess gasped, bringing both hands to her mouth. Could it be possible? She frowned, narrowing her eyes.

"Why are you lying to me? My uncle is gone forever. Maybe Mr Barrett is the only one who can help my aunt now."

"I am not lying."

"I don't believe you." Tess crossed her arms and glared at him.

"Suit yourself." Henry ran toward Front Street.

Tess hesitated then ran after him. "Wait for me."

They ran the length of the boardwalk past the construction and the Dufour Bakery to the other end of town.

Sawdust floated in the air, and wood piles lined the fence of a large lumber yard and mill. A sign beside the office door read "Bruin Mill."

Henry motioned to Tess to follow as he climbed the four-foot tall fence built of narrow wooden boards and posts.

Tess crossed her arms and shook her head.

"Come on, it's okay. No one will see us." Henry glanced toward the front of the lumber yard then back at Tess. "See? All clear."

Tess sighed, grasped one of the posts, stepped onto a slat halfway up and pulled herself over.

Henry led her to a towering pile of logs at the back of the yard, sneaking behind piles, staying out of sight of the workers. He searched behind a stack of wood then ran around to the front.

"I swear I saw a body back there."

"I don't see anything." Tess craned her neck to look, not keen on getting closer but stepped forward to scan the area. "I don't believe you."

"It's true. I saw a man lying face down on the ground. It could have been your uncle."

"Maybe it was a worker on his break, sleeping."

"Nope, this guy was dead, stiff as a board."

Tess shivered. "That is horrible. Stop lying. Why did you bring me here? You are giving me false hope, and I think it is cruel." She kicked the pile of logs.

The pile shifted slightly.

"I'm telling the truth." Henry protested.

"I have never known you to tell the truth yet. Let's get out of here. It's a waste of time looking for something that's not here." Tess stomped towards the front of the yard.

"Hey, kids get outta here." A stocky man waved his arm as he lumbered towards them.

Tess and Henry ran out of the yard toward the river.

At its edge, Tess put her hands on her hips and gasped for breath.

The Yukon River flowed past without a sound, ominous in its silent refusal to give up its secrets.

"Do not get me in trouble again, do you hear me? We must do this properly and go over the clues again. I wrote them in my notebook. We haven't properly tailed Carl yet."

"Carl is always in the kitchen washing dishes. I never see him leave except for breaks out back." Henry pulled a branch off a willow and whipped it around like a floppy sword.

"How would you know?"

Henry ran towards town. "Who cares?"

Tess sighed and ran after him.

They stopped to take a breath and sat on the edge of the boardwalk near the docks.

Tess pulled out her notebook and scanned her notes. "I don't have much. Someone told Carl to get a job done. So far, nothing suspicious has happened. Old Bert told us about two men fighting at the river. I overheard Fred selling wood to the guy building a store on Front Street. Did you know he was a salesman for a mill? It sounded like their wood cost less but was of poor quality."

"You are the worst detective I have ever met."

"How many detectives have you met?"

"One." Henry grinned. "Who do we tail first?"

Tess chewed the end of her pencil. "I don't know."

They sat, dangling their legs off the boardwalk.

A whining sound filled the air, increasing to an ear-piercing siren that stopped people in their tracks.

"Fire!" Someone yelled.

Tess and Henry jumped to their feet and looked around.

A white plume of smoke rose in the air near the river.

They ran toward the smoke until they reached a crowd of people assembled across the road from the Bruin lumberyard. The fire wagon arrived, speeding into the yard.

Henry motioned to Tess to follow him. They crept around the side and climbed the fence.

Tess's eyes grew wide.

The pile of lumber they had been standing beside was consumed by a wall of fire and smoke. The piles on either side were fully engulfed and sparks landed on neighboring stacks.

Tess inhaled the fragrant smell of wood smoke. She missed their old stove and wished she was home filling the box with firewood. She would never again grumble at the daily chore if it meant they could return to Vancouver.

The memory quickly faded, replaced by a new vision of the fierce and destructive nature of fire as it devastated a thriving business, leaving it in a pile of hissing embers.

"We have to tell Aunt Molly." Tess yelled over the roaring inferno and the shouts of men working to contain the damage.

"I'm sure she already knows. Word travels quickly in a small town."

"I have to go." Tess jumped off the fence and ran, gasping for breath, stopping for a few seconds before carrying on toward the hotel. At one point she looked behind but Henry had not followed. Figures, she thought. He bails at the first sign of trouble.

Breathless, with her leg muscles screaming, she burst through the door into the lobby and down the hall into the parlor.

Anna paced across the floor while Molly sobbed into her handkerchief. They both looked up as Tess flew into the room. She ran to her mother who wrapped her arms around her.

"The lumberyard is on fire. I saw it. The wood is burning." Tess cried.

"Are you alright?" asked Molly clutching her handkerchief.

"Why were you at the lumberyard?" asked Anna.

"I finished late at the bakery and…" Tess hesitated. "I heard the siren and ran to see what was happening." She decided not to mention Henry or the fact they had been spotted playing in the back of the lumber yard before the fire began.

"Thank goodness you weren't hurt," said Molly.

"What will you do? Your business is ruined." Tess rubbed tears from her cheeks, smearing the soot into streaks.

"We will carry on, as usual," said Molly. "Wood can be replaced." She hugged Tess.

"You, on the other hand, are irreplaceable. I will not allow you to continue running free in the streets of Dawson. What were you thinking?" Anna placed her hands on her hips and shook her finger at Tess.

Tess frowned. "I was curious."

"You could have been hurt."

"I was careful. Besides, you've been too busy to care about what I do with my time. Why are you suddenly worried about me?"

"Tess, that was uncalled for."

"Anna, what's done is done. She knows the dangers and will continue to learn from her mistakes." Molly patted Anna's arm to calm her.

"Aunt Molly is right. How am I going to learn about life if I stay cooped up in our room? You cannot keep me safe by locking me away."

"Well now, that is a turn of events. You refused to leave the hotel for days upon our arrival in Dawson. Do I detect a softening to your view of our new home?" Anna raised an eyebrow.

"Never. I miss our home in Vancouver. I miss my friend Sally and building sandcastles on the beach. Father is a million miles away and I fear we will never see him again. I hate it here. I will hate it wherever we go because without Father we have no real home." Tess stomped her foot and ran from the room.

She glared at Theo as she ran out the door.

SIXTY

As Fred and Earl sat in the saloon, a man burst through the doors. "Fire!"

"Where?" Fred stood.

"The Bruin Mill."

Earl leaned back in his chair and raised his glass toward Fred.

Fred finished his drink in one gulp and headed out the door. He left Daisy hitched to the rail and strolled toward the fire, blending with the crowd. His eye twitched, and he fought to keep a smile from forming as he approached the disastrous fire engulfing the Bruin mill and lumberyard. He had been wise to hire his brother.

Fred stood next to Floyd Gardall, the bank manager. "Mrs Bruin has had enough tragedy and now this. What a shame." He shook his head slowly.

"Maybe it was for the best. Without a husband to manage operations it would have collapsed, eventually. Women don't have a head for business," said Floyd.

"We can't say that about every woman. Mrs Bruin was courageous to carry on after the loss of Beau. The hotel is thriving with the help of her sister."

Floyd pursed his lips and stared at the flames leaping into the air. "Not for long. I heard Mrs Bruin has been suffering from food poisoning. They kept it quiet so the restaurant would not be affected."

"Unbelievable. Who has been spreading vicious rumors? I will have you know the Golden Grizzly dining room serves the best meals in town." Fred folded his arms and shook his head.

"Maybe, but you can't dispute the evidence. Mrs Bruin is laid up in bed with no signs of recovery."

"Mr Gardall, you, of all people, should know better than to believe malicious gossip. The Bruins were a leading couple, beloved by all, and we should stand in support of the grieving widow and choose to ignore the lies. You wouldn't want Mrs Bruin to withdraw the millions they have deposited in your bank because of your scorn, would you?"

Floyd raised an eyebrow and stared at Fred. "I'm not sure what Beau told you but they do not keep their money in my bank."

"Forgive me, I assumed wrong." Fred pulled out his pocket watch with trembling hands and checked the time. "Two o'clock already. My goodness, where does the time go? I have an appointment I cannot afford to miss. Good day, Floyd."

"Good day, Fred. I will keep your words in mind and do my best to counteract the rumors."

"Mrs Bruin would be most appreciative."

Fred tipped his hat, turned his back to the fire and strode toward town picking up the pace to get to Daisy as quickly as possible. A plan was simmering, and he needed a quiet spot to figure out the details.

He patted Daisy on the neck. "Hello beautiful." He hopped into the buggy, clicked his tongue and set off down the road to his office.

SIXTY-ONE

Tess sat on the bench outside with her head cradled in her hands, her mind reeling with confusion. Why would Henry lie about seeing a body? Had the man been sleeping? Had he woke in time to escape the fire? Or, did he start the fire?

"Excuse me young miss, may I have a word with your mother?"

Tess held her breath, staring at the polished brown leather boots in front of her. Her gaze slowly followed the yellow stripe up dark blue trousers to the scarlet jacket and stern face of Sergeant Roberts.

"You must mean my aunt. Her mill burned to the ground."

"I will follow you," said Sergeant Roberts as he opened the door and motioned for Tess to enter. She slowly walked into the lobby, shrugged her shoulders at Theo's questioning look and led the officer to the parlor, her spine bristling with awareness of the towering man following behind.

Molly and Anna gasped as the two appeared in the room.

"Dear me, what has Tess done?" Anna fanned herself with her hand.

Sergeant Roberts bowed and removed his stetson. "No need to be alarmed. I am here to inform you your mill and lumber yard are a complete loss. The fellows battled the blaze with courage and determination but were unsuccessful in extinguishing the fire before it caused considerable damage. The neighboring properties were saved."

"Thank goodness no one was hurt, and the surrounding businesses were not damaged." said Molly, ringing her handkerchief into a tight ball. "Thank you for your prompt visit to inform us of the disaster."

"Our investigation is in the early stages but a man has been killed. And, there is one other problem." Sergeant Roberts turned his stetson in his hands. "Your niece and a young boy were seen running from the yard moments before the fire began."

"Tess told us she was at the bakery when she heard the siren." Anna glanced at Tess with a worried look in her eyes. "Tess? Tell the officer."

Tess lowered her chin and stared at her feet.

"The foreman at the lumber yard described the two. A little girl with long dark braids and a boy who seems to fit the description of our resident mischief maker."

"Henry?"

"What? You know him?" Tess whirled around to face her aunt who failed to hear her.

"I wouldn't doubt it. But, certainly Tess wasn't involved. She was helping out at the bakery," said Molly. "She told us."

Sergeant Roberts tilted his head and raised an eyebrow at Tess.

Tess nodded, but as her eyes met the officer's steely gaze she burst into tears.

"We didn't start the fire, honest. We were looking for a dead body Henry said he saw earlier." Tess looked at her aunt and clamped her mouth shut. Mentioning the possibility it was her uncle would be heartless and cruel without solid proof.

Anna cried out.

Molly gasped and buried her face in her handkerchief.

"How did you know about the body?" Sergeant Roberts knelt on one knee in front of Tess, his hand gently resting on her arm.

"I didn't see it. Henry saw it earlier. I didn't believe him."

"You kids were lucky you weren't caught in that fire. A man was found under a pile of sawdust. It will take time to identify his remains."

Tess felt her legs give out, and the room swirled into a black void as she lost consciousness.

SIXTY-TWO

Fred changed his mind and decided to visit Molly before returning to his office. Best to offer his sympathies and assistance before too much time elapsed. Madam Molly would be most appreciative to hear he had done his part to squash the rumors about her restaurant. He chuckled and made a mental note to add a bonus to Earl's pay. He had outdone himself this time. Although, if it were up to Fred, he would have spaced the acts of sabotage further apart. Fred didn't want Madam Molly too devastated to accept his offer, sufficiently lower now that the mill was no longer an issue. The land was valuable, ideal location for his next business venture. All he had to do was find out where Beau kept his gold.

He approached the Golden Grizzly as Sergeant Roberts emerged. Fred continued past the hotel, avoiding eye contact. After he directed Daisy to turn the corner he kicked himself for not stopping and making conversation. Sergeant Roberts might grow suspicious if Fred avoided him.

Fred drove to his hotel and saloon through near-empty streets enjoying the unobstructed journey. The town needed a good fire now and then. It cleared the streets for a short time, and his lumber business would enjoy a much-needed boost.

After Daisy was handed over to be brushed and fed, Fred entered his saloon with a hearty wave to the bartender who nodded as he poured a drink for a customer.

Inside his office, Fred poured himself a drink, swirling the whiskey in the crystal glass as he stood at the window surveying the lingering wisps of smoke above the buildings.

SIXTY-THREE

An hour later, Tess opened her eyes. She was in her bed. Her mother sat against the headboard and smiled as Tess turned to look at her. She pressed a cool damp cloth against Tess's forehead.

"How are you feeling, dear? Are you hungry? It is almost dinner time."

Tess pulled herself up and leaned against her mother.

"I had a horrible dream."

"Unfortunately it was real, and you are lucky to be alive. What on earth were you thinking? I should never have allowed you to leave the hotel unsupervised. It is my fault." Anna sobbed.

"No, it's not. I should have known better not to listen to Henry. He was a bad influence, leading me into trouble and abandoning me. Henry is the one who knocked over Miss Clara's display."

"He is a troubled youth." Anna shook her head slowly.

"I don't understand. Who is he? Where does he belong?"

Anna started to speak but stopped.

"Mother. He told me he was a ghost."

"Oh honey. He is a normal little boy with an overactive imagination."

Tess jumped out of bed and pulled on her boots. "I have to find him and make him tell me the truth." Before Anna could stop her Tess ran down the stairs and out the door.

She put her hands on the railing and inhaled deep breaths, waiting for her heart to slow down and stop beating against her rib cage. The roaring in her ears drowned out the noise and voices of the street. A few men and women glanced up at her then quickly carried on. She wanted to scream at them. How could they carry on normal lives when a man had been killed? Her aunt's business had just been burned to the ground. And her only friend in this stupid town may have been the instigator.

How could she face her aunt, or her mother? Where was Henry? Tess had no idea where he would go if he knew he was under suspicion.

Tess stared at her hands clenched in tight fists, her knuckles white as her fingernails pierced her palms. She took a deep breath and opened her hands, staring at the short red lines left by her nails.

Henry did not start the fire. Tess knew it in her heart. They had to do their own investigation and prove their innocence. Someone had moved the man's body to the sawdust pile after Henry saw it. The man had been dead before the fire. She had to tell Sergeant Roberts. But, first she had to find Henry.

SIXTY-FOUR

Fred ordered liver and onions at his restaurant. He spit out a half-eaten mint into his napkin before eating. In order to keep the food poisoning rumors alive he would refrain from dining at the Golden Grizzly.

After dinner he lit a cigarette, blowing smoke rings as he watched the diners. The dining room was full for the first time in months.

He placed his napkin on his plate and left the restaurant, walking through the hotel to the dance hall.

Earl sat on a red velvet upholstered bench with a raven-haired beauty on his lap.

Raucous piano music and a cacophony of voices made Fred's head throb as he approached Earl.

Earl waved his drink in the air. "Fred, you and I have some celebrating to do." He slurred his words then took a drink, spilling half down his shirt.

Fred grabbed his arm and pulled him to his feet, knocking the woman unceremoniously off his lap onto the bench.

"We gotta talk." He yelled, but Earl grinned and staggered over to the bar.

Fred followed, stomping out his cigarette on the floor, and signalled for his usual whiskey, watching the oddly matched couples crowd the floor as prospectors paid to dance with smiling women dressed in festive gowns.

He sipped his drink and gave up trying to talk to Earl. After a top-up he made his way to a table in the back, motioning for Earl to follow. Along the way, his gaze met the eyes of a woman and he bowed slightly, waving his arm toward the table. She gathered her shawl and handbag, following Fred.

The four sat and Fred allowed himself to relax and enjoy the evening. They had plenty of time to compare notes tomorrow.

Under penalty of law, drinking establishments remained closed on Sundays. A useful rule for Fred to utilize as a day of rest and recuperation from another frantic, drink-filled Saturday night.

SIXTY-FIVE

Tess headed to Old Bert's cabin. "Did you hear what happened down at the Bruin Mill?" Tess asked Bert as he sat in the wooden rocker on his sagging porch.

"Heard the racket, wondered what happened. Not surprised. There's a fire in Dawson every other day. Oil lamps, wood stoves, flimsy buildings."

"The police found a body."

"They did?" He leaned back and rocked. "Not surprised."

"They think Henry and I started it."

"Not…"

"If you say you're not surprised one more time, I will scream. You and I both know Henry would never do something so horrible."

"True. I wonder where he is hiding. He does that when he is scared."

"Do you have any idea? I need to find him. We have to go to the police and tell them what he knows."

"And what might that be?"

Tess hesitated. She didn't think Old Bert was a bad person, but she didn't want to tell too many people about her suspicions either.

Trust was a difficult thing to give away, especially to an adult whom she didn't know well, but Henry knew Bert and trusted him.

"Henry said he saw a body in a different spot before the fire started. Sergeant Roberts said they found the body under a pile of sawdust."

"Interesting. Men don't usually walk around once they're dead. Was Henry sure the guy was dead?"

Tess thought for a moment. "According to Henry, the guy looked stiff as a board. Maybe the man was sleeping and moved to the sawdust pile to stay warm."

"Hah, funny. Smart move, but he got a might too toasty."

"Ew, that's not funny."

"If I was Henry I'd hide out in my favorite spot."

"Where's that?"

"I don't know. It's his favorite, not mine."

Tess groaned. She was getting nowhere. She had no idea where Henry lived, where he hid or hung out, other than the junk yard. He loved playing there.

"The junk yard."

"That's his favorite spot."

Tess took a deep breath, let the air out slowly to calm her nerves and thanked Bert for his help. "I must go."

"Go where?" Bert blinked and tilted his head. "Isn't it kind of late for you to be out? Get on home."

Tess ignored him and ran down the road searching the junk yard for a dark head moving among the rusted bed frames and spindly bushes.

"Henry, it's me. Where are you?"

A soft breeze blew across the tall grasses and weeds, whispering in Tess's ear. 'Miss Tess, sour puss, go home.'

"I have no home. I don't belong anywhere. Henry, I know you're here somewhere. I'm not leaving without you."

A raven cawed from the top branch of a trembling aspen.

Tess waded through the tall grass, dragging her feet so she would not trip on a hidden piece of rusted metal. She zigzagged around an old wood stove, a claw-foot bathtub and broken furniture until she was at the back of the lot, unable to see the road from where she stood.

The air was colder among the thin stand of trees at the base of the mountain and Tess shivered. She knew Henry was here. Somewhere.

"Henry, I need you. I thought we were friends."

She waited, straining to hear Henry's voice, but the silence pressed down on her. "Have it your way. I'm leaving." She turned toward the road and stepped on a piece of corrugated metal twisting her ankle. She lifted her foot and hopped before falling onto a tuft of grass, narrowly missing the edge of a pitted axe.

Then she heard it. Or was it the wind? A muffled sound. She turned her head to listen.

A rain drop splashed onto her nose, then another. Droplets clanged against the metal and pattered amidst the trees, adding a glistening, otherworldly sheen to the junkyard.

"Help."

Tess narrowed her eyes. She couldn't tell where the sound had come from.

"I'm down here." Henry's voice was faint against the deluge of rain.

"Keep talking and I'll find you." She stood and hobbled back and forth, moving toward his voice.

"Careful where you walk. I'm in an abandoned mine shaft."

"Out here?" Tess placed one foot in front of the other, wincing at the pressure on her ankle, carefully watching for a depression in the grass. She used her sleeve to wipe the rain from her eyes.

Then she saw it. A patch of weeds had been flattened. She peered over the edge. "Henry, are you alright?"

"This is my hideout. I'm not hurt. The ladder busted and the sides are too high. I can't get out."

Tess lay on her stomach and reached her hand as far as she could into the hole but could not touch Henry's outstretched fingers.

"Wait here. I'll look for something you can climb."

"I'm not going anywhere."

Tess searched the piles of junk for anything that looked usable. She spotted a dented stove pipe and dragged it to the opening.

"Move out of the way." She pushed it over the edge and let it fall into the hole with a deafening clang. It landed upright but reached halfway up the side of the hole. "Can you shimmy up the pipe? Maybe you can grab my arm once you get to the top of it."

"Yeah, I'm strong as a bear cub. Watch me." Henry grasped the pipe and using the dents as footholds he worked his way up to the end of the pipe slick from the rain. "I can't let go of the pipe or I'll slide back down."

Tess spied a chair missing two legs, pulled it to the hole and lowered it down settling it on top of the stove pipe. "Try that."

Henry pulled his weight onto the seat, repositioned then stood on the rickety tower, steadying himself against the dirt wall. His head rose out of the hole and he lifted his arms to grab a tree root.

Tess grabbed his arms and pulled as he wiggled his way out then rolled onto his back and lay in the wet grass, gasping for air.

"You could have died. I'm sorry. I didn't mean to take you there." Tears mixed with raindrops dripping down the sides of his face.

"Where?" Tess sat beside him not caring that her dress was wet and muddy.

"The mill. It was dangerous."

"You never mean to cause trouble, but, no matter how hard you try, it follows you everywhere."

Henry sighed, shrugging his shoulders. "I didn't mean to hurt you."

"Stop saying that. You did not hurt me. I know you didn't start the fire. We have to tell the police what you saw. They think the man died in the fire."

"Will you forgive me?" Henry looked at her with wide eyes.

"What are you talking about? It was my fault as much as yours. I chose to follow you, knowing full well you would lead me to trouble." She dabbed her handkerchief at a cut on his forehead.

"I couldn't save my friend."

A chill settled along Tess's spine. She held her breath then exhaled slowly. "What do you mean? What friend?"

"My best friend in the whole world. It was my fault he died." Tears brimmed in Henry's eyes.

Tess gently touched his arm. "The man was your friend? What happened?"

"No. I don't know who that guy was."

"What happened to your friend?"

"We were playing on a pile of wood. We shouldn't have been there, but no one was around. The pile wasn't secured, but we didn't know. I jumped and Henry was buried under the logs."

"Your friend's name was Henry?"

"Yes, that's why he was my best friend in the whole wide world. We were the same age and shared the same name, Henry Smith."

"So, that's who is buried on the mountain. Why did you tell me you were a ghost?"

"I should have died instead. If I can keep him alive, we can both live." Henry stood then pulled Tess to her feet.

"What about his parents?"

"They left town. His ma couldn't take living here anymore."

"Where are your parents? Do they know you are pretending to be Henry?"

"The doctor said it was best to play along with my fantasy. He said I would grow out of it." Henry kicked the dirt with his mud-caked boot.

"How sad. I don't know what to say. I'm sorry." Tess tested her ankle. She found a broom handle to lean on. "We should go home."

Henry put his arm around Tess and helped her walk. The journey back to the hotel was long and slow. The rain changed to a drizzle. Cold and tired, Tess limped along, stopping to give her ankle a rest every few minutes.

They arrived at the hotel and Tess turned to her friend. "Are you ready to tell where you live? Who are your parents?"

Henry pointed at the hotel. "My ma's name is Nellie and my pa's name is Elmer."

Tess's mouth fell open. "Elmer? Nellie called Chef Pierre by that name. Your father is Chef Pierre?"

"Yeah. His name is Elmer Smith."

"Did you come from France?"

"Nope, he says that because it sounds better. He used to cook for a roadhouse near Whitehorse."

Tess sat on the step and held her head with her hands, processing the new information. "Why didn't Nellie tell me?"

"You never asked."

"How would I know to ask such a question? I didn't know Chef Pierre was her husband. I can't believe this."

"What did you talk about when you cleaned rooms?"

Tess shook her head. "Traveling. Prince Charming. I don't know, I don't ask questions because adults never give straight answers." None of what Henry said made sense but in a crazy way, it did. Kids had a different way of coping with traumatic events. Wrinkling her forehead she looked up at Henry. "That's how you knew when I was on the verandah and popped out of nowhere."

"Me and Henry used to play tricks on the hotel guests."

"Very funny. I'm sure they loved that. Where is your room?"

"We stay in the cabin behind the hotel, near the storage shed, but I used to help Ma before you came. I think she likes your help better."

"Does Aunt Molly know about Chef Pierre? He shouldn't lie."

"She knows." Henry folded his arms, standing tall and proud.

"Mother and Aunt Molly didn't tell me." She clenched her fists. "They never tell me anything."

"My folks don't talk much either."

"What happens if people find out he's not a French chef?"

"They'll never find out, because he is the best in town, and it doesn't matter where he studied cooking. I better get home."

"Me, too. I'll see you in the morning."

SIXTY-SIX

The next morning, Fred arrived at the Grizzly Hotel, and without stopping to check with Theo charged down the hall to the parlor. He paused to put on an appropriately upset face before entering.

Tess sat in the wingback chair with her arms crossed, scowling.

Anna and Molly stood over her shaking their fingers.

Henry sat in a chair beside her with Nellie and Elmer berating him. "How could you, Henry? What were you thinking?" Nellie cried.

"We didn't do it." Henry said, but stopped when Fred entered the room.

"What is this I hear about young Tess?" He strode over to Tess and took her hand. "Are you alright? I will have those men fired for not adhering to the safety rules. No children should be allowed to run around in a fully operational mill."

Molly turned and faced him. "I appreciate your concern but it took place at our lumber yard. I or Anna will look into the incident. Human error was most likely the cause."

Everyone turned to stare at Henry who sobbed. "Henry died because of me. I could have killed Tess. It was my fault."

"No, it's not. I followed you and am as much to blame as you," said Tess, patting his arm.

Fred crossed his arms and confronted Elmer. "Your son is a menace, and I expect you will take the appropriate actions and commit him to the crazy ward at the hospital. Allowing a boy to run wild in the streets of Dawson City telling people he is a ghost is no way to heal from the tragic loss of his friend. He is the talk of the town."

"Mr Barrett, if you please. This is no concern of yours," said Elmer, moving to stand behind his son and placing a hand on his shoulder. "You have no right to speak that way in front of my son."

Fred lunged toward Elmer, but Anna stood between the two men. "Why are you here, Mr Barrett?"

Fred looked at Anna and Elmer. "I was concerned for Mrs Bruin's well-being. A tragic accident at her business should be the least of her worries at a time like this."

"I am fine, Fred." Molly sighed. "You needn't worry about me."

"Nevertheless, I will look into it." Fred straightened his lapels. "Best keep a closer eye on these two. It's not safe for young children to run around town unsupervised. Who knows what hazards could befall them?"

Nellie dragged Henry out by the ear, alternating between scolding and hugging him.

Elmer bowed to Molly and Anna. "Your ongoing patience with our son has been appreciated. We will consult with the doctor to discuss our options."

Molly nodded.

"I will talk to you shortly," said Anna, in a low voice as Elmer passed by her.

Fred raised an eyebrow. "Is something wrong?"

"Just a slow period at the moment. Chef Pierre believes a misunderstanding has occurred. A rumor has been circulating that someone suffered food poisoning. There is no cause for alarm," said Molly.

"That is ridiculous," said Fred. "I will ask around, see if I can find out who is to blame."

"I'm sure it's nothing." Molly sighed, visibly growing tired and impatient. "Fred, we can handle it."

"I am merely offering to lighten your load, but will graciously step aside if you prefer." He turned to leave but stopped. "I almost forgot, in light of the recent events. I have been meaning to offer you an invitation, but this is not the time."

"An invitation? What is the event?"

"The annual summer dance. My church choir will be singing. It would be a great opportunity to hear me sing." Fred tilted his head and smiled.

Molly looked at Anna. "You would love the summer dance. It is a lot of fun. If my health holds up, we will be there. Thank you for the reminder."

"Can I go, too?" Tess sat upright.

"If you behave." Anna grunted as Tess threw her arms around her.

"Am I free to go to Miss Clara's? I am late."

Anna nodded and Tess ran out of the room.

Fred held his hat. "Please reconsider my offer, Mrs Bruin. If the businesses become a burden, I am pleased to help. It is too much to put onto your dear sister." He gestured toward Anna. "My offer to purchase your enterprise at a handsome sum still stands. Why not make a new life for yourself, maybe back in Vancouver?"

Anna's eyes brightened as she glanced at Molly.

"Take your time." Fred brought his hands together. "Think of this as an opportunity to make a new start."

"We are not destitute. I will rebuild the mill." Molly dabbed her eyes with a lace-trimmed white handkerchief. "I can't leave Beau, although I do miss Vancouver."

"No pressure." Fred held his breath as he lifted Molly's hand to his lips. "My other offer remains open, if you would have me." He held her gaze until she lowered her eyes and pulled her hand away.

Molly set her lips in a thin line. "You are a good man, Fred, but I will never reciprocate your feelings for me."

Fred held his composure and smiled, his eyes glittered with menace. No one rejected Fred Barrett.

"Give me time to change your mind."

Molly shook her head, avoiding his steely gaze.

"You need an astute businessman to handle your affairs. I insist on investigating the carelessness at the lumber yard. Men will speak candidly with another man." Fred bowed.

Molly glanced at Anna. "That will be appreciated. Thank you. Please report your findings to me as soon as possible."

Fred nodded. "Consider it done."

As he marched along the corridor, a smile played at the corners of his mouth. **Fred tipped his hat toward Theo then left.**

SIXTY-SEVEN

As Tess stood on the staircase she watched Mr Barrett leave. She rubbed her ear. Had she heard properly? Was Aunt Molly considering selling and returning to Vancouver? Food poisoning? Tess realized that may have been her fault if the doctor had mentioned her inquiry to someone else. She caught Theo staring at her. Or, was Theo the culprit? He had heard her talking to the doctor.

She wandered past Theo without meeting his gaze and peeked into the dining room. One old man, a regular, sat at a table drinking coffee. The rest of the dining room was empty.

Tess had to find a way to stop the rumors. Maybe it was for the best. Would Mr Barrett help them return to Vancouver? She could not believe her luck. No, she couldn't allow her aunt's business to fail because of her suspicions.

She left the hotel and went around back to find Henry. He was in the cabin.

"I'm not allowed to leave. Ma says I'm grounded."

"She's busy. Won't notice you're gone."

"You're starting to sound like me." Henry laughed.

"I have to talk to Sergeant Roberts. I think I started the rumour about your Pa's food thinking he was trying to poison Aunt Molly."

Henry laughed. "Forget about becoming a detective and become a writer. You've got one heck of an imagination."

"You're probably right. I'm not good with details, or finding clues, or watching suspicious people."

"Where to?" Henry pulled on his boots.

"We have to find a policeman."

SIXTY-EIGHT

Back at his office, Fred poured a drink and leaned back in his chair. Pleased the authorities had not come looking for him, he looked forward to talking to Earl about yesterday's incident. He would talk to the men at the Bruin mill later to see if anyone was suspicious.

He poked his head out of the door and caught the bartender's eye. "Have you seen Earl?"

"Mentioned he'd be back later. Had something he had to take care of."

"He's a busy man these days, efficient and productive." Fred tried to remember what he had said to light the fire under Earl.

Fred relaxed in his chair with his drink and listened to the sounds on the street, his window open to the boardwalk below.

SIXTY-NINE

Tess and Henry ran down the boardwalk, dodging people along the way. Tess slowed as they approached the Eagle Saloon, not realizing it was Fred's place.

"Wait, I have to catch my breath." Tess leaned forward and rested her hands on her knees. "We have to figure out what we will say or the policeman will interrupt and tell us to go play. I know the way adults think." Tess sat on the edge of the boardwalk.

"We start out by telling him the guy they found under the sawdust pile was already dead. That'll get his attention."

SEVENTY

Fred balanced his chair on the two back legs and tapped his fingers on his glass.

"You got my attention." He said under his breath.

He had hoped the authorities would assume the man was in the wrong place at the wrong time, burned beyond recognition, written off as a down-on-his-luck prospector.

Problems would arise if it was discovered the man had been dead before the fire started. A full investigation would certainly begin with a search for someone who might be missing a man.

Fred couldn't wait for Earl. He had to get out to the dredge site and make sure mouths stayed shut.

He reached for the telephone, spoke into the mouthpiece and talked to the constable on duty, and then grabbed his hat and rushed out of the saloon. Fred glanced toward the post office and saw Tess and the weird kid. Of all the kids in Dawson, she ended up becoming friends with him? Fred shook his head.

SEVENTY-ONE

Sergeant Roberts exited the post office, a grim look darkened his eyes as he strode past the children.

Tess jumped to her feet and hurried over. "Excuse me. May we have a moment of your time to speak with you?" Tess said as he rushed past.

"Can't talk, there's an incident down at the docks."

Tess and Henry watched the sergeant hurry toward Front Street.

"Great, we should follow him, see what's going on," said Henry, ready to run.

"No. This could be our chance to check out the mill. Everyone will be at the docks."

"Now you're thinking like a detective. I'm the only one who saw the body in its original spot. Maybe he left something behind before he got dragged to the sawdust pile. We can help Sergeant Roberts with his investigation."

"Our investigation." Tess reminded him. "We have to find out who did this, or they'll blame us and be done with it."

"Let's go."

Tess and Henry ran to the mill, avoiding Front Street.

Piles of logs barricaded the entrance to the lumber yard. Tess and Henry ran to the side and climbed over the burnt wooden fence.

Soot coated the wet dirt turning everything black and stuck to their boots.

Henry ran with Tess following, picking her way through the mud and ash. "Mother's going to kill me."

"We can wash off at the river. She'll never know."

Henry searched the base of the burned pile of lumber. "This is where I saw the body."

Tess bent forward to get a closer look at the ground, kicking at clumps of dirt with her boot. She picked up a stick and raked the earth while Henry lifted a half-burned two-by-four out of the way.

"Look at this." Henry picked up the burnt remnants of a leather boot half-hidden in the mud.

SEVENTY-TWO

Fred hopped into his buggy and rode out to Bonnet Creek. An unsettling silence enveloped the area as he neared the dredge camp.

A massive dredge stood motionless in the stagnant pond.

Its crew was nowhere to be seen.

The wooden behemoth was Fred's baby now that Beau was gone. His jaw clenched. He should be listening to the sweet sound of mining, deafening sounds of metal scraping against rock as the dredge inched along, a hideous screeching that pried at the protective walls of a man's soul and drove him close to madness, but instead Fred's ears rang with fury, pounding in unison with his raging heartbeat.

Time was money, and his dredge should be chewing up everything in its path, nonstop. Jets of water should be washing the contents in the trommel, its monstrous iron belly digesting then dropping the gold onto sluice boxes while spewing out gravel. Tailing piles transformed the landscape in the dredge's wake into undulating hills of scoured rocks and pebbles.

Since Beau's disappearance, Fred enjoyed sole access to the collection room where the gold settled onto mats in the sluice boxes. If the crew mutinied, they may have taken off with his gold.

He urged Daisy over to the entrance and looped the reins onto a discarded dredge bucket before rushing into the wooden structure, up the ladder and past the trommel to the gold room. His heart lurched in his chest and he swallowed hard to push back the acidic taste in his mouth.

The metal door was intact and the lock untouched.

Fred took out his gold cigarette case and opened a secret compartment, letting a key drop into his hand. With shaking fingers he turned the key in the lock. It opened easily. He held his breath. As he opened the door, he breathed a sigh of relief.

The mats sat undisturbed and salted with gold. He picked out a few nuggets the size of a pea and dropped them in his pocket. He went to work washing the mats and collecting the gold into a jar, tucking it into his pocket.

After he finished in the dredge, Fred marched over to the crew's living quarters, a dilapidated building covered in rusted metal plating. "What is the meaning of this? Why has the dredge been stopped?" He peered into the murky interior, waiting for his eyes to adjust, and jumped as a mouse skittered across the dirt floor. The bunks were empty.

He strode over to the cook shack and yanked the door open.

A man in a grease-stained white jacket whirled around, a meat cleaver in one hand. The buttons strained against his belly. "Oh, it's you." He lowered his hand.

"Where is everyone? Why aren't they working?"

"The last of them quit this morning. Your guy was out here but he couldn't make them stay. They were sick of working for nothing, afraid of dying from fatigue or worse."

"Where is he?"

"He left hours ago. Didn't say where he was headed. Figured he'd be out looking for you, seeing as you're the boss with Mr Bruin gone." He crossed himself. "May his fine soul rest in peace."

Fred whirled around and slammed the door. If the dredge guys were riled up, they might be willing to talk to the authorities. Fred kicked himself for leaving the dirty work to Earl. Some jobs needed a delicate touch, a convincing pep talk to soothe the men's worries, and a quiet burial of an accident victim with reassurance that the man had been careless, nothing more. Earl was a thug. No one knew that better than Fred.

He jumped into his buggy and snapped the whip. Daisy snorted then galloped down the road, quickly tiring and slowing to a canter. "Come on, Daisy, let's go." She refused to go faster. Fred sighed and set down the whip. "You're a town horse, I know. My apologies to you, my duchess." He took off his hat and wiped his forehead, and settled in for the long twenty mile trip back to town, plenty of time to stew about the consequences of trying to hide a workplace accident.

He found Earl waiting for him in his office. "Where've you been?"

"I went out to Bonnet Creek looking for you. What happened to the crew? Where were you?"

"They quit. Decided to find reliable employment with the other mines."

"Did you threaten them to keep their mouths shut?"

"About what?"

"The dead body. What did you think I meant?"

"Told them it was an accident, and they were not to blame, but if the authorities came sniffing around, it would look bad for them. They should've been looking out for their fellow workers. Looking the other way has created a permanent kink in their necks and they'll have to live with it the rest of their lives. Nothing to worry about. Our problem went up in smoke."

"Nothing to worry about except those two brats."

"I'll put the scare into them. Maybe a near miss that'll have their mothers locking them in their rooms for the rest of the summer."

"Do not hurt them."

Earl laughed. "Look at you, the bleeding heart all of a sudden."

"That's enough. Tell me, what were you thinking when you dragged that guy's body to the Bruin Mill? How did you manage to avoid being seen?"

"Told the guys I'd take him to town for a proper burial. As far as they know he's with the mortician getting gussied up so they can pay their last respects. Not that any of them would show up. They didn't take too kindly to him going to the boss and begging. Made them look bad."

"Pride. Keeps a man silent and out of the way." Fred chuckled.

"As for getting the stiff over to the lumber yard, I got him over the fence near the back of the lot while the crew went on their noon break."

"I overheard the kid say he saw the body."

"I had to hide for a minute so he wouldn't see me."

"Idiot. He saw the body then ran to get the girl."

"By the time they got back, I had it hidden under the sawdust. Had to yank on it. Dang thing got stuck on a log, lost his boot. No time to grab it. The fire would have taken care of it."

"You better hope so."

"Aren't you going to thank me?"

"For what?"

"Covering up the accident at the dredge and using the guy to sabotage the Bruin Mill. They'll blame the arson on him."

SEVENTY-THREE

Tess and Henry went down to the river and cleaned their boots as best they could. The acrid scent of smoke clung to their clothing.

"Mother will think it's from yesterday," said Tess, brushing off the ash on her skirt.

Henry washed the mud off the boot then wrapped it in his jacket.

They hurried back to the hotel, leaving the stinking boot under the verandah.

"Let's see what's to eat. I'm hungry. Get to work, Theo," he called as he ran past.

Theo rolled his eyes.

Tess passed the reception desk slowly to wave and smile at Theo, who nodded. She followed Henry into the kitchen.

"Hey, Pa, what's for lunch?"

Chef Pierre sat slumped on a chair with his chin resting on his hands, staring at a lumpy potato. He gestured toward the counter without speaking.

"Toasted bread? That's all you got? Where's the soup?"

"No customers. We are doomed. I will have you know my food is fit for kings."

Tess gulped as she backed out of the kitchen.

Henry peeked out, munching on the toast. "Aren't you hungry?"

"No. We should find Sergeant Roberts. I need to talk to him."

"Pa, you got a bag we can use?"

Chef Pierre flopped his arm towards the back of the door and sighed, not moving his eyes from the potato.

Henry grabbed a burlap sack and ran from the kitchen.

They hurried past Theo and pulled open the door.

"Hey, you kids cut the racket, will you?" Theo stood with his hands on his hips. "What are you up to?"

"None of your business," Tess said, sticking out her tongue before slipping outside, letting the door slam shut behind her.

Henry removed the boot from under the verandah and put it into the sack. They ran, not stopping until they arrived at the town station of the North West Mounted Police.

Tess opened the door, held it open for Henry and stepped inside. She sighed as the refreshing cool air enveloped her.

A young constable sat at a simple wood desk. Perfectly aligned stacks of files and papers covered a long shelf to his right. "May I help you?"

"We are looking for Sergeant Roberts. Is he here?"

"He is. Is it important? He is a busy man."

"Please, it'll only take a minute."

Sergeant Roberts emerged from behind a partition, folding his arms and tilting his head as he towered over the two children. He chuckled. "Master Henry and his accomplice. I apologize for dismissing the two of you at the post office. Turned out to be a false alarm. Come to confess?"

Tess shook her head vigorously. "We didn't do it."

"We have evidence." Henry held up the burlap sack.

Both men coughed and covered their noses with their hands as the smell of burnt leather wafted through the air.

SEVENTY-FOUR

Fred stood behind the bar. The saloon was closed for the day. He took an amber bottle from the shelf and glasses clinked together as he picked one from the rack. "Six days of the week this place vibrates with the sound of money, and although I'm losing a day's take by honoring the Lord's Day, I could get used to the peace and quiet."

"You'd get jumpy. Silence has a way of bringing forth ghosts from the past, I always say." Earl glanced around the empty room.

The red velvet seats clashed with the gold and blue swirls of the wallpaper. Specks of dust floated through the fingers of sunlight that found their way through the dirty windows.

"I promised Mrs Bruin I would question the mill workers. Safety was the number one priority when Beau was in charge. No matter what Madam Molly says, she and her sister are not adept at handling a business of that nature. The sooner they realize it, the better for me."

"Why would Beau's workers talk to you?"

"I have the ear of their dear employer, Mrs Bruin, and shortly I will be the new owner, either through purchase or marriage. It doesn't matter to me."

"You're an arrogant son of a…"

"I create opportunities for my business to grow. No harm in that. With the disposal of the body taken care of, and Bruin's mill and restaurant in ruin, we need to discuss another matter that has come to my attention. Beau's gold."

"Too many links will lead the NWMP right to you, Fred. Greed will be your undoing."

"They have nothing on me. My hands are clean."

"What's your plan?"

"Madam Molly would certainly know where their gold is hidden," said Fred. "She won't use it unless she is in dire straits. We will take a breather for a couple of days. See how she's doing before adding another act of sabotage."

"Got it."

"I've got the summer dance coming up and don't want any surprises."

"You can't be serious, a summer dance?"

"What can I say? I am a well-rounded person, helpful, generous and handsome. My efforts have not gone unnoticed around town. They love me. I am above suspicion."

"You are delusional."

"I'm not discounting a visit from the authorities. They'll be checking every business to find out who's missing a worker."

"Nothing will go wrong. You lie like a fancy rug made of cheap burlap."

"Maybe so, but let's not get complacent." Fred narrowed his eyes.

"You're on your own. I'm lying low for the day. You may enjoy staying in town on a Sunday afternoon but I'm heading out to do me some gold panning."

"You're the one who will need the luck. Most of the claims are worthless. Except the one I sold to you, big brother." Fred chuckled.

"Of course." Earl formed a finger pistol, aimed his index finger at Fred and pretended to pull the trigger. "See you tomorrow."

Fred sat at the bar and nursed his drink for a while. The mill would be closed today. He didn't feel like talking to Beau's men. He would make something up and report his findings to Madam Molly.

He drained the rest of his whiskey, left the glass on the bar for the staff to deal with tomorrow and headed into his bedroom beside the office for a nap.

SEVENTY-FIVE

Henry held up the bag and Sergeant Roberts took it from him.

"We didn't start that fire," said Tess. "Henry took me to see a dead body, but it was gone when we got there."

"We went back to search for clues and found the boot. It must have come off when the body was moved." Henry pointed to the bag.

"What makes you think that boot came from the body? It could have been there for a long time." Sergeant Roberts wrinkled his brow as he questioned the kids.

"It does look old," said Tess, wrinkling her nose.

"What did the body look like?"

"At first I thought he was sleeping, but when I poked him with a stick he didn't move." Henry lowered his eyes, whispering. "I know what a dead person looks like."

"I believe you, Henry." Sergeant Roberts laid his hand gently on Henry's shoulder. "The body under the sawdust pile had one boot. We found it odd. Your discovery proved the man was dead before he was moved, which means someone else started the fire. I do not condone your actions but you have been helpful to the investigation."

Tess pressed her lips together, hesitating. "If we are no longer suspects, I have a problem and need your help. There is a rumour spreading through town food poisoning was reported at my aunt's restaurant. It's not true. It was my fault. I thought the chef was poisoning my aunt, so I asked the doctor about a strange herb. The doctor laughed at me and said it was saffron. Maybe he thought it was funny and told someone else and they misunderstood. I don't know what to do."

"Where did you get that awful idea? Chef Pierre would never harm your aunt. I'm sure no one believes the rumours. Your aunt has the finest restaurant in Dawson."

"The dining room has been empty since yesterday. The mill burned down and the restaurant is slow. My aunt is grieving for Uncle Beau and this should not be happening to her."

"I agree. I will put the word out it is safe to eat at the Golden Grizzly due to a misunderstanding."

Tess let out a sigh of relief.

Sergeant Roberts held up the boot. "Thank you for bringing in this piece of evidence. If we can identify the body, our findings should lead us to the culprit who started the fire, and a possible cover-up of a heinous crime."

Tess shivered. "Henry, we should go. I don't think it's safe to run around town anymore."

Henry twirled around and headed for the door.

"I am heading downtown to speak with someone. Walk with me." Sergeant Roberts guided them out the door, into the bright sunshine.

SEVENTY-SIX

Half an hour later, Fred woke from his nap, grabbed his hat and emerged into the sunlight, closing the large door across the swinging saloon doors.

"Afternoon, Mr Barrett. Mind if I talk to you, in private?"

He froze and turned toward Sergeant Roberts who waved to him from the corner of the building.

Fred nodded and stood motionless while Sergeant Roberts approached.

"Not at all, Sergeant. My office is right through here." He gestured with his hand to the officer to follow him as he unlocked the door and led him into his office.

"I have a few minutes to spare. I have a previous engagement helping prepare for the annual summer dance, and we have choir practice today. Can't keep Judge Wright's wife waiting. What seems to be on your mind?"

"I'm sure you heard about the fire at the Bruin Mill."

"Yes, a tragedy of epic proportions added to the already tragic circumstances of our dear Mrs Bruin. Have you found the scoundrel responsible?"

"We have not discovered the identity of the perpetrator yet, no. Just following up on leads in the meantime. You own a number of businesses in town, do you not?"

"Yes, I own this hotel and saloon, and the dance hall next door. I was co-owners with Beau in the dredge operation on Bonnet Creek. Why?" Fred left out mention of his hidden ownership of the mill. It didn't look good to be associated with a poor quality product, shady business dealings, and a possible motive. He owned it and two other disreputable places, in a roundabout way with links broken and reconnected in a maze of paperwork.

"Are you missing any workers of late? Anyone failed to show up for work in the past few days? Had trouble with any employees, soaking their troubles in the drink, or worse?"

Fred furrowed his eyebrows and tapped his finger against his chin. "There haven't been any reports of missing employees. I will certainly let you know if I hear otherwise."

"I appreciate your cooperation. We are narrowing down an identity on the body pulled from the fire. It looks like a case of arson, possibly by a disgruntled employee of the Bruins."

"That would be most likely. Poor Mrs Bruin must be having a terrible time keeping up with her husband's business ventures, possibly she forgot about the payroll for the mill."

"Can't see that happening. They have a fine foreman in charge, and Mrs Bruin's sister has been most efficient in keeping everyone paid up. I talked with her earlier."

"Ah, yes, Mrs Douglas has been a great help."

"I won't keep you any further. If you hear of anything, contact me at the station. Good luck."

Fred blinked. "Luck?" He swallowed hard. What was the sergeant getting at?

"Your choir practice. That is a feat in itself gathering the great voices of Dawson together for a sing-along. I will have to make myself available to witness the event." Sergeant Roberts chuckled.

Fred laughed, rubbing his neck. "It takes all kinds of singers. You should think about joining." It was smart to keep your enemies close, he thought.

"My singing would deter the most hardened criminals, but I won't expose jailbirds to that kind of punishment. Afternoon, Mr Barrett." Sergeant Roberts touched the tip of his stetson then left the saloon.

Fred cringed at the thought of being part of a captive audience. Mrs Wright was enough punishment. Half-smiling, he watched the officer's departure through narrowed eyes. He admonished himself for letting the sergeant's presence affect him. He had no reason to feel guilty, having done nothing wrong. That was the difference between him and his brother. Earl was reckless and would be caught red-handed eventually. Fred would be more than happy to let Earl take the credit, and the blame. No one knew they were brothers, merely acquaintances. The bartender was paid handsomely to keep his mouth shut. Fred would take his rightful place in high society without a backward glance. Earl was disposable. Fred had no respect for a man who neglected staying in touch with his mother and who had no idea she had passed away three years ago. Fred was the good son, staying by her side until the end.

SEVENTY-SEVEN

Tess's rumbling stomach woke her up. She looked over at her mother, asleep in the bed next to her. Even while she slept she looked exhausted with her mouth slightly open and snoring softly. Tess giggled, covering her mouth with one hand. She got up slowly to avoid making noise that might awake her mother. Pulled on her dressing gown and crept out the door, rubbing sleep from her eyes as she made her way downstairs to the kitchen.

Tess had no idea what time it was. There was a low light outside which didn't give any hints. In the Land of the Midnight Sun it could be two in the afternoon or two in the morning.

She glanced at the front desk, empty for once, then tiptoed past, hoping no one would notice.

"Morning Miss, you're up early."

Tess jumped, letting out a squeak.

"Sorry, didn't mean to startle you." Theo said, talking with his mouth full as he emerged from the kitchen with a plate piled with toasted bread and a chunk of cheese.

Tess's eyes grew wide. "What are you doing here? Don't you ever sleep?"

"I gave up my room at the boarding house, too noisy and a waste of money as I was never there."

"Does Aunt Molly know you're staying here?"

"Of course, I told her it was no problem for me to sleep at my desk, when necessary."

"I thought my Mother covered for you at night."

"She used to, but now that I live here, she can sleep."

"That is kind of you, but how…" Tess had a dozen questions about washing up and wardrobe but blushed instead. Some things were better left unsaid. She yawned. "What time is it?"

"A quarter past four."

"I can't sleep. Is there any toasted bread left?"

"No, but check in the ice box. There is cheese left, and those flat pancakes Chef Pierre made for dessert last night. Creeps, I think. Kind of limp if you ask me. Can't hold the syrup for nothing."

"They sound horrid. I'll grab some cheese." Tess headed toward the ice box and opened the door, scanning the contents, shivering in the icy draft.

Through the open window, a loud crackle followed by a snap caught Tess's attention. She frowned and stood on her toes to peer out of the window. Fingers of grey smoke escaped through the roof of the storage shed. An angry orange flame reached for the sky.

"Fire!" Tess yelled, throwing open the back door to the porch and running down the steps.

Embers floated over to the log cabin next to the shed lighting the sod roof on fire in several spots.

Tess pounded on the cabin door. "Henry, wake up! Your house is on fire. Chef Pierre. Nellie. Open the door. You have to get out now." She continued pounding until Chef Pierre pulled open the door, pulling his suspenders up and hooking them over his shoulders.

"What's going on? Why are you up this early, Tess?"

"Fire!" She pointed to the storage shed.

Chef Pierre peered out the door then ducked back inside. Moments later Nellie hurried out, clutching a bundle of belongings in a blanket. Henry ran into the alley toward the storage shed.

"Henry, run and get the fire brigade," yelled Chef Pierre. He spotted Theo on the porch. "Start filling buckets." He sprinted toward the stairs.

Moments later they emerged with buckets of water and threw them on the sod roof to protect the cabin. They hurried back for water and re-emerged, a few men followed with sloshing buckets. They managed to save the cabin, but the storage shed fire was out of control. By the time the fire brigade arrived, the building was gone and charred. Wisps of smoke rose in the air from a pile of crates.

A few guests crowded onto the porch, and others leaned out their hotel room windows to watch the disaster.

Anna pushed her way through the crowd on the porch and screamed. "Tess, where are you?"

Tess had been standing with Henry and Nellie. "I'm over here, Mother. I'm alright."

Anna grabbed Tess and hugged her tight. She stared at the smoldering wood, her shoulders dropped, and she buried her face in Tess's hair. "What will I tell Molly?"

SEVENTY-EIGHT

The next morning, Fred banged his fist on the desk. "Carl was supposed to wait for my signal."

Earl leaned back in his chair holding a cup of black coffee with both hands. "Called in someone else to do the deed. Carl's been unreliable. I didn't agree with your decision to wait. If you want to sink someone you gotta strike quickly and often. Don't give her a chance to breathe. She'll be forced to use her gold to get out of the mess."

"Too much, too soon. The mill fire was a random incident. The food poisoning was fortuitous, but not our doing. The authorities will know someone is targeting the Bruin businesses, and won't stop until they find the link."

"Relax."

"No, I will not relax. You're forgetting who is boss around here, who makes the decisions, and who calls the shots."

"I decided to go ahead." Earl leaned towards Fred, placing his hands on the desk and glaring. "What are you going to do about it, little brother?"

SEVENTY-NINE

Tess entered the kitchen to look for breakfast, rubbing her eyes, scratchy from smoke, and heavy from lack of sleep, too excited to go back to bed after the fire.

She checked the ice box and lifted the cover on the flat pancakes Theo had mentioned, picking up a rolled, cigar-shaped crepe with her fingers.

Tess wrinkled her nose, sniffing the unappetizing, rubbery roll, detecting a pleasant mix of sugar and vanilla. She took a bite. Creamy strawberry filling oozed out the end. Tess grabbed another, searching for a plate while holding one in her mouth and bouncing the other between her fingers.

Tess headed onto the porch as she munched on the crepe.

Her mother leaned against the railing.

Sergeant Roberts and another officer combed the debris looking for clues.

"I hope they find who is responsible. First, the mill, and now this."

"How is Aunt Molly?" Tess bit into the second crepe.

"I'll be fine. It can't get any worse. Thank goodness no one was hurt," said Molly, appearing in the doorway. "We can rebuild the shed. The mill will take time, but we have overcome setbacks before." She wrapped her arms around Tess's shoulders from behind, and Tess touched her hand. It felt cool and clammy.

"You should be in bed. I will handle things."

"No, it is time I started helping, especially now."

"I'm going to see if Sergeant Roberts found anything."

Tess finished the last bit of crepe, wiped her mouth then jumped down the steps and hurried over to him. "I didn't do it."

Sergeant Roberts straightened his back and laughed, glancing at Tess. "That's the first thing a guilty person says. Don't worry. This was the work of an adult."

"How do you know that?"

"We found a cigar inside the shed. They used it to start the fire."

"The dishwasher, Carl, smokes cigars. I heard him talking to someone a few days ago, out by the shed." Tess felt like a tattletale but Carl made her nervous. He never acknowledged her when she was in the kitchen and constantly looked gloomy. He had to be up to something.

"Have you seen him this morning?"

"No, the kitchen was empty. The restaurant is closed."

"We'll find him."

Tess ran back to the porch. She couldn't bear to see the sadness and defeat in the two women's eyes. "I'm going to the bakery for a few hours."

"Are you sure? You didn't get enough sleep last night," said Anna.

"I'm fine. I'll be back by Noon." Tess ran across the street and up to Front Street, relieved to get away from the hotel. She could tell that her mother and aunt were devastated, but in front of Tess they pretended everything was fine. Why couldn't grownups admit their weaknesses? She had a mind to tell them she knew when they were worried or fearful, and it made her feel invisible to be left out of the discussion.

She skipped along the boardwalk and into the bakery through the front door. Clara was serving a customer in a hat covered in bright orange and yellow feathers.

Tess imagined an exhausted bird flopping dramatically across the crown with its wing thrown over one beady eye of a hat pin.

She snuck past into the back room, pulling her apron from the hook and tying it around her waist. Pans of bread covered the counters and a sheet of cinnamon rolls sat waiting for frosting.

Clara came into the back room. "My goodness, Tess, you have certainly been in the center of the action these past few days. You needn't have bothered coming in today. I'm surprised your mother allowed it."

"I had to get away for a while. Mother and Aunt Molly are pretending they are not upset by the fires, saying they can rebuild, start over. Aunt Molly looks pale and weak. She should not be walking around worrying."

"Your aunt is a strong woman. She is no stranger to loss and hardship."

◇ ◇ ◇

Tess frosted cinnamon rolls in the peaceful kitchen then decorated cakes until Noon.

She headed to the hotel and ran around back to check on the site of the fire. Sergeant Roberts was talking to Carl. She held back and hid behind a bush to listen in.

"I didn't do it, honest."

Sergeant Roberts held up the cigar. "Is this one of yours?"

Carl stared at the remains. "Looks like one of mine, but I'm not the only smoker in town."

"You're the only person who smokes them around this hotel, am I correct?"

"I don't know. Maybe. What about the guests?"

"I questioned the guests, and no one smokes the same brand. Also, they don't have a motive."

"Why would I burn the storage shed? I need this job."

"You tell me." Sergeant Roberts held Carl's gaze and waited. The silence stretched between them and Carl shifted from one foot to the other kicking at a piece of blackened wood.

"I got nothing to say."

"Do you owe money to anyone?"

Carl blinked and stared at the officer. "What? How did you know about that?" He clamped his mouth shut.

"They gave you one job and your debt would be forgiven, is that correct?"

Carl hung his head. "You gotta believe me, I didn't start the fire. They wanted me to, but I kept putting it off. Mrs Bruin is a nice lady and I couldn't do that to her, not after what's happened lately. I'm not a monster."

"Can you tell me who did?"

"I don't know. Maybe it was the guy who talked to me the other night."

"Why do you say that?"

"He was a shifty character. Probably got tired of waiting."

Sergeant Roberts nodded. "Would you recognize him if you saw him again?"

"He had his hat pulled down over his eyes, couldn't tell what he looked like."

"Where did you accumulate said debt?"

"If I tell you, you can't say where you got the information. I'd be dead before the day is out."

"If you obstruct justice by not cooperating, I guarantee you will find safety behind bars."

"There's an illegal gambling hall behind the Eagle Saloon. I play poker real good, but someone cheated. Took me for all I got, and more."

"Why didn't you report it?"

"You don't know those guys."

"Would you recognize the other men involved in the poker game if you saw them again?"

"What're you going to do? Round up every man in Dawson?"

"Just the mean and desperate ones."

"Half the men in Dawson. That will go over well."

"What else can you tell me?"

"I heard a lot of guys were looking for work. Turns out the whole crew quit out at Bonnet Creek, shut down the Bruin dredge."

"Mr & Mrs Bruin had a dredge operation?"

"That's what I heard."

"Don't go anywhere while this is under investigation." Sergeant Roberts folded his arms and studied the hotel.

"I wash dishes for a living. Can't afford to go far."

Sergeant Roberts walked toward the front of the hotel.

Tess crouched lower behind the bush as he passed.

"Miss Tess, walk with me."

Tess gulped then giggled as she stood and fell in beside the sergeant. "Is Carl in trouble?"

"Too soon to tell. He may be our only link to who set the fire. Keep an eye on him for me, will you?" He turned his head and winked.

"I will."

They entered the hotel lobby and Theo lifted his head, smiling, expecting a hotel guest. The smile disappeared as he saw the sergeant and Tess. He jumped to his feet.

"Sir, how may I help you?"

"I'm looking for Mrs Bruin."

"In the parlor. Tess can take you." He motioned toward the hallway with a shaky hand.

Tess glanced back at Theo as they headed toward the parlor. He looked like he could use a nap. She wondered how much sleep he was getting now that he was at the hotel all day and all night. She had a feeling Aunt Molly did not know of the new arrangement.

Molly looked up from her knitting as Sergeant Roberts entered the parlor. A concerned look shadowed her face.

"No need to worry. I've got two men on the case and we will find the perpetrator as soon as possible. My gut instinct tells me the two fires are linked. Can you think of anyone who might want your businesses to fail?"

"Goodness, no. Beau didn't have an enemy in the world."

"Did Beau have a partner in the dredge operation?"

"Mr Barrett. He is an upstanding gentleman and has been helpful since Beau..."

"What happens to the dredge now that Beau is gone?"

"Co-ownership falls to me. Fred has been kind to take on the day-to-day operation until I am fit enough to step in."

"How well do you know this man?"

"He and Beau had been friends for years. He has many fine businesses in town, and he sings in the church choir."

"I heard." Sergeant Roberts snickered. "They will be singing at the summer dance."

"Yes, he was rather proud of the fact." Molly laughed. "Trying to impress me, I believe."

"He is sweet on you?"

"He feels badly about not being able to save Beau and believes he is responsible for my well-being. Nothing could be further than the truth. I have Anna, and my staff." She smiled at Tess who stood behind the sergeant. "And, my Tess." She raised her arm and motioned for Tess to sit near her.

Tess moved past the sergeant and sat next to her aunt. "Mr Barrett is annoying my aunt."

"Why do you say that?"

"He keeps bringing her cinnamon rolls and barging his way in on matters that don't concern him."

"Tess, come now. Don't speak like that. Mr Barrett was trying to be nice."

"He is being too nice. It is not normal."

Sergeant Roberts interjected. "If he is bothering you, I will have a word with him."

"He was a friend and partner to Beau. I think highly of him, especially after he almost drowned trying to save Beau. He feels terribly guilty. He offered to buy me out to ease my worry and is prepared to pay handsomely."

"Interesting." Sergeant Roberts tipped his hat. "I'll see myself out."

EIGHTY

Fred sat at his desk examining his ledgers. His lumber business had picked up considerably.

Loud conversation leaked through the door, signifying a full house despite the morning hour. Amazing what a case of food poisoning could accomplish. Buoyed by the recent improvements to his business, he felt like celebrating. He would mingle with the customers later, possibly buying a round for his customers.

His heart jumped into his throat as someone knocked on the door. He was not expecting anyone.

"Who is it?"

"Sergeant Roberts."

Fred sighed as the sergeant walked into his office.

"Pardon the interruption, the bartender said you were here."

"What can I do for you?" Fred motioned for the sergeant to have a seat.

"I'll just be a few minutes," said Sergeant Roberts as he lowered himself onto the wooden chair.

Fred realized not many men had sat in that chair since Earl had wiggled his way into becoming his confidante and right-hand man. It didn't sit well with Fred. He'd have to remedy the situation before Earl took more liberties. He was going to get them both in trouble if they weren't careful.

"I have a few questions for you, if you can spare the time."

"Certainly. Happy to help. Can I get you anything? Coffee, whiskey?"

"No, thank you. How was choir practice?"

"Excuse me?"

"Yesterday, you said you were on your way to choir practice."

Fred shifted in his seat. "Oh that. Turns out we had to reschedule. Mrs Wright is feeling poorly with a sore throat. Will wonders never cease?" He laughed.

"I am intrigued more than ever. I am looking forward to hearing our dear Mrs Wright and her charming nightingale voice. When did you say the dance was being held?"

"In four days."

"Do you know a man named Carl?"

Fred furrowed his brow. "Can't say that I do. Should I know him?"

"No." Sergeant Roberts leaned back in the chair. "I hear you lost the crew out at Bonnet Creek. Have you informed Mrs Bruin of the incident?"

"I didn't want to worry her. I have been working on hiring a new crew. We should be up and running in a few days."

"Has the pay been decent?"

"The pay?"

"I hear the dredges pick up a lot of gold. Have you cleaned out the mats since the shut-down?"

Fred licked his lips. "I haven't been out there recently. No."

"Half is Mrs Bruin's. I don't think it is wise to leave it unattended."

"I will send one of my men to collect it."

"And, to ensure his safety, I will send one of my men with him. Can't have your man be a sitting duck for a disgruntled employee who didn't get paid."

"They quit. None of them asked for their earnings. I can't be held responsible for their mutiny."

"Mrs Bruin tells me you kindly offered to look after things until she got back on her feet. Mrs Bruin will need funds to rebuild her mill and storage shed. You will see that she gets her share."

"Yes, absolutely."

Sergeant Roberts stood and placed his hands on the desk. "It is your responsibility to make sure nothing happens to Mrs Bruin, do I make myself clear."

"Of course. My goodness, I have nothing but the greatest admiration for Madam Molly."

"Make sure you remind your hired help, as well."

Fred straightened in his chair and frowned. "My hotel and saloon employees are trained to serve my customers. What kind of hired help are you referring to? Are you threatening me?"

"Certainly not." He stood, straightening to his full height, towering over Fred. "Unless you have something to hide. Guilty men tend to see things that are not there, filling in the blanks with knowledge only they know."

"I don't know what you're talking about." Fred calmly laid his hands on the surface of the desk and met the sergeant's eyes.

"Then it doesn't concern you." Sergeant Roberts moved toward the door and turned the handle. "Good day, Mr Barrett."

As the door closed with a click, Fred glowered. It was Earl's fault the sergeant was snooping around. His way of dealing with a problem was messy and unnecessary as far as Fred was concerned.

EIGHTY-ONE

Tess sat on the bench and watched the people and horses go by, gathering comfort in the comings and goings of the citizens of Dawson City. The businesses were closed but people were strolling about town enjoying the day.

Out in the open, no one looked suspicious, the streets were safe, but she wondered if everyone had a secret they kept close, pretending in broad daylight they were not conspiring to destroy an enemy's happiness. Secrets were harder to hide in the Midnight Sun.

"I see you." Tess turned her head catching Henry creeping toward her. "Now that I know your secret, you can't sneak up on me anymore."

"I wasn't sneaking up on you." Henry flattened his feet and sauntered over to Tess, a tattered stub of an unlit cigar between his teeth.

"That thing is disgusting. It looks like a shriveled up toe in your mouth. Spit it out."

Henry spit out the mangled cigar, stooped to pick it up off the wooden floor of the verandah and placed it in his pocket next to another one.

Tess shook her head from side to side, scrunching her face and sticking out her tongue.

"What do you want to do today?"

"I don't know," said Henry kicking the railing with his scuffed boot.

"It should be something that won't get us in trouble."

Henry laughed. "Trouble is my middle name."

Tess jumped to her feet. "Let's visit Bert."

"Why? He doesn't know anything."

"I think he does."

They grabbed their sticks and dragged them across the slats of the boardwalk as they headed toward the landslide.

Bert's cabin came into view and he sat on the porch writing, in deep concentration, muttering under his breath.

"Good afternoon, Bert," said Tess, stepping through the rundown gate hanging on one rusted hinge.

Bert threw up his hands, the pencil and notebook went flying and he jumped out of the rocking chair sending it moving back and forth. "You kids shouldn't sneak up on an old guy. Can't a man have peace and quiet in his own home anymore?"

"We're sorry. I thought you saw us. Why are you jumpy?"

"I'm not jumpy. I don't appreciate my privacy being invaded that's all." Bert scanned the road behind Tess and Henry.

"You are outside, where everyone can see you. Not what I would call private."

"You walked through my gate without knocking."

"I said good afternoon. What more could I have done?"

Bert picked up his notebook and pencil and eased back into the chair. "What are you kids up to? Looking for something else to light on fire?"

"We did not start those fires. It's a matter of time before the culprit is caught."

"Or culprits," added Henry.

"Probably the same person." Bert scratched his nose with the pencil tip.

"Why do you say that?"

"Both places owned by the same person. Somebody's gotta be pretty dang low to target a gentle lady like Mrs Bruin."

"Do you know anything? Something you're not telling us?" Henry folded his arms and glared at Bert.

"If I did, I wouldn't be shooting my mouth off. Desperate characters stop at nothing to get what they want, and they don't like loose lips."

"What are you writing?" Tess stood on her toes to peer at his notebook.

"Been working on a few stories." Bert laid his hand over the cover.

"Any related to recent murders or fires?" Henry pulled an intact cigar from his pocket and held it toward Bert.

Bert's eyes widened as he spotted the cigar. "Don't tease me, boy. I'm not a snitch but I am fond of a good cigar."

"Give us something to go on, and we'll get out of your hair." Henry dropped it in Bert's open hand.

"Where did you get that?" Tess whispered. "You best not have stolen it."

"I earned it."

Tess folded her arms, tilting her head to the side. "Sure, you did."

Bert put the cigar in his shirt pocket and grinned. He stroked his matted, grey beard and pursed his lips. "All I can tell you is someone's watching me, and if I say a word, my body will be the next one found under a pile of wood shavings."

"No fair, you promised you'd help us."

"I said nothing of the sort. I advised you to look around and take notice of who is watching you."

Henry raised his arms then slapped them against his legs. "Thanks a lot, Bert. Let's go, Tess."

Tess and Henry headed back along the boardwalk towards town and down to the river's edge.

"What do you think he meant?" Tess poked her stick in the water, watching a partly submerged log float past in the silent current.

"Who knows? Bert doesn't care. He wants to be left alone with his crazy ideas. We can't believe a word he says."

"Where'd you get that cigar?"

"Someone left it in the lobby. I grabbed it while Theo was away from his desk."

Tess looked at him. "You stole it from Theo?"

"Possibly."

"I didn't know he smoked cigars."

"He doesn't. Probably got it from a hotel guest."

"Who do you think would be watching us?" Tess picked up a rock and threw it into the water creating a ripple that quickly disappeared.

"Nobody notices kids. We are practically invisible."

Tess nodded. "We could spy on the adults."

"Mr Barrett?"

"He thinks he's smart but we can find out what he does when he thinks no one is watching him."

"Where do we start?" Henry picked up a large rock with two hands and heaved it into the water. It landed two feet away splashing him and Tess.

Tess jumped back brushing at the wet spot on her skirt. "All I know is he visits the bakery every morning to get cinnamon rolls for Aunt Molly. She is looking better but she should be eating healthier foods." She groaned. "I sound like my mother."

Henry laughed. "If I had to eat those every morning I'd get tired of them."

"I love helping Miss Clara at the bakery but the smell of yeast makes me ill sometimes. Too much of a good thing quickly turns it bad."

"We can't do anything today. We'll have to wait for him at the bakery tomorrow morning and follow him."

"You will. I'm staying to help Miss Clara for an hour."

"Working off the destroyed baking display?"

"No, I help because I like feeling needed."

"You're not mad at me for getting you into trouble?"

"It worked out for the best. I help customers sometimes and speak without making a fool of myself." Tess thought back to the first time she encountered Miss Clara. She had been a cowering little mouse, unable to say a word without feeling intimidated. Her father would be proud. If only he were here. She had so much to tell him, along with words of apology.

They climbed the river bank and wandered along Front Street. Men unloaded crates and barrels from a wooden barge moored to the dock, gesturing and shouting at one another. The sound of hammering and sawing added to the noise.

"It's near dinner time." Tess's stomach growled in agreement.

"I hope Pa made something better tonight. He is down in the dumps about the slow business. He's never happy. Complaining when it's busy and when it's slow."

"I feel awful. It was my fault the rumour started."

"Things will turn around. People have short memories when it comes to their stomachs. They'll be rolling in soon enough."

Tess and Henry arrived at the hotel and took the steps two at a time, laughing as they burst through the front door.

Theo glanced at them then returned to his paperwork.

"What do you do all day?" Henry approached the reception desk.

"I keep account of the hotel and restaurant receipts, report to Mrs Douglas, check in guests, and ensure their happiness. More than you two do around here." Theo pointed his ink pen at them.

"We are kids," said Tess. "I'm barely eleven."

Henry patted her on the back. "Feels good, don't it?"

Theo raised an eyebrow and snorted. "Wish I was a kid again."

"I wonder if you ever were a kid." Henry smirked.

"All I can say is, don't grow up too fast. Adults have to worry about things like housing, employment, where their next meal is coming from. No one takes care of them. My parents had enough problems. Didn't want to be a burden, so I left home. I'm not complaining, mind you. I could be out drinking and whooping it up, but I'd rather be saving my earnings."

"What fun is that?" Henry snorted.

"Did you think I plan on being a hotel clerk all my life?"

"You are doing a darn good job," said Henry.

"Too good, if you ask me," said Tess.

"Why do you say that?" Theo raised an eyebrow.

"It's almost as if you are afraid to leave your post."

Henry peeked around the reception counter as Theo slammed his hand down on the ledger. "That is none of your business."

A tantalizing smell of cheese and bacon caught Tess's nose. She sniffed, wrinkling her nose like a mouse. "Let's go," she said, as Theo scowled at her.

She grabbed Henry's arm, pulling him into the dining room following her nose.

EIGHTY-TWO

The next morning, Fred emerged from his room, strode across his office out into the saloon.

"Where's my coffee?" He barked at the bartender.

"Morning, Boss. What's got your goat?"

"Why do you and Earl think I'm in a bad mood all the time?"

"Never seen you in a good one. You save that for those genteel folk you're trying to fool, getting on their good side so they'll welcome you into their uppity ranks." The bartender avoided Fred's glare and moved to the far end of the bar, sorting glasses. "They're not worth the effort, if you ask me."

"Did I ask for your opinion?" Fred drank the steaming black coffee in three gulps, slammed the cup on the bar and stormed across the saloon floor. "I am a businessman, and a gentleman."

"Could've fooled me." The bartender snickered.

Two men at the bar drinking coffee chuckled.

"I heard that." Fred patted his hat onto his head and pushed through the doors.

Fred stood on the boardwalk for a moment, tipping his hat to two women as they passed him and nodded demurely.

He watched their progress, dainty steps, slender frames, and white feathers bouncing on their stylish hats.

Decent folk. Fred had made up his mind as a young lad that he would claw his way up from the bottom of the dank alleys of Toronto and make something of himself. His Pa had no ambition, but Ma instilled in Fred a sense of pride and determination, wrangling four sons and a lazy husband, taking in laundry and sewing to support the family.

Fred strolled past the post office and crossed the street, weaving in and out of the oncoming horse traffic, annoyed at the muck attaching to his boots.

He had an early appointment with a prospector about a claim purchase. Daisy would attract attention.

EIGHTY-THREE

Tess stopped in to see her aunt for a few minutes before going to the bakery.

Molly quickly dabbed at her eyes with a handkerchief.

"You can cry all you want, Aunt Molly. You don't have to be strong all the time."

"Thank you, Tess, but I have to be strong for Beau. I thought I knew what he would have wanted me to do, but this has been too much for me to handle." She sniffled and touched the handkerchief to her eyes as tears flowed.

"Maybe a change of scenery would do you good. If Mr Barrett's offer is generous, you could return to Vancouver with us and start a new life."

"I have been thinking about that option. We have enough gold that I could rebuild here, but if someone has made up their mind to ruin me what is the point?"

"Henry and I..." Tess started to tell Molly her plan to find Beau, but decided it was best not to. She didn't want her mother and aunt to worry, or to stop her. "Henry and I are going to the bakery would you like anything? Something other than a cinnamon roll for a change?"

Molly laughed. "You are sweet, but Mr Barrett will be along shortly."

Tess scrunched her face.

Molly put her index finger to her lips then Tess's nose. "I can handle him."

"I know." Tess moved toward the door.

"Enjoy your time at the bakery."

Tess smiled as she skipped along the corridor and out the hotel door. She loved helping Miss Clara. It made her feel good to give of herself. Her confidence had increased as Miss Clara's trust in her grew, and her baking skills along with it. As she walked, Tess wondered why she was suspicious of Mr Barrett. He hadn't done anything noticeably wrong, and Molly seemed to trust him, but Tess couldn't shake the feeling he was hiding something.

"Good morning, Miss Clara." Tess entered the bakery and headed into the kitchen to grab her apron.

"Not so fast, young lady," said Clara, putting a floury white hand up in front of her.

Tess paused, gulping as an immediate feeling of guilt flushed her face, even though she had done nothing wrong. Confrontation made her feel that way, and she hated it.

Clara glared at her.

Tess stepped back, shaking her head. "What's wrong?"

EIGHTY-FOUR

Fred checked the mining claim then tucked it in his pocket. He had been successful with the miner who had decided it was time to head to Alaska to try his luck.

The man's mining supplies had been junk but his claim was close to town and he could sell it for twice the amount. It never ceased to amaze him how easy it was to convince the men he was their only hope.

Fred thought about Sergeant Roberts and his strong suggestion that Madam Molly was in need of half the gold he found in the dredge.

At first, Fred had been taken aback but the more he thought about it, the better he liked the idea of giving Molly the gold. She would probably hide it with the rest leading him right to it. She would be so grateful to Fred for his honesty and integrity, she wouldn't be able to help but fall for him.

The thought appealed to him so strongly he went to his safe and pulled out the jar he had filled. No escort needed, he would tell Sergeant Roberts. He would explain that he had gone quickly last night and brought it back himself, handing half over to Mrs Bruin.

He filled a smaller jar, carefully measuring exactly half, minus a nugget or two, no sense shorting his own profit.

With the jar safely hidden inside his jacket, Fred drove to the bakery to pick up cinnamon rolls.

EIGHTY-FIVE

Clara gestured to Tess to sit in a chair at the table while she sat in the chair opposite.

"What's this I hear about you and Sergeant Roberts?"

Tess blinked twice, staring at Clara. "I don't understand. I'm helping him with his investigation. What's wrong?"

Clara leaned closer. "What is he like? How old is he?"

"He is nice. I don't know. He seems to be around your age, whatever that is."

"Never you mind."

"Why are asking me about Sergeant Roberts? Are you sweet on him?"

"He came into the shop the other day." Clara's eyes sparkled, and she brought her hands together in front of her. "One look in those dreamy eyes and I nearly dropped the cake."

"That is exciting. Where is he taking you for dinner?"

"Dinner? We just met."

"Do you want me to talk to him for you?"

Two magenta spots bloomed on Clara's cheeks. "Land sakes, don't mention a thing about me."

Tess giggled. "Are you sure?"

"If you happen to see him, you may put in a kind word. Nothing obvious. Let him know my bakery gives discounts for men in uniform."

"If he asks, I will tell him you like him a lot." Tess stood and reached for her apron.

Clara's eyes widened with terror.

"Just kidding." Tess laughed.

Tess and Clara were in the kitchen finishing up the frosting on the final batch of cinnamon rolls when Fred entered the shop.

"Good morning, Miss Clara. I see your little helper is here. Good morning Miss Tess."

"Good morning, Mr Barrett." Tess fumed.

"I am off to see your aunt. She loves her cinnamon rolls." Fred laughed as he picked up the basket.

"Why don't you bring her something else for a change, like a strawberry tart? Did you ever think to ask if she might be getting tired of the same old thing every morning?" Tess was irritable, frustrated that her aunt was going through so much and she was unable to help. She knew Mr Barrett was up to something but she and Henry couldn't prove it.

"Now that you mention it, I do have a little surprise for her." Fred patted his jacket.

Clara's eyes widened. "Is that what I think it is?" She wiped her hands on her apron and approached Fred. "Let's see it. You are a scoundrel aren't you? Are you sure she's going to say yes?"

"What are you on about?"

"The ring. Let me see it."

"What ring?"

Clara laughed. "You said you had a surprise for Molly. I assumed you were going to ask her hand in marriage."

Tess gasped. "Never. She would throw you out of the parlor."

"I don't think she'd be that angry." Fred shook his head, throwing a dark look Clara's way. "You are exasperating. I do not have a ring. I would not presume to ask Mrs Bruin's hand in marriage. It is far too soon."

Clara folded her arms and nodded. "You best remember that. Molly is not available. I will not have the likes of you taking advantage of my dearest friend."

"Miss Clara, how dare you say that in front of the child? I would do no such thing." Fred glanced at Tess who licked the frosting spoon and gazed out the window.

"Maybe I will take her a couple of those strawberry tarts as well." He wasn't sure, but he thought he saw the corner of Tess's mouth curl into a smile.

Tess hurried to the front window as Fred left the bakery and waved to Henry as he sneaked past the building.

EIGHTY-SIX

Fred wiped his brow as he guided Daisy down the road, turning corners until he was in front of the Golden Grizzly.

How could Clara jump to such a preposterous conclusion? He searched his memory trying to figure out when he had ever mentioned his intentions with regard to Madam Molly.

Was he that transparent? Did calm, cool and collected Fred Barrett carry his heart on his sleeve for all to make fun and laugh at him?

Clara was his closest friend, but she had crossed the line in front of Molly's niece. Who knows whether she would run home and tell her aunt of his intentions.

Maybe Clara knew something he did not. Maybe Molly would say yes if he asked. This was a dangerous town, not safe for a delicate woman on her own, despite her insistence she was not alone.

Fred's heart pounded. He would be the perfect husband and take care of Molly, with love and tenderness, as he did with his mother in her final years.

He carried the basket into the hotel, nodded to Theo, and headed to the parlor without asking if Madam was available. His heart knew she was waiting for him.

He knocked gently on the door, and Molly's soft voice said, "Come in."

Molly sat in her usual chair with a pink blanket covering her legs. "How lovely, thank you. You are thoughtful to take time out of your busy schedule each morning." She lifted the cloth and exclaimed. "Strawberry tarts. My goodness, how did you know those were my favorite as well?"

Fred tilted his head. "Your niece mentioned it, as a matter of fact." He furrowed his brow. Maybe Tess was on his side after all. He did help her out of a few predicaments, and he wondered if that was what a loving father would do. He wasn't sure. His own father had never shown the slightest affection to anyone in his family, including his mother. Fred frowned.

"What is the matter? Is everything all right?" Molly brought a hand to her heart with a look of concern.

"I apologize. My mind was elsewhere for a moment. It pleases me that your niece was kind enough to suggest I bring tarts. She thought you might be getting tired of cinnamon rolls."

Molly laughed. "Never. They are my favorite. Although, I probably should not be eating them every day." She patted her stomach. "I am feeling a bit round these days."

Fred took a seat opposite her and settled his plate on his knee. He dug around in his pocket and pulled out the jar. "I was out at the dredge the other day." He handed the jar to her.

Molly took it in her hand and immediately dropped it in her lap. "My goodness, it is heavy."

"The efficiency of the dredge is beyond expectations. If I can convince our investors, we can bring in another dredge and double our profits."

Molly stared at the dull gold flecks and nuggets. "Has the crew been paid well for their hard work?"

Fred smiled. "That is the beauty of the operation. The dredge does most of the work. We hardly need a crew at all."

Molly looked up at him, her eyes searching his.

Fred straightened in his chair, holding her gaze. His heart fluttered, but he sat motionless.

"That's not what Beau used to tell me."

"Of course we need men to work the dredge. I meant to say it is a different type of operation than sluicing or, say, running a saw mill or a hotel."

"Of course." Molly bit into the tart and closed her eyes. "Mmm, delicious. I must pay Clara a visit soon."

"How are you feeling? I could escort you if you wish. Choose a day and we will make it happen."

"You are too good to me, Fred."

Fred shifted in his seat and patted his jacket, wishing he had a ring. He would fall to one knee right then and there and beg her to become his wife. He fought the urge with all his might as he stared at Molly. Her glossy dark hair fell in waves around her shoulders, soft brown eyes hid under long feathery lashes, and a delicate blush of pink colored her cheeks.

"Molly."

"Yes?"

"If I asked you to marry me, would you say yes?"

Molly brought her hand to her lips and gasped. "Fred, please don't. I…"

Fred took her hand in his and kissed it.

Molly pulled her hand away and clasped both together in her lap. "This is much too soon. A year is too soon. Ten years even." Molly's eyes filled with tears that splashed onto her cheeks. "I am sorry if I gave you the wrong impression. I had no business accepting your gifts each morning. It was horrible of me to take advantage of your kindness. I will never love anyone the way I loved Beau. He was my one and only. My heart belongs to no other. You are a good friend. That is all." Molly buried her face in her hands and sobbed.

Fred stood abruptly, his plate dropping to the floor. He stared at the strawberry sauce and crust mashed and camouflaged against the pattern of the oriental carpet. Mortified, he hurried from the room and left the hotel, stopping to compose himself on the verandah.

"What are you looking at?" He snarled at the crazy boy who stared at him, snickering.

"I'm not sure. Is your face usually beet red?"

Fred raised his hand toward him then lowered it as the boy cowered using his hands to protect his head. Fred whirled around and stomped down the steps, hopping in his buggy, cracking the whip and sending Daisy into a mad gallop down the road.

EIGHTY-SEVEN

An hour later, Tess hung up her apron. "I had a lovely time, Miss Clara. The oat cookies are cooling on the counter."

"Thank you for your help." Clara waved from behind the counter.

Tess closed the door behind her and hurried to the end of the road, past the construction.

Henry sat on a boulder twirling a piece of grass.

"What did you find out?"

"Wow-wee. I don't know where to begin." Henry jumped up. "Mr Barrett went to the hotel. I peeked through the window. He gave Mrs Bruin the basket of rolls and tarts. They talked about something and he gave her a jar of gold. It all fell apart after that. He asked her a question and she started crying. Got the front of her dress all wet, blew her nose a bunch of times. You should have seen it. He looked embarrassed when she shook her head back and forth a million times. Boy did he leave in a hurry. He saw me on the verandah. His face was so red it looked like his head was going to explode. He almost hit me."

"He did what?"

Henry waved his arm as if to strike Tess. "Like this. I lost track of him after that."

"He must have taken Miss Clara seriously and asked Aunt Molly to marry him. All this time we thought he was trying to ruin her businesses and he has been madly in love with her." Tess shook her head. "That explains a lot."

"We should follow him."

"If we can find him."

"Let's go home first. Maybe if I ask Molly a few innocent questions I can find out if he has a routine or something."

Moments later they stumbled through the door and Theo put a finger to his lips shushing them.

"I'm going to see Pa, get us something to eat."

"I'll talk to Aunt Molly."

They split up and Tess tip-toed down the hall, peeking into the parlor. A clicking sound filled the room, and Tess giggled at the sight of her aunt ferociously knitting, the needles flying back and forth in a blur. A cup of tea on the table beside her. She looked up when Tess entered.

"Hello, dear. How was the bakery?"

"It was fun. I love decorating cakes."

"We will have to get you to make a few for the restaurant one of these days. Chef Pierre will be happy to let you share his kitchen."

"Are you sure?" Tess raised an eyebrow.

Molly laughed. "I'll talk to him."

"How did you like the tarts?"

Molly blinked rapidly and smiled, her lips quivering. "Mr Barrett told me it was your suggestion. They were lovely." She touched her handkerchief to the corner of her eye.

"Anything wrong?"

"I had something in my eye." Molly placed the handkerchief on the table next to the jar of gold.

Tess's eyes widened. "Is that…?"

"Gold. Yes. Mr Barrett brought it from the dredge we own together."

"Will that be enough to rebuild the storage shed?"

"I believe so. Until then I will keep it with the rest of our savings." Molly gestured with her hand to the piano. "Would you bring me that stack of music books?"

Tess looked at her aunt, puzzled. She put her hands around the foot-tall pile and lifted it. It was light.

Molly chuckled, holding out her hands as Tess settled it on her lap.

Tess moved closer. "What is that?"

"It was your uncle's idea. A box made from hollowed out music books. No one would think to look in there."

Tess nodded. The parlor was full of music books, yet Molly never played the piano.

"What if someone wanted to play a song from one of those books?" Tess pointed to the stack in Molly's lap.

"The sides of the books do not give enough information. Even the most bored reader would not bother to look twice. Besides, Beau was the only one who played. I should get rid of it. It is taking up space and causing painful memories."

"I never noticed that stack of books."

"See? Beau's idea was brilliant."

Molly lifted a fine gold chain from around her neck with a key attached. She pushed the key into a hidden lock on the bottom of the box. Molly lifted the lid and peered inside. She gasped.

"Oh, no. It can't be." She placed a hand to her neck. Her eyes widened in fear.

"What is it, Aunt Molly? Are you alright?"

Molly shook her head back and forth, her eyes blinking rapidly. "It's gone. Our gold is gone. It should have been much heavier when you picked it up."

Tess jumped up and looked inside the box. "It's empty."

Molly mumbled. "It can't be." She turned the box upside down and shook it.

"Was there a lot in there?"

"I should have noticed you were able to carry it with very little effort. Gold is heavy. How is this possible?"

"What are you going to do?"

"I have no choice." Molly held the small jar that Fred had given to her, staring into space. "I will have to sell everything."

"Who would do such a thing?"

"I don't know. Beau and I always believed the best of people."

"My mother and I believe the worst in people."

"You are in Dawson now."

"You should call the police."

Molly gave the North West Mounted Police officer the information, along with a list of her employees and former guests of the hotel. The officer left, and Molly leaned her head back against the chair.

Tess sighed, thinking of the catastrophes she had seen since her arrival. "No one is safe. It is no better up here."

"We must continue to think highly of others. What would life be like if we gave in to our darkest thoughts? Focus on the goodness of our town, the friends you have made," said Molly.

"I like it here. Henry was a nuisance, but he ended up becoming a good friend. Miss Clara scared me at first, now she is my friend. Even Old Bert."

"Old Bert?"

"The crazy prospector who talks to himself and writes."

Molly wrinkled her forehead in confusion then her eyes brightened. "You must mean Bertram, Nellie's father. Didn't Henry tell you?"

Tess shook her head. "What?"

"Bert is Henry's grandfather."

Tess let her mouth drop as she digested the news. After a few moments she laughed.

"That explains a lot. They seem to be close, but Henry called him Crazy Old Bert."

"The poor man has had a difficult life, was never the same after his wife passed on, and took to the drink. Henry has seen him at his worst. He didn't meet his grandfather until they moved to Dawson during the gold rush."

"Do you know if he is a good writer? Has he had books published?"

"I do not believe so. Some writers never allow others to see their work."

"Thank you for telling me about Henry's grandfather. I must be going. Henry and I are…" Tess paused. "Going on a picnic down by the river."

"How lovely. Have fun but be careful." A shadow passed over Molly's eyes as she clutched the small jar of gold flakes.

Tess stopped. "What will you do?"

"Don't worry. We will be fine. Your mother and I will think of something."

"I was wondering where Mr Barrett works."

"He owns the Eagle Hotel. It has a restaurant and dance hall connected to it."

"What does he do for fun?"

"Why are you asking about him all of a sudden?"

"I don't know. He seems interesting."

"He sings in the choir, but you know that. He is also helping with preparations for the upcoming dance."

"I forgot. Maybe Henry and I should offer to help."

"The dances are held in the Palace Grand. You could ask Mrs Wright. I wish I could help."

"There's always next year." Tess watched her aunt's reaction. After Mr Barrett's embarrassing behavior, maybe her aunt would decide enough was enough and leave Dawson for good, if it meant getting away from him.

Molly sighed, and stared at the framed black and white photos that adorned the wall. "I can't even think ahead to next week."

Tess hugged her aunt. "I should go. Henry is waiting for me."

"I'm glad you made a friend. Henry is a good boy. Your friendship is helping him get over a great deal."

Tess left the parlor in a daze, passing Theo's desk into the dining room without acknowledging him. As she entered the kitchen Henry sat at the center table sticking his finger in a bowl of jam.

"There you are. Pa made us sandwiches."

Tess glared at Henry, but her mouth spread into a broad smile. "You are a menace."

Henry's mouth quivered calmly meeting her stare. "What did I do? Something terrible, I hope." He snorted.

"Why didn't you tell me Old Bert was your grandfather?"

"You never asked." Henry doubled over and laughed until tears ran down his cheeks. "You never ask the right questions."

Tess stomped her foot, whirled around and stalked out of the kitchen, through the dining room and into the lobby. She glared at Theo as she left the hotel, finding her favorite seat on the verandah.

Henry appeared beside her moments later. "Sorry, I didn't tell you. It didn't seem important. The nice part about being a child is you don't have to know everything that goes on. I like being able to live my life and not worry all the time. You worry too much. It's making you old before your time."

"There is a lot to worry about that may affect all of us."

"Let the adults deal with it."

"Sometimes you sound like a wise old man." Tess sniffled. "Despite everything you've been through, you manage to have fun in life. I wish I could be like you."

"Hey, you and I are alike. You didn't have to follow me that first time, but you trusted your instinct and probably figured you'd never have fun sitting on this old bench all summer."

"I used to have fun in Vancouver," said Tess, remembering how content she felt reading under the oak tree, playing on the beach with her friend Sally, and having tea at each other's houses while their mothers visited. Her mother must miss her friends, too, but was probably relieved to be far away from that bossy lady, Agatha's mother. They had both fled from bullies. "Sometimes you have to move away and make a new start," said Tess, thinking about her aunt.

"Let's find out what Mr Barrett is up to."

Two streets back from the hotel, Tess and Henry arrived at the Palace Grand. Pots of red and white flowers lined the front of the building. A large cloth banner advertising the upcoming dance flapped in the breeze.

Three horses and buggies were hitched to posts, their owners inside. A speckled white mare contentedly munched from a feedbag hanging from her neck.

"There's Fred's horse," whispered Tess, blushing. Social settings made Tess nervous and shy.

Henry pulled open the door and let Tess pass him into the entrance hall.

Two doors were propped open, and voices echoed from the spacious hall. Two men on ladders held a banner across the stage, securing it in place. Three women chatted as they sat at a table stringing flowers on strings. One red-breasted woman strutted around the gleaming pine floor barking orders at anyone who moved, her black taffeta shirt swishing around her ankles as she marched. The cherry red shirt matched the color of her cheeks.

"That's her," said Henry, ducking behind Tess.

Tess whirled around trying to push him to the front, unwilling to engage the demanding woman whom she recognized from the bakery. Why had she not remembered the woman's name before this?

"Bad idea. Let's get out of here." She turned to leave.

"Miss Tess, what are you doing here?" Mr Barrett strolled toward them, his eyes hard and glittering. "Come to laugh at me?"

Tess stepped backward. "Of course not. What are you talking about?"

"Your sneaky little game, suggesting I take strawberry tarts to your aunt, knowing full well she loves them." He turned to glare at Henry. "And, you, spying on me. You are both in big trouble."

Henry twirled his finger around his ear. "What a nutcase. Come on, Tess." He pulled her arm and they ran for the exit.

Tess looked back. Mr Barrett stood motionless, hands on hips, with cold eyes narrowed to slits. She felt his anger stab through her, chilling her to the bone.

They didn't stop until they were around the corner on the next block.

"What the heck happened?"

"It sounds like he thinks I set him up."

"Woo-wee, good job. That was brilliant."

"I did not."

"Whatever. He sure is mad. We should go back and wait for him."

"What if he sees us?"

"Remember, we're just kids. Adults don't notice children."

Tess tilted her head. "He will be looking for us."

"We will hide around the side of the building. He's bound to come out sometime. Here, have a sandwich."

Henry pulled a mangled sandwich wrapped in cloth from his pocket and handed it to her.

They stayed low behind a stand of spruce trees near the corner of the building.

It wasn't long before Fred left, smiling and waving to others inside, but as he headed toward Daisy his face contorted into anger, his jaw clenched and his movements stiff as he jumped into the buggy.

As the horse and buggy started down the street, Tess and Henry stayed low, hurrying from bushes to openings between buildings, keeping watch on Fred's progress. He ignored waves from passersby, who dropped their arms and shrugged their shoulders, continuing to stroll along the boardwalk.

They followed him for four blocks before he turned into an alley.

"Don't stand near any open doors," said Tess, cringing as she remembered her embarrassing encounter when she tried to follow Carl.

Halfway down, Fred pulled up to a seedy-looking building, jumped out and tethered Daisy to an old discarded potbelly stove. He rapped his knuckles against a red door three times, knocking off pieces of peeling paint. A face appeared in the four-inch square window, then the door opened enough to allow Fred to slip through before slamming shut with a bang.

"What do you think is in there?" Tess gulped, scanning the alleyway for danger.

"We probably have time to go around front and see if there is a sign on the door."

Tess nodded and they both ran out of the alley, breathing sighs of relief as they jumped onto the boardwalk and ran half the block before stopping in front of a pleasant-looking boarding house, painted white with green trim around the windows, and baskets of red and white flowers hanging from the porch that led to the welcoming forest green door.

"This can't be it." Tess paced back and forth in front of the building, checking the structures on each side, a barber shop and a bank.

"It's gotta be. Let's get back to the alley and watch for him."

They ran into the alley and found a hiding spot behind a garbage barrel, holding their noses while they stared at the red door.

Soon, the door opened and Fred emerged. A slender arm wrapped around his waist and held him tight. He smiled and turned toward the owner.

The door swung wide open. Tess and Henry could see the arm belonged to a voluptuous young woman with cascading blond hair to her waist that covered a red velvet corset, a shockingly short skirt revealed her ankles and bare feet.

"Freddy baby, don't go. Let's have dinner and you can take me to the Palace Grand for a show."

"Another time, doll. You know, I will. I got business to attend to, a few annoyances I have to take care of."

The beautiful woman pushed her full red lips into a pout and she batted her eyelashes.

Fred laughed and kissed her nose. "You drive a hard bargain, love. I'll return in an hour."

The door closed and Fred hopped in the buggy and steered Daisy down the alley.

Tess and Henry gawked at each other, their mouths hanging open.

"Didn't he profess his love to Aunt Molly?"

"He did indeed."

"The scoundrel. I'm telling Aunt Molly as soon as we get home. You lead the way. I'm lost."

Fred stopped at the far end of the alley as a man jumped out from the shadows and grabbed Daisy's harness.

"What the…?" Fred stood up in the buggy then lifted his boot to push the man away as he tried to climb in.

"You cheated me, you no-good thief." The man yelled.

People scurried past averting their eyes. Scuffles were common and no one looked too closely at the men involved.

"What are you going on about? I paid you fair and square." Fred stood in the buggy glaring down at the man rubbing his shoulder where Fred's boot had connected. "I am a businessman and a gentleman. I never cheat my customers. Ask anyone and they'll tell you."

"I'll not be asking. I'll be telling who ever will listen what you truly are." The man stepped closer to Fred who hit him with his boot hard enough to knock him over.

Fred jumped from the buggy and stood over the man lying on the ground. "I reckon you might want to hit the road to Alaska sooner than later. The gold is waiting, but for every man who leaves Dawson before you, that's one more you'll have to wait behind in line before you get a chance to grab it. Get out of here." Fred kicked the man in the ribs then wiped the bottom of his boot on the man's pants.

Tess gasped.

Fred turned his head, locked eyes with Tess and glowered.

He adjusted his hat, pulled himself into the buggy, whipped the reins and drove into the street disappearing around the corner.

Tess couldn't stop shivering, folding her arms tightly as she tried to stay calm.

Henry crept toward the injured man lying on the ground and nudged him with his boot. "Are you okay, sir?"

The man mumbled something and groaned.

"Let's go," whispered Tess, pulling at Henry's sleeve.

"No, I have to make sure he's not dead." He leaned over, peering close to the man's closed eyes.

Tess's stomach lurched as she feared the worst, and how this was going to affect Henry. She put her arm around his shoulder. "He's not dead. He will be fine."

Henry jumped back as the man opened his eyes, blinking furiously as he tried to focus.

"What did that man do to you?" Henry asked.

"None of your business," he growled. "You best stay away from the likes of him. The sooner I leave this town the better." He struggled to get up.

Henry offered his hand and the man took it.

Tess grabbed his other hand and the three of them worked together to get the man on his feet and staggering down the alley.

Tess rubbed her hands on her skirt and stared after him, scared and shaky, shocked at the brutality Mr Barrett had displayed. The real person surfaces when they think no one is watching. She had seen enough to know her aunt was in grave danger. Possibly she and her mother were, too, if they stood in the way of Mr Fred Barrett.

She looked down and spied a shiny wet mint lying in the mud. "Let's go home."

EIGHTY-EIGHT

The morning began with sunshine streaming through the dingy window in Fred's office. He sprawled in his chair staring at the cup of coffee on his desk, tracking the steam as it rose in the air.

He was in his black velvet smoking jacket. No sense getting dressed. He had no intention of going to the bakery to pick up cinnamon rolls this morning. He had made a fool of himself and could not show his face around the Golden Grizzly until he had cleaned up his mess and figured out how to smooth over yesterday's misunderstanding.

Fred thought about the events of yesterday, his mood worsening as the day progressed. Anger simmered beneath the surface and every muscle tensed as he plotted his next move, unaware the door had opened.

"Whoa, you're here? Thought you'd be at the bakery by now." Earl stopped in his tracks spilling his coffee.

"Sneaking in here and pretending you are the boss while I'm away, is that it?" Fred growled.

"Angrier than usual this morning." Earl lowered himself into the chair and set his coffee on the desk. He chuckled as he leaned his arms on the surface. "Come on, tell big brother what the problem is and I'll go beat up the bully for you."

"Turns out, I didn't need your expertise yesterday. Took care of matters myself for a change. It felt good." Fred rubbed the stubble on his cheeks and scratched his chin. "Didn't even get my hands dirty."

Earl raised an eyebrow.

"Used my boot." Fred chuckled.

Earl stayed silent, waiting for him to elaborate but Fred continued to stare at his cup.

"I take it that wasn't the worst of your day?"

"Nope. I can't take it back, no matter how hard I imagine a different scenario."

"What happened? It can't be that bad."

"Think of the absolutely worst possible thing I could have done and double it."

"You're not making sense. What are you going on about?"

Fred shook his head slowly from side to side. "I forgot to watch her hide her gold."

EIGHTY-NINE

Tess stared at the ceiling, listless, with no desire to face the day. Whatever doubts she had about Mr Barrett's good intentions toward her aunt disappeared the second he had emerged from the red door. Witnessing him beat up the man in the alley horrified and sickened her. She could not stand by and allow that man to pretend he was anything but a bully and a criminal.

Tess swung her legs over the edge of the bed and sat contemplating her options. She had to tell her aunt. Maybe Mr Barrett stole the gold. He had certainly been in Molly's parlour enough.

Tess had to let Sergeant Roberts know what they had witnessed. She had forgotten to keep an eye on Carl. What if Carl had stolen the gold?

She threw on her brown muslin dress with the white lace collar and tied the laces of her black leather boots, scuffed and dirty. She smiled. Her boots had become a satisfying symbol of the fun and excitement she finally had in her life.

She skipped down the stairs, waved to Theo before heading into the parlor where her aunt worked on her knitting.

"Good morning, Tess. How are you this fine day?"

"You must tell Sergeant Roberts Mr Barrett is up to no good," said Tess.

"I will do no such thing. He meant no harm. I feel badly about how I reacted."

"He beat up a man in an alley yesterday."

"Heavens, what were you and Henry doing in an alley?" Anna entered with a steaming cup and set it on the table beside Molly.

Tess gagged. "Are you drinking Chef Pierre's horrible concoctions?"

"How rude." Anna glared at her. "What is this I hear about you and Henry?"

"We didn't do anything wrong. We were tailing Mr Barrett and we witnessed him hugging and kissing a beautiful woman, and he beat up a man who yelled at him."

Both women gasped and Anna fell into the nearest chair fanning herself with her hand.

"Children should not be spying on adults. I am sure there is a legitimate reason for his actions." Molly's voice quivered. "Is it a terrible thing he wants to marry me? He could make all our problems go away."

"You can't be serious," said Tess, her mouth dropped.

Molly stared past Tess with a glazed look in her eyes. "I am so tired. Where is Beau?"

Tess placed her hands on her hips. "I will find evidence and you will see that I am right. You will have to listen to me once and for all." She ran out of the room.

Minutes later she burst into the bakery gasping for breath.

Clara motioned with her head for Tess to go into the kitchen while she finished up with a customer.

Tess flopped in a chair, elbows on the table, and rested her chin in her hands, kicking the table leg with her boot.

"Now, now, don't chop down my table leg, missy. What has gotten into you?"

"I hate it here. I hate that no one listens to me. Henry and I see things no one else does and they don't believe us."

"What kinds of things? Tell me." She sat next to Tess and touched her arm.

"Did Mr Barrett show up today?"

"As a matter of fact he did not. This will be the first morning in over two weeks. Strange."

"You didn't hear what happened?"

"No. He took strawberry tarts." Clara chuckled and threw her hands up. "What was I thinking shooting my mouth off like that?"

"Turns out he went crazy and asked Aunt Molly to marry him. Later, he blew up at me and Henry, threatening us because he thought I tricked him up by suggesting the tarts."

"That's not right." Clara frowned.

"We followed him to a boarding house, and he went in the back door, and when he came out a woman was hanging onto him and they kissed. How could he do that after asking Aunt Molly for her hand in marriage?"

"Wicked man. Can't stop being the arrogant, selfish rogue for one minute." Clara's face reddened.

Tess lowered her head, afraid to continue. Mr Barrett was a good friend of Miss Clara's. Her next words might destroy what was left. "We saw him kick a man. In the alley." She peeked out from under her eyelashes waiting for Clara's reaction.

Clara inhaled deeply then slowly let out her breath, frozen and still as a church mouse. "He said he would never get his hands dirty, insisted he would never stoop so low. Wait till he shows his face in here. I'll have a few words to say to that man. I am so disappointed I cannot see straight. His arrogance and greed have gotten the better of him. There is no going back."

"We have to tell Sergeant Roberts."

Clara pinched her nose and sighed. "There goes that romance out the window. He will think I was in cahoots with Fred."

"Why?"

"Fred lent me the money to open this business. I wonder what kind of money my bakery was built on." She lowered her head and covered her face with her hands sobbing.

Tess gently stroked her back. "Why did you believe me when Mother and Aunt Molly did not?"

"You didn't tell me anything I didn't already know, just thought I could forget and carry on with my new life."

"Don't worry. You will. I'm going to find the evidence we need to get rid of Mr Barrett. You'll see."

"He's a slippery snake, be careful. Let Sergeant Roberts handle things."

Tess ran out of the bakery and back to the hotel.

NINETY

Earl leaned in his chair and threw his head back howling with laughter.

"What's so funny?"

"You're moping around here whining because you forgot to spy on Mrs Bruin? How were you planning to pull that off? Hide behind a curtain and wait, hoping she wouldn't notice?"

"The verandah. Her window faces the street."

"Idiot. Forget about the gold for now. Let me handle the sabotage, and when I'm done you'll be able to buy her hotel for less than the cost of that bottle of whiskey." He nodded his head toward the side table.

"I asked her to marry me." Fred said in a low voice. "I didn't mean to. It spilled out before I could contain myself."

"She must be quite the woman to have that effect on you."

"She is a fine, gentle woman with spirit and character."

"You have been known to admire fine women, I'll give you that."

"This is different. I have been in love with her since the day we met."

"No surprise there. You enjoy the challenge of an unavailable woman."

"Be quiet."

"Did you kill Beau so you could get to Molly?"

Fred picked up his coffee cup and took a sip, swishing the bitter black liquid around in his mouth before swallowing, taking his time before he answered. "It was an accident. I tried to save him but childhood survival instincts kicked in. He was a threat to my way of doing things, blocking my path to success. Ma would have been proud."

"Of you killing your friend?"

"Taking what should be mine."

Earl whistled through his teeth. "Ma wanted you to succeed but not like this. She taught me to stand up for myself. I'm not sure what she taught you."

"Ma made sure I knew I had no one to depend on but myself."

NINETY-ONE

Tess and Henry sat opposite Sergeant Roberts in the NWMP station watching him search through files. He pulled one from the pile and reviewed its contents.

"Mr Barrett filed a report of attempted robbery. He claims a man tried to steal his horse and buggy. He acted in self-defense."

Tess shook her head back and forth. "That's not what we saw."

Henry looked at her. "The man grabbed hold of the harness and yelled at Mr Barrett."

"Whose side are you on?" Tess turned to stare at Henry.

"Unfortunately, it says here the man left town and Mr Barrett decided not to press charges."

"That is convenient. It's our word against his." Tess sighed. "No one will believe us." Miss Clara had believed her. She knew Mr Barrett better than anyone, it seemed. Tess was reluctant to tell the sergeant and ruin her friend's chance for romance. "Let's go."

Henry pulled open the door.

Tess stalked past him but paused, turning toward Sergeant Roberts. "Henry found cigars on Theo's desk after the shed fire, and we know for a fact that Theo does not smoke."

"Interesting. What brand?"

"Same as Carl's."

"Carl said he was missing some from his box in the kitchen," said Sergeant Roberts. "Great job, kids. We will look into it."

Once they were outside, Henry and Tess walked back to the hotel.

"What about the woman?" Henry asked. "What did your aunt say about that?"

"She and Mother think I made up the whole thing. They didn't believe me."

"Main thing is we know what we saw."

"What good does that do?" Tess kicked a rock as they walked.

"We know something Mr Barrett does not."

"What's that?"

"He is not as nice as everyone thinks. We gotta figure out how to show it to the people who count."

"It could take forever," said Tess, whining as her impatience kicked in.

"We're kids. All we have is time."

Tess stopped and stared at her friend. "Are you sure you're only ten?"

NINETY-TWO

Later that evening Fred strode into the Palace Grand eager to impress. He caught Floyd Gardall's eye and nodded as he took his place in the back row.

Floyd nodded briefly, flexing his fingers as he sat at the piano.

"Attention, please. We must stay focused tonight and make the most of the last practice before our performance at the dance. Perfection is the goal," said Mrs Wright.

She took Mr Percy's baton and waved it as she spoke, pointing to several men and women at random.

"We have two days to prepare for our debut. I am sure I don't have to remind you how important this is to our city."

Mr Percy bounced up and down waving his arm as he tried to grab his baton so he could signal Floyd to begin playing.

Fred chuckled then brought his hand to his mouth to stifle the noise as Mrs Wright's eyes darted his way. He could not figure out whether she had super-sensitive hearing or had honed in on his movement with her eagle eyes.

"Mr Barrett, this is not a laughing matter. Being a part of this choir is a privilege not given to many. I advise you to treat your fellow members with the utmost respect."

Fred lowered his chin, feeling like a chastened schoolboy. "Yes, Mrs Wright. I was wondering if Mr Percy might like to have his baton returned in order for us to proceed with the serious business of singing."

A low rumble of laughter rolled through the group but stopped as Mrs Wright glared. She handed the baton to Mr Percy then took her position front and center clasping her hands together.

"Begin."

Floyd's nimble fingers coaxed cheerful tunes from the piano keys. The choir voices came together in erratic harmony and eventually produced recognizable melodies.

An hour later, the group dispersed and Fred stood near the piano conversing with Floyd and Mr Percy.

Mrs Wright approached the trio.

"Mr Barrett, may I have a word with you before you go?" She gestured toward the stage.

"Most certainly, Madam." Fred shook the men's hands then proceeded to the stage.

He watched Floyd and Mr Percy leave the hall. "How may I help you?"

Mrs Wright puffed up her chest like a mother hen, rustling the multiple layers of white lace as she held her hat in front of her. "You have done enough, Mr Barrett."

Fred frowned slightly but continued smiling. "I don't understand."

"Despite your disruptions at inappropriate times, I have come to like you. You have been a great help with the dance preparations, and you have shown great improvement in your voice and in your demeanor."

"I am pleased you think highly of me, Mrs Wright. Thank you."

"My husband and I are hosting a luncheon on Sunday, and we would be delighted if you would be our guest. It has become an annual tradition to hold a refined social function after the summer dance. Only the upper levels of society are in attendance. A bit of fresh air as they say."

Fred's eyes lit up. "I would be honored to attend. Please give Judge Wright my sincere best wishes."

"Wonderful. I will have a social card delivered to your residence tomorrow. Good evening, Mr Barrett." Mrs Wright smiled, affixing her hat to her head with a pearl-topped hat pin.

Fred gave a deep bow then strode from the hall, patting his hat on his head as he approached Daisy. He hopped into the buggy and headed down the road, smiling broadly. He tried to calm his breathing that bordered on hyperventilation by inhaling the cool evening air deeply into his lungs.

An invitation to the Judge's home for a luncheon was a golden opportunity, and he had to make the most of it. Soon he would be hobnobbing with the proper people and making friends in high places. Someday he would run for mayor.

"What a night, Daisy." He laughed as Daisy whinnied and swished her mane from side to side.

NINETY-THREE

Tess placed a chocolate cake garnished with cherries on the shelf in the window next to another example of her skills, a layer cake with fluffy white frosting and delicate pink roses circling the top. As she turned from the window, Fred entered the bakery.

His eyes narrowed and his lips flickered as he sneered at Tess.

"Good morning, Miss Tess." He removed his hat and bowed. "I am feeling rather cheerful this morning despite our unfortunate misunderstanding the other day. Please accept my apologies for allowing my anger to get the better of me."

Tess folded her arms ignoring him as she walked toward the kitchen where Clara was whipping cream.

Fred stepped forward blocking her path. "A good baker's assistant does not ignore her customers."

"How may I help you, Sir?" Tess continued to glower at him.

"You can help by staying out of my business. Stick to playing with dolls and your strange little friend. You are children, a nuisance as far as I'm concerned, and you cannot stop me from getting what I want."

"I will never let you marry Aunt Molly. Henry and I saw you with that woman yesterday."

Fred wrinkled his brow. "What woman?"

"In the alley, at the boarding house with the red door."

Fred laughed. "I own that building. It was time to collect the rent."

"You kissed her."

"People are drawn to my handsome looks and charisma. What can I say?" He stroked his chin and chuckled.

Tess straightened her back and glared at him. "You have no business playing with Aunt Molly's emotions. I know what you are up to. Henry and I will be watching you." Tess trembled, fighting to return Fred's steely look.

"Watch me all you want but you'll never be able to do anything about it. I could make your life miserable, so be forewarned." Fred folded his arms against his chest and smirked.

Tess stood her ground, fuming. As much as she tried, she couldn't run away from her problems, from bullies like Agatha. They merely continued to appear in a different form. If she didn't stand up to Fred, she would continue to be bullied, letting it erode her confidence, and give in to a life of defeat.

"Stay away from me, Mr Barrett, or I will scream. We will see who Miss Clara believes when I tell her you threatened me."

Fred glanced at the kitchen then left the bakery without a word, slapping his hat on his head.

Clara emerged from the kitchen. "Was that Fred?"

Tess nodded, shivering uncontrollably as she forced her wobbly legs to move, thankful she was not carrying a cake. "Yes. He came in to inform us he will no longer need to pick up cinnamon rolls."

NINETY-FOUR

Fred clenched his fists at his sides as he stomped along the boardwalk towards Daisy. He couldn't think straight. Frustration and anger clouded his thoughts. If he didn't take control of his emotions, he would continue to make mistakes, calling attention to his schemes. He prided himself on staying in control, exerting confidence and superiority in every situation. How had he allowed a child to antagonize him so easily?

"It's Earl's fault," he mumbled under his breath.

NINETY-FIVE

Tess walked back to the hotel in a daze. Her mind whirled with excitement and fear. After allowing the humiliation of Agatha's bullying to haunt her for too long she felt exhilarated standing up to Mr Barrett, but, in doing so she had awakened a dangerous foe. She glanced over her shoulder as she picked up her pace and hurried home.

Minutes later, Tess walked into the parlor.

Molly wept as Anna sat beside her on the settee.

"I am at my wits end, Anna. Sergeant Roberts believes someone is targeting our businesses. If I were to rebuild, they might be destroyed again. She shuddered as she looked at Anna. "I can't do this without my Beau." She sobbed. "He is not coming back, is he?"

Anna shook her head slowly from side to side, tears sliding down her cheeks, ignoring them as she held Molly's hand. "I fear not."

Tess knelt in front of the two women. "We can't give up."

Molly smiled and patted Tess's head. "It is merely a business transaction selling to Mr Barrett. I will never regard it as giving up. We could start anew in Vancouver, the three of us."

"I think you're wrong. If you sell to Mr Barrett he wins."

"It is not a contest, Tess."

"He certainly thinks it is."

"I thought you wanted to move back to Vancouver," said Anna, stroking Tess's hair. "You could see Sally again. Go back to your old school in the fall."

"Of course, but it seems like a lifetime ago. I don't think I would fit in anymore. I feel free, no longer a fearful, timid child."

"Has it only been less than two weeks? So much has happened to you. I feel responsible."

"This move was good for both of us."

"It's true, I haven't missed Vancouver as much as I thought I might," said Anna.

"If they don't find who set those fires, will Henry and I be blamed?" Tess asked voicing a fear she had held deep inside, worried that saying it aloud might make it come true.

"Your aunt and I know you were not responsible. You would be able to put it behind you if we returned to Vancouver."

Tess nodded, her eyes widened as she fought back tears, unable to speak for a moment.

"We never once believed you and Henry would do such a thing. Sergeant Roberts and his men are working hard to find out who did," said Anna. "Despite what you may think, I am here for you."

"I know. I apologize for being childish and expecting you to entertain me when you had to keep the hotel running and care for Aunt Molly."

"She has been a godsend," said Molly. "You both have saved me."

"If we moved back to Vancouver James could join us. We would be a family again," said Anna, her eyes welled up with tears and she lowered her chin, dabbing at her eyes with a corner of her apron.

"I don't think we will be happier in Vancouver. What if Father doesn't return? We can't live a rewarding life while pining for a different one." Tess surprised herself with her words, realizing they were true. "It has been exciting here in Dawson and is beginning to feel like home." Tess pulled herself up and stood in front of her aunt and mother. "I hardly recognize myself. I refuse to be the girl who let bullies win."

Molly and Anna glanced at each other, smiles flickering at the corners of their lips.

"We don't have to make a decision yet," said Molly. "Let's wait to hear from Sergeant Roberts."

"Would you excuse me? I must find Henry." Tess kissed her mother and aunt on their cheeks and skipped out of the room.

She peeked in the dining room. It was the lunch hour yet a handful of guests occupied a few tables. She popped into the kitchen. Chef Pierre stirred a steaming pot on the woodstove, throwing in chopped herbs, tasting with a spoon.

"Hello Tess, are you hungry? Can I entice you with a bowl of mushroom soup?"

Tess made a face and shook her head. "Thank you, but I already ate at the bakery. It smells good." She smiled. "Have you seen Henry?"

"He is helping his mother with an errand. They should be back soon."

"I'll wait for him outside." She went through the back door and down the porch steps. Startled, she spotted Carl sitting on an overturned barrel smoking a cigar. Tess stopped, searching for a place to hide but he saw her.

"Hey," said Carl, staring at her through the lock of hair covering his eyes.

"Hi. It looks like a few people are eating at the restaurant."

"Mostly new guests from out of town who haven't heard the rumors."

"I'm glad Aunt Molly didn't fire you."

"Why would she do that?"

"The restaurant has been slow."

Carl puffed on his cigar.

"I'm sure no one believes you started the fire," said Tess, in an attempt to make conversation, uncomfortable with silence yet worried she might say the wrong thing.

Carl snorted. "Yeah, right. I've had the police breathing down my back ever since that night."

"I don't think you did it."

"Gee, thanks. Get your friend the sergeant to back off if you're so confident. I told him a couple of cigars were missing from my box in the kitchen, but I can't prove it."

Tess moved a rock around with her foot, avoiding Carl's glare. She clamped her mouth shut, tempted to tell Carl about Theo, but afraid of his reaction. She let out a sigh of relief as Henry appeared in the doorway.

Henry jumped off the porch. "Pa says you were looking for me. What did you find out? Hey, Carl."

Carl stared at the pile of rubble that used to be the storage shed as he nodded to Henry.

"Tess and I think we know who burned the shed, but can't prove it yet. The two fires are connected somehow. Me and Tess are going to figure out how."

"You two? Good luck." Carl snorted.

Tess grabbed Henry's arm. "Let's go."

"Where?"

"I'll tell you on the way."

NINETY-SIX

Fred rode up to the front of his saloon and jumped off the buggy, securing Daisy's reins to the post.

Sergeant Roberts and two of his men approached.

"Are you an owner of the gambling hall situated behind your building? We have a complaint that it has been operating on Sundays, and threats have been made to gamblers who don't pay up their losses. There are suspicions of other criminal activities from that vicinity as well. We have enough evidence to shut him down."

"Certainly not. My businesses are run honestly and fairly."

"You know the owner. Interesting you both have the same last name."

Fred frowned. "We do but his is spelled with one 't' instead of two. What will happen to him?"

"He will be handed a blue ticket and put on the next boat out of here, with a warning to never return."

"Marvelous. It will be my privilege to help. I commend you and your men for keeping our city safe from undesirables."

Inwardly he congratulated himself. Soon after Earl had showed up in Dawson City, Fred saw his opportunity to add him to the ownership maze.

He purchased the building adjacent to his hotel, filing the necessary paperwork, stating it would be a sewing shop and laundry service with Earl as the owner, without his knowledge.

His anonymous complaint to the NWMP was the perfect opportunity to get rid of Earl and take back his growing empire, avoiding the unpleasant task of soiling his hands.

"He and I discuss business over drinks now and then. I don't know him that well, but as luck would have it we planned to meet for lunch in my restaurant."

"What a coincidence," said Sergeant Roberts squinting at the position of the sun high in the sky. "It is lunchtime."

"Follow me, gentlemen."

Fred led them into the restaurant, and spying Earl lounging in one of the chairs at a table in the back, pointed him out. "It's best if I am not seen. I trust you no longer need my assistance."

Sergeant Roberts nodded, and Fred slipped out the front door and casually walked toward the river.

NINETY-SEVEN

Tess ran along the boardwalk towards Bert's cabin. Henry followed.

"He's not going to talk."

"I want to confirm something."

They arrived, breathless, outside Bert's cabin. The door was closed and Bert's rocking chair empty.

Tess hesitated, remembering the last time they visited and scared him out of his wits. "Maybe we shouldn't disturb him."

Henry snorted and pushed past her up the steps onto the porch, rapping his knuckles against the door. A board creaked as Henry stepped back and waited.

"Bert, are you in there?" Henry yelled through the door then peeked in the window. A tattered navy shirt blocked his view.

They waited then Henry knocked again. "Bert, it's me, Henry."

He jiggled the doorknob, unlatching it, and the door swung open.

The interior of the cabin was dark. The front window let in little light.

Tess pulled the old shirt to one side, allowing a ray of light to infiltrate the darkness. Dust particles floated in the light beam that landed on a shabby brown rug covering the floor in front of a sagging wooden bed.

Bert lay on the rough grey blanket, eyes closed, his breathing ragged and shallow.

The two children rushed to his side.

"Bert, are you alright? Say something." Henry poked his arm and Bert groaned.

"What are you kids doing, trying to scare an old man to death?" He struggled to sit but clutched his chest and fell back onto the pillow.

"What's wrong? Does your chest hurt?" Tess asked, fearful of his answer.

"It's nothing you kids need to be concerned about. Can't I get a wink of sleep around here?"

"You are not fooling us. There is something wrong with you. You need to see the doctor."

"Forget that business. He won't tell me anything I don't already know."

Henry caught Tess's eye and whispered. "You stay here. I'll get Pa."

Before Tess could answer, Henry ran out the door towards the hotel.

"Bert, stay awake for me, will you? We can visit until Henry returns."

Bert nodded but kept his eyes closed. "You're a feisty one, young lady. You didn't know it when you arrived, but I did. One tough egg, but you let others get your goat too easily."

"You didn't even know me."

"I could see through you. A ghost of a child, uprooted and lost. The last place you wanted to be was Dawson City, far away from everything familiar."

"I didn't want to abandon Father."

"Where is he?"

"He is missing in action in the Boer War, on the other side of the world. I was afraid if we left he would never find us, especially in the middle of nowhere."

"And, now you've changed your mind?"

"In many ways Dawson City is more advanced than Vancouver."

"During the gold rush this place was rolling in gold and money, enough to buy the best in the world, from the finest china to the latest in advancements. I'll bet you we've got more telephones here than in Vancouver. They called this the Paris of the North."

"The hotel has a few telephones. Theo uses one all the time."

"They are a handy gadget if you feel like talking to people. I don't see the necessity. I hate people in general."

Tess poked Bert's arm. "You do not."

"I especially hate tough eggs poking me in the arm." He winked, then moaned as he placed a hand on his chest again, closing his eyes.

Tess giggled but stopped as Bert's breathing quickened. "Bert?"

Bert lay motionless on the bed.

Boards on the porch creaked as footsteps landed with a thump. Elmer and Henry burst into the room, followed by Nellie who rushed to Bert's side and took his hand in hers.

"Papa, it's me, Nellie. Can you hear me?" She spoke into his ear.

"Of course I can, I'm not deaf." Bert opened his eyes. "Nice of you all to visit but I'd like to have a nap. Come back tomorrow."

"We are not leaving until you tell us what happened," said Elmer, standing at the foot of the bed with his arms crossed.

"I was writing in my journal when an elephant pinned me down and walked across my chest, so I decided to lie down until he left."

"That's it we are taking you to St. Mary's Hospital. Nellie, grab his arms. I'll get his legs. We'll carry him out to the wagon."

Bert pushed their hands away and pulled himself up, leaning against the headboard. "I'm not a rag doll. I can walk on my own." He moved his legs to the edge of the bed and with the help of Elmer and Nellie he stood, teetering for a moment before putting one foot in front of the other. He stopped. "Wait. Henry, get my boots. They're beside the stove."

Henry grabbed the worn leather boots. He and Tess put them on over Bert's stocking feet before jumping up and pinching their noses shut with their fingers. "Pee-ew, your feet stink."

"My feet are clean enough. Just had my bath last month."

Together the four of them helped Bert out to the wagon and hauled him to the hospital. The two-storey log building was a welcome sight, built on a level patch of land below the ancient landslide, a defiant symbol that provided hope and healing to the townspeople.

Nellie and Henry stayed while Elmer took Tess back to the hotel.

"Tell your aunt I'm back. Dinner will be ready on time, in case people decide to show up." Elmer grumbled on his way to the kitchen.

Tess ran to the parlor. She burst into the room which sat empty and silent.

"In here, Tess." Molly called from the bedroom.

Tess entered and stood by the bed. "Nellie and Henry are at the hospital. Elmer... I mean Chef Pierre is back in the kitchen preparing dinner."

"How is poor Bert?"

"As cranky as ever but something is wrong with his chest."

"We are all thankful you and Henry discovered him in time."

"He will be okay, won't he?"

"We must hope for the best." Molly laid her head back among the pillows and closed her eyes.

"I will leave you for now. Try to get some rest."

"I should help in the kitchen," Molly mumbled as she rolled over and stared out the window.

"No, you need to get your strength back. I can help Mother and Chef Pierre if needed."

Tess tip-toed out of the room, hurried to the dining room. Her mother was going over an inventory list.

"If you don't need me I think I'll go to my room for a while."

"Go ahead, dear."

Tess ignored Theo and climbed the stairs to their room, thinking about Bert, Henry's grandfather. Families suffered losses and were expected to continue living, but she didn't want to think about carrying on without her father. What if he didn't return? She did not have the heart to consider the possibility of never again playing at the beach and building sandcastles with him.

Tess lay on her bed. Grief pressed down on her, heavy and suffocating, sobs racked her body and she gave into hopelessness. She cried herself to sleep and drifted into the world of dreams.

Tess hurried toward the river. She pushed through trees emerging onto the sandy beach.

A thick stand of birch muffled the sounds of Front Street, and a slight breeze whispered through the leaves. The Yukon River flowed in silence, broken branches bobbing up and down as they passed Tess standing at the water's edge. Water gurgled against rocks but left the beach untouched.

Tess knelt on the black sand, the same color as her heart filled with overwhelming feelings of sadness and loss. She gathered the sand together in a pile with her hands. Black suited her mood. The beach in Vancouver had been lighter, speckled with tiny bits of white shell. She patted the wet sand into walls of the castle and formed a turret on each corner. She dug a protective moat around her sandcastle.

The strong current of water flowed downstream ignoring the moat, leaving it empty. No hissing, crashing waves crawled up the beach to pull apart her castle. The Yukon River was a benign force of nature, uninterested in destroying it. Tess had a feeling the river was not responsible for taking her uncle's life.

"Our family is stronger than Mr Barrett." She picked up a branch, removed all the leaves but three and stuck it in the highest tower.

Something blocked the sun, casting a shadow over her handiwork. Before she could look up it smashed down on her castle leaving it in ruin, a soggy pile of sand.

NINETY-EIGHT

Fred headed for the Palace Grand to help finish setting up for the dance. Earl was capable of escaping custody or may refuse to leave Dawson, but Fred had faith in Sergeant Roberts to handle him. He knew Earl would tell the sergeant Fred was behind the fires and the crew member's death, but there was no evidence pointing to Fred.

The dredge was operating once again with a new crew in place. Fred had destroyed all signs and paperwork showing the man had worked there. He planned to stay away from his office for a while just in case.

Outside the Palace Grand a woman sat on a wrought iron bench twirling a white parasol.

Fred slowed his pace, but he was unable to avoid her.

"Freddy, baby, I've been looking all over for you." The woman rose from the bench with grace and dignity and casually smoothed her skirt.

"Florrie, what are you doing here?"

"You promised you'd take me for dinner but you never came back."

"I've been busy. Give me a few days to straighten things out and we will definitely have a night on the town."

"You always say that, then I don't see you for days." Florrie stamped her foot. She stepped toward him and placed her white gloved hand on his chest.

"Not here." Fred lowered his voice scanning the area for people who might recognize him. "Go back to the dance hall and I'll meet you there later. I promise."

Florrie pouted then spun on her heels and flounced down the boardwalk, her parasol bobbing in the air.

Fred set his mouth in a grim line as he entered the darkened entrance of the Palace Grand Theater. He blinked, waiting for his eyes to adjust as he escaped the glaring sunlight that threatened to expose his other life.

"Hey Fred, do you know of any good singers?"

Fred jumped, startled at the voice that had come from the shadows. "What do you mean by that?" He scowled.

Floyd emerged from behind the door to the hall. "Nothing. Mrs Wright asked me to find a replacement for Miss Winsome who has taken ill. We will be short one soprano for the dance."

"You startled me. I'm afraid I don't know any singers who might be a good fit for the choir." Fred shook his head, knowing Florrie could put the entire choir to shame with her magical voice. Unfortunately, in a ridiculous set of circumstances, a woman like Florrie would never be considered, despite her talent. "Shame about Miss Winsome."

Fred threw himself into the final preparations, setting up rows of benches on stage where the choir was to perform. The piano was on the floor below the stage.

Tables lined two sides of the hall, covered in lace tablecloths and adorned with mason jars filled with pink fireweed, blue lupins, and baby's breath.

Three hours later, Fred left the theater and headed toward his hotel, taking the alley to avoid passing in front of the dance hall.

As soon as he started down the alley, he realized his mistake. Out of sight of the respectable citizens he was at the mercy of the seedy aspect. He quickened his pace, passing a dark figure sitting on the ground leaning against a building with their hat over their eyes.

He reached the back door to his saloon and ducked through the door. His pulse raced with fear which turned to anger as he entered familiar territory, ignoring the bartender and patrons as he went into his office.

Fred removed his hat and tossed it on the empty chair that Earl no longer occupied. He poured himself a drink and sat behind his desk with his feet resting on its surface. Muffled voices and music from the saloon seeped into the room amplifying the silence. Fred raised his glass to the empty chair. "Here's to my new life."

A knock at the door made Fred jump, his feet dropping off the desk with a thump. He spilled a few drops of whiskey down his shirt.

"Who is it?"

The door opened and Fred let out the breath he had been holding as the bartender popped his head through the crack. "Someone here to see you, Boss."

NINETY-NINE

Tess opened her eyes, her heart racing as the last remnants of her dream faded, leaving her trembling. She stood on shaky legs, holding the bedpost until she regained her balance.

Tess made her way downstairs and entered the restaurant.

"Just in time." Anna waved her arm gesturing Tess to sit.

Tess hugged her mother and Molly, a burst of love mixed with anxiety made her hold on longer than usual, causing the two women to exchange glances after Tess sat in her chair.

The dining room was empty except for a few hotel guests. No one approached their table.

"I could get used to this," said Molly, scanning the room. "It was lovely to see our friends and customers, but Beau and I never had a quiet meal with just the two of us unless we ate in the parlor."

"Why didn't you build a separate little dining room in your suite?" Tess asked.

"At the time we didn't think it was necessary."

"It would have been terribly impractical," said Anna. "The kitchen staff would be running back and forth through the lobby with hot food and dirty dishes."

"Wise words, dear sister. Your assistance has been invaluable and words are not enough to express my gratitude." Molly pulled a red velvet box from her pocket and handed it to Anna.

Anna's eyes grew wide as she took the box and opened the lid. A pea-sized gold nugget lay inside a coil of delicate sparkling chain.

"It's beautiful." Anna exclaimed as she lifted it up to examine the necklace. "You didn't have to do this, Molly."

"I wanted to show my appreciation."

"It will be perfect with my gown for the dance tomorrow. Thank you." Anna touched Molly's arm and smiled.

Anna handed the necklace to Tess.

"I have never seen anything like this. That chunk came out of the ground? This place is amazing." Tess gazed in wonder at the nugget twirling before her eyes. "We should go hunt for gold sometime. Maybe have a picnic."

"We still have our claim. That is a marvelous idea. Beau would have dearly loved to be the one to teach you how to pan for gold."

Tess lowered her head. "Never mind. It was a silly idea."

"No, it is not. It is time we move forward and make a life for ourselves. Beau wanted the best for us. I will teach you." Molly inhaled deeply and lifted Tess's chin to gaze into her eyes. "Let's eat. Chef Pierre has prepared your favorite dessert."

"Chocolate moose?"

"Of course." Molly laughed.

After dinner, Tess went with Henry and Nellie to visit Bert at the hospital.

Bert lay on the white metal frame bed. His eyes were closed.

"He looks ancient." Tess whispered to Henry.

Bert opened his eyes and glared at the two children for a moment. "I heard that but will take it as a compliment. Anyone over the age of twenty looks old to you two. I don't regret a single minute of my life, and you best remember to make yours count."

"We won't stay long," said Nellie, leaning toward her father and kissing his cheek.

"Doc says I don't have long."

"What?" Nellie gasped.

"He's kicking me out of here tomorrow." Bert chuckled. "Always could get a rise out of you."

Nellie playfully slapped his arm. "You are incorrigible."

Tess moved closer to Bert. "I want to ask you something."

"If I knew what it was, I could give you an answer."

"I haven't asked you yet." Tess rolled her eyes toward the ceiling. "Did Mr Barrett ever talk to you about my uncle?"

Bert scratched his clean beard, no longer speckled with bits of food and ash from his cigars. "I reckon there ain't much he hasn't talked about. He's a big talker, likes to brag. Thinks he's better than all of us, but he's a two-bit con artist. I know the type."

"What does he know about Uncle Beau's accident?"

"I was too far away when it happened. He says they were talking business when Beau tripped. I didn't see what happened after that. That was all I could tell the police."

"I don't understand why Uncle Beau did not swim to shore."

"Good chance he hit his head on something. Lots of debris in that river."

Nellie pulled the blanket over Bert's chest and tucked in the edges. "Get some rest, Papa. We will see you in the morning."

Tess and Henry followed Nellie out of the hospital and they walked home.

"I'm positive Mr Barrett had more to do with Uncle Beau's death than he admits. My uncle was a strong man."

"The only people who know what happened are Mr Barrett and your uncle, but he's dead."

"That leaves Mr Barrett. I have to find a way to get him to talk."

"Good luck. Nothing will make him admit to you he murdered his friend and partner."

ONE HUNDRED

Fred's gut lurched as Florrie pushed past the bartender who hesitated for a moment raising his eyebrow in a silent question.

Fred sighed then nodded with reluctance.

The bartender's raised eyebrow disappeared behind the door as it closed.

"I told you I would meet you later."

"It is later," said Florrie, as she gathered her ivory silk skirt close, picked up Fred's hat and set it on the desk before settling into Earl's chair. She pulled off her white gloves one finger at a time as she glanced around the room. "I'd love a drink."

Fred rose and moved to the side table. "I've got whiskey here or I could get you something from the bar."

"That's fine."

Fred poured whiskey into a crystal glass and handed it to her before returning to his chair.

"Where shall we go for dinner?" Florrie curled her ruby lips into a smile before taking a sip of the amber liquid.

"I thought we could have an intimate dinner in here. The Palace Grand is closed. Preparations for the summer dance."

"Dinner in your office? You certainly know how to treat a lady." Florrie sniffed. "I hear the Golden Grizzly is fabulous. Their chef is the best in town."

Fred was not prepared to be seen about town with Florrie a common dance hall girl. She may be his star singer but was an anchor when it came to high society.

"There was a recent case of food poisoning. The owner is recovering. We will eat in tonight."

ONE HUNDRED ONE

Tess ran to the bakery late, her hair rolled in rags. Her mother didn't want her to remove them until right before the dance that evening.

"Thank you for coming. I have been baking rolls all morning and we need another ten dozen. You can help me wrap everything for delivery to the theater." Clara placed a pan into the oven.

"Are you going to the dance?"

"I will probably fall asleep in the punch but I'll be there." Clara laughed. "I'm hoping a certain someone will be, too."

The door to the bakery opened and Sergeant Roberts entered. "Anyone here?"

Clara's eyes widened, and she mouthed the words to Tess. 'It's him.'

Tess giggled as Clara pinched her cheeks to make them rosy and patted her hair leaving white streaks of flour wherever she had touched.

Clara casually strolled to the front of the bakery. "Why, hello Sergeant Roberts. What a pleasure to see you this fine morning."

Sergeant Roberts removed his hat and tucked it under his arm. He bowed slightly before moving to the display shelves. "I am a great lover of your cinnamon rolls. Have you got any left?"

"You are in luck. I have one. My shelves are a little sparse, working on getting the rolls and baked treats ready for the dance. Tess and I must deliver them this afternoon."

"Are you going tonight?" Sergeant Roberts asked, staring intently at the empty shelf in front of him.

Clara nodded. "Never miss it. We will see you there, I hope?" She placed the roll in a napkin and tied it closed with a string.

"I'm on duty but will pop in for a spell. Seems the church choir is the hot ticket, want to see it for myself."

"I'm never sure if it was supposed to be serious or a comedic intermission. No one dares laugh for fear of the wrath of the judge's wife."

Sergeant Roberts chuckled. "I look forward to watching the shenanigans." He took the napkin and winked at Clara before exiting the shop.

Clara twirled on her heels and clasped her hands together as she faced Tess. "It's a date."

Tess wrinkled her nose in confusion but smiled at Clara's excitement, following her into the kitchen.

Tess stood at the table placing cookies into boxes while Clara packaged up the cakes. She thought about Bert's comment. "Do you think Mr Barrett would tell you if he killed Uncle Beau?"

"Oh honey, he will never admit that to anyone, not even me. He is careful about his image. When you see him doing something wrong, come tell me and I will go with you to the police. If Sergeant Roberts likes me, he will understand my position. If not, too bad. He'll have to find another baker."

"That is the nicest thing anyone has ever said to me." Tess looked over at Clara, her friend. She swallowed the lump in her throat, fighting back tears. If they moved to Vancouver, she would never see Clara or Henry again, and for the first time Tess realized she would fight to stay in Dawson City, to become a part of the community and make new friends.

ONE HUNDRED TWO

Later that afternoon, Fred hummed to himself as he exited the barber shop. He nodded to passersby as he strolled along the boardwalk toward his office.

He agreed with the idea of community dances. Events that brought the community together made the residents happy, giving them a sense of belonging and trust between neighbors. He counted on using that trust to further his own ambitions.

Soon the days would become shorter and cooler, and autumn would arrive at least a month before it did down south.

Fred didn't want to think about the coming winter but the lack of sunlight made it easier to do business without being seen.

He whistled a quiet tune as he nodded and smiled to the patrons in his saloon. He nodded to the bartender who stopped wiping a glass and stared.

Everything was going his way, and Fred had decided he didn't need Molly Bruin. He had an exclusive invitation to the judge's home. Too bad Florrie was not going to be a suitable companion. He would remedy that soon enough. There were sure to be plenty of young women at Sunday's luncheon.

Fred put on his tuxedo and straightened his tie. Popped his top hat on his slicked back hair and checked his pocket watch. Daisy was clean and groomed.

Minutes later he pulled his buggy up to the Palace Grand Theatre.

ONE HUNDRED THREE

Later that afternoon, Tess sat in a chair while Anna removed the rags and brushed Tess's hair into ringlets. She fastened a large pink bow on Tess's head.

Tess stood and twirled her white cotton dress gathered at the waist with a rose pink sash. She loved the lace sleeves and lace appliqué on the skirt that hung to the top of her black leather boots.

"I had Theo polish your boots as best he could. We will have to purchase a new pair for school. You were never this hard on your clothes when we lived in Vancouver."

"Will there be other girls at the dance tonight?"

"Of course. I am surprised you haven't met any of them yet. We will have to throw a luncheon once Molly is feeling better and invite their mothers."

"We don't have to. I'm happy spending the summer with Henry. I can wait for school."

"Don't be shy at the dance. I'm sure you will meet a few who will become great friends."

Tess's stomach clenched as she remembered Agatha. There were sure to be a few of those in Dawson but she must think on the bright side, there might be girls like Sally.

Anna stood back. "You look lovely. There is a sparkle in those eyes I haven't seen in a long time."

"If Father were here…"

"Hush. He would be here if he could. Let's go downstairs. I'm sure Molly will need help."

Anna lifted the skirt of her rose taffeta gown with one hand while she grasped the stair rail with the other and descended with a swish of her skirt. The necklace sat at her collarbone. Her hair was pulled up in an elegant chignon.

"You look beautiful, Mother."

"Thank you, my dear. I feel wonderful. And, excited. How about you?"

"Very excited. This is my first dance."

They entered Molly's parlor and proceeded to her bedroom.

Molly sat on the edge of the bed. She sighed.

"What's wrong?"

"Too much lying in bed and doing nothing. The dress I wanted to wear tonight has become too tight."

Anna immediately searched through Molly's wardrobe pulling out other dresses. "How about this?"

Molly turned to look at Anna's choice then shook her head. "I will have to wear one of my everyday skirts, certainly without a corset."

"I hear the latest fashions are doing away with corsets. You will be perfectly in style."

"I am scandalized." Molly brought her hands to her mouth and her eyes grew wide. She threw her head back and laughed. "It will have to do."

"Are we walking or riding?" asked Tess, twirling in her dress, eager to arrive at the dance as quickly as possible. Her aunt's infectious laughter brought joy to Tess's heart, adding to the excitement, and bringing a sense of normalcy to their little family.

"Chef Pierre and his family will join us in the hotel wagon. We will arrive in style." Molly stood behind the wood-framed paper partition, decorated with painted fireweed blossoms.

She emerged dressed in a long skirt and white blouse.

They met Henry and his family in the lobby.

"Aren't you coming to the dance?" Tess asked Theo.

"I'm working. Someone has to stay and look after the place."

Tess tilted her head. "Enjoy the peace and quiet."

They left the hotel and soon were bouncing along in the wagon toward the Palace Grand Theatre.

A crowd mingled outside the theatre slowly filtering into the building, a buzz of voices hummed in the perfumed air.

Tess whispered to Henry. "Is everyone going to fit in there?"

"There are fewer people in Dawson this year so I'm sure there's room. I'll show you around."

"Do you have butterflies in your stomach, too?" Tess bounced on her toes.

"Are you crazy? What did you eat for lunch?"

"I didn't mean real butterflies. Aren't you nervous or excited?"

"Nope. I went last year, and it's not a big deal. It's fun to run around and eat all the cookies."

"I refuse to run in this dress." Tess pulled at her sleeves. The lace scratched her arms. Why did she think dressing up would be fun?

ONE HUNDRED FOUR

Fred stood outside the theater graciously talking with as many people as possible, complimenting the women on their gowns and laughing with the gentlemen. He felt dashing and debonair.

As he entered the theatre he stuck out his chest and strolled across the floor toward Mrs Wright.

She was talking to a woman, dressed in a white silk taffeta gown with pink chiffon flowers attached at the bodice and along the hem. She tossed her head in laughter, auburn curls catching the light.

He stopped as he overheard Mrs Wright talking.

"I invited Mr Barrett to the luncheon on Sunday, but forgot to ask if he plays tennis. I'm sure he does. You will like him, dear, he is a true gentleman. He owns quite a few businesses in town."

The young woman giggled. "I look forward to meeting him."

Fred squared his shoulders, popped a mint in his mouth and stepped forward with a bow.

"Good evening, Mrs Wright. You are looking lovely as always."

"Mr Barrett, flattery will get you nowhere." Mrs Wright tilted her head and smiled. "May I introduce my niece, Miss Gwendolyn Wright."

Fred bowed low and took the young woman's hand, brushing his lips against her white lace glove. "A pleasure greater than I deserve. It is my honor to make your acquaintance Miss Wright."

"I hear you will be joining us on Sunday. Do you play tennis?"

"I have wielded a racket or two in my time but you will outplay me swiftly and surely."

"We shall see." Miss Wright giggled, bringing her hand to her mouth. "Until Sunday."

"Until then." Fred bowed. "Please excuse me. I must see if my assistance is required at the punch table."

He left the two women. A smile flickered under his mustache as Miss Wright continued to giggle. Sunday couldn't come soon enough.

ONE HUNDRED FIVE

Tess followed Henry as he wove his way through the crowds of people. He headed for the front of the room where a group of women and children surrounded the piano as a man played cheerful tunes.

Henry went up a set of stairs at the side of the stage.

A man and woman were talking near benches that had been set up in the center.

Henry walked up to the heavy red velvet curtain, pulled them apart and peeked out the opening. He motioned Tess closer so she could do the same.

Tess looked out on a sea of faces, not one person looked her way. She felt anonymous, powerful. As a child she was expected to be seen and not heard. On stage, behind the curtain she was unseen but the acoustics of the hall would insure she was heard if she so desired to belt out a song or two.

Tess laughed. She could never sing in front of a crowd, even if someone gave her ten gold nuggets.

Fred stood at the top of the stairs peering onto the stage. "Hello, Mr Percy."

"Fred, good to see you. We are set to go on in about ten minutes. Miss Smith and I will gather the others." Mr Percy moved past him down the steps, and the woman he had been talking to followed dabbing her lips with her handkerchief and avoiding Fred's gaze.

Fred looked around the stage, checking the benches then stopped.

Tess froze grasping the edges of the curtains in her fists.

Henry moved out of sight as Fred sauntered toward the front of the stage.

"Spying on the entire population, are you?"

Tess shook her head, letting go of the curtains that fell closed and stepped away from him to the side of the stage. She glanced toward the stairs and moved toward the curtain as she considered jumping through the heavy fabric.

"You shouldn't be back here." Fred looked through crack in the curtains. "The problem with children is they are constantly sneaking around meddling in people's business that does not concern them."

"We were not bothering anyone. Henry was showing me around."

Fred glanced at Henry who had shrunk into the shadows.

"When I'm mayor of this town, children will not be allowed to run free in the streets creating havoc for hard-working citizens."

"You'll never become mayor. They won't let you."

"Says who?"

"Me. I will do everything in my power to stop you."

"You are a mere child and no one will listen to you. I can do whatever I want. Stay out of my way or else."

"I will tell Sergeant Roberts if you do anything to hurt my family." Tess moved in front of Fred who turned to stare her down, his back to the curtain.

Fred stepped forward, closing the gap between them.

Tess wrinkled her nose, turning her head away from the foul odor of tobacco, onions, and peppermint. Her stomach lurched as he spoke.

"If you make trouble for me, I will see to it that you join your uncle at the bottom of the river."

Tess gasped. "What did you do to him?"

"It was an accident."

"I don't think so. Uncle Beau was big and strong."

"Even a large man can be cut down to size when he's not anticipating an attack." Fred raised his arm, forming a fist toward Tess before lowering it again.

"You hit him?"

"He tripped."

"I don't believe you. You're too weak to beat up Uncle Beau."

"I can, and I did."

"Why?"

"It's none of your concern."

"You made it my concern when you killed my uncle. I know you killed him."

"I told you, it was an accident. Not my fault he fell off the dock."

"You told Aunt Molly you jumped in to save him."

"I did, but he struggled. It was him or me."

"You are a monster."

"I had everything under control until you arrived in town. You and that weird kid sticking your noses in where they don't belong." Fred lunged forward and grabbed Tess's shoulders with both hands.

Tess screamed, grasping at his hands, twisting to free herself with no luck.

"Shut up." Fred moved his hands to encircle her neck.

Tess fought but she was no match for him. With one last bit of strength she brought her hands down, formed them into fists in an attempt to punch him. Her hand caught on the edge of his pocket, ripping it. A small bag fell. Mints rolled across the floor.

A loud gasp echoed throughout the hall.

ONE HUNDRED SIX

Fred turned to face the crowd who had gone silent, his hands around Tess's neck.

Tess coughed and wheezed, gulping the air with rasping breaths. She pulled at his hands with no success, her feet barely touching the floor.

Henry stood, motionless, tears glistening on his cheeks as he held the ropes he had used to open the curtains.

Fred frowned for an instant then backed away from the front of the stage dragging Tess.

"Nothing to see here, folks." He moved towards the back of the stage.

"What happened to Beau Bruin, Fred?" Mr Percy yelled.

"Who started the Bruin lumberyard fire?" Floyd's voice called from the back of the room.

Fred hesitated, then yelled to the crowd.

"The child is lying. Who's going to believe a little girl who has been in trouble since she arrived, over me, an upstanding member of this community?"

"Why, Fred?" Molly's voice was clear and strong before ending in a sob. She leaned against the snack table for support.

"What was I supposed to do? Beau demanded to know what was going on. He threatened to expose me."

"He was a far better man than you."

"Doesn't matter. Your businesses are in ruin. How's your restaurant? Has your chef been locked up yet?"

While Fred was distracted, Sergeant Roberts rushed to the steps at the side of the stage, taking them in one leap.

"Let go of the girl, Fred." He approached with caution, his arms out, palms open. "We can talk about it. Figure out how to fix this."

Fred pulled Tess in front of him, holding one arm across her neck. "Too late for talk."

A dozen men stormed the stairs and jumped onto the stage advancing on Fred as he pulled Tess toward the stage door.

"Don't come near me or this girl will join her uncle at the bottom of the river."

Tess dug her heels in but she had no leverage. Maybe he would let her go if he made it out the door. She tried to breathe but his arm pressed against her neck. He had too much to lose, and Tess had seen the fury in his eyes. He would never be able to let go. She grunted and moaned, pulling at his arm. Her ears rung, stars danced in front of her eyes. It was too late for him, and soon it would be too late for her.

ONE HUNDRED SEVEN

Fred didn't see the mints until it was too late. His feet slid out from under him. He fell backward hitting his head on the floor.

Tess fell on him, gasping for breath.

Anna rushed to gather Tess in her arms and moved her away from Fred.

Sergeant Roberts grabbed Fred, yanking him to his feet. "I am placing you under arrest." He escorted him off the stage.

The crowd, silent and wide-eyed, moved aside to allow them through the hall.

Fred caught Mrs Wright's eye, and she clicked her tongue, shaking her head. He winked, tilting his head slightly.

"Well, I never." Mrs. Wright gasped.

"This is all a mistake. I will set things right and see you at Sunday brunch."

"You will do no such thing, young man. You are a menace to society and not welcome in our home."

Fred's eyes darkened. He jutted out his chin and held his head high. He opened his mouth to speak but Sergeant Roberts pushed him forward.

"We decided to keep Earl in town instead of shipping him off to create havoc on another fine community. Turns out Earl can sing, too. He told us everything. Did you know he kept copies of pay stubs for the dead man, just in case his own brother double-crossed him? Of course, you didn't."

"He's a liar. You can't hold me. What's the charge?"

"You are both being charged with one count of involuntary manslaughter and indecency to a body in the unfortunate death of the dredge crew member. You will also be charged with one count of murder in the death of Beau Bruin. A new charge of assault and attempted kidnapping will be added to the list. We have a room full of witnesses that will attest to your despicable behavior tonight."

Judge Wright stepped forward. "I will meet you at the detachment."

Tess leaned against her mother with trembling legs. Her frantically beating heart roared in her ears.

Distorted voices rose and fell as the dance floor moved beneath her feet like a boat caught in a storm cresting each wave before diving into the ocean depths. Tess swayed slightly.

In provoking Mr Barrett Tess had unleashed a terrifying monster that lurked beneath the surface. His tightly coiled evil had become more difficult to control, and Tess had tricked it into revealing itself. She shivered uncontrollably as reality seeped in reminding her how close she had come to death's door.

Anna wrapped her arms around Tess, moving closer to Molly who stood by the snack table weeping.

Fred sneered at Molly as he passed. "Beau is fish food. You would have been wise to marry me when you had the chance."

"Greed was your undoing. You would have been wise to appreciate what you have." Molly glared at him, then glanced at Tess and Anna. "Never underestimate a child."

ONE HUNDRED EIGHT

The group arrived back at the hotel after the dance. Tess and Anna twirled as they crossed the verandah and entered the hotel.

"I wish they had dances every month." Tess sighed, ignoring her sore feet. "Are children allowed in the dance halls?"

Anna and Molly gasped.

"No, dear, adults only. The prospectors need a break from children running loose around the hall." Anna cast a glance at Molly, who rolled her eyes.

"I think there should be more dances."

"We have one every few weeks during the winter to keep away boredom and cabin fever."

"Are we staying?" Tess asked, wondering if the answer would disappoint or excite her.

"Due to the recent development I declare we stay and call Dawson City home." Anna ruffled Tess's hair, undoing the bow.

"I agree with your mother," said Molly. "This is your home as long as you want. I can't imagine my life without you. We will go panning to find the gold we need to carry on."

Molly hooked her arm through Tess's and strolled across the lobby then stopped. She turned toward the reception counter.

"It is awfully quiet. Where is Theo? I don't know how or why but he is behind the counter all the time. He must be in the kitchen."

Tess ran to check, scanned the empty kitchen then ran back into the lobby.

"No." She peeked behind the reception desk. "His stuff is gone."

Molly gasped. "It must have been Theo."

She gathered up her skirts and hurried into the parlor, with Anna and Tess following.

"I am positive Theo took the gold."

"But, how did he know where to look?"

"He was always around, watching us, listening. He must have seen Beau removing gold from the box one day."

"We must call the police." Anna cried.

Molly hurried to the telephone. Within seconds she spoke into the mouthpiece.

"I have new information regarding the robbery at the Golden Grizzly Hotel. We returned home after the dance to find one of my employees has disappeared. He may have been the one who stole our gold. His name is Theo. He is on the list I gave to the officer."

She listened for a moment. "No, we have no evidence, but his belongings are gone."

Molly lowered her head slightly then nodded, speaking into the mouthpiece. "He will have the evidence on him, I can assure you. He will be carrying a lot of gold that is not his."

She paused while the officer spoke. "Yes, officer, we will wait to hear from you." She hung up the earpiece.

"Well? What happens now?" Anna asked, wringing her hands.

"They will watch the docks and stop him from boarding any boats."

TESS

Tess gasped. "Do you think he started the fire in the storage shed as a distraction while he grabbed the gold?"

"Of course, it would have been the perfect opportunity to gain access while everyone was focused on fighting the fire. We were ignorant to think a secret box sitting on a piano bench would be a safe place to hide our entire savings." Molly fell into a chair with both hands on her cheeks.

"I did think it was odd. But, you told me you made a point of seeing the good in people," said Tess.

"It was naïve of us to believe in the goodness of others."

"Your world will turn dark if you become mistrustful of everyone. But, it might be best to keep temptation out of sight and mind. Not everyone is who they say they are." Tess placed her hand on Molly's shoulder.

"You are wise beyond your years."

"I wonder if that's the reason Theo moved into the hotel." Anna said. "I thought it was rather strange of him but he told me he had lost his room at the boarding house and needed a temporary place to stay until he could find another."

"Do you think they were all in it together? Maybe Theo was working for Mr Barrett. When Carl refused to burn down the shed, Mr Barrett probably told Theo to do it. We found Carl's cigars on Theo's desk."

"I don't believe Theo would have told Mr Barrett or Carl about the gold. He wanted it all for himself." Tess shook her head.

ONE HUNDRED NINE

Tess finished her breakfast. "I'm going with Henry and Nellie to see Bert. He gets out of the hospital today."

"Tell him there is a room made up for him here at the hotel until he is feeling better," said Molly.

"I will, but he will probably growl at us and say his cabin is better just to annoy us."

"Of course he will. You be firm with him, Tess." Molly chuckled.

The trio arrived at the hospital and found Bert sitting on the edge of the bed in his tattered clothing which had been cleaned.

"Get me out of this place. It's noisier than Dead Man's Saloon in here. Didn't get a minute's peace with the new guy." He pointed to the bed beside his.

A figure lay in the bed, face covered in bandages, moaning.

"Who is he?" Tess whispered.

"Nobody knows. They found him in West Dawson crawling along the river's edge. His knees were raw and bleeding. They say his nose was smashed in and his skin was covered in insect bites."

TESS

Tess peeked at the man and shuddered. Prospectors were a tough and hardy bunch but it sounded like this man had fought against nature and barely survived.

The man's arm dropped out from under the blanket.

Tess jumped. She stared at the hand covered in angry red bites and screamed.

"Hush, this is a hospital. What are you going on about?"

"Look at his hand. He has a scar."

"It looks old. Nothing to be afraid of." Henry rolled his eyes.

"Aunt Molly told me a story about the time they fought off a bear at the creek. It took a gash out of Uncle Beau's right hand."

"The ghost is alive." Bert said in a low voice.

"I have to go." Tess ran as fast as she could, ignoring her screaming leg muscles. She burst into the hotel calling out to her aunt.

Chef Pierre appeared in the doorway to the dining room.

"What is all the fuss? Your mother took your aunt to the hospital. She took a turn for the worst."

Tess gasped for air. "I have to go."

She ran back to the hospital. Anna sat on a chair in the hallway.

"Where's Aunt Molly?" Tess gasped, bending over to catch her breath.

Anna pointed toward a canvas door. "She is not well. You can't go in there."

Tess ignored her and ran toward the door before Anna could stop her. She found Molly lying on a bed with her eyes closed while a nurse took her pulse.

"Aunt Molly, I think I saw Uncle Beau."

"Hush, child, you mustn't disturb her. Her heart cannot take the stress." The nurse frowned. "You should not be in here."

"But, this will heal her heart. I promise."

The nurse ushered her out of the room. "Nonsense. Please wait in the hall." She closed the door in Tess's face.

Tess stood in shock, staring at the door for a moment then pushed her way through. "No, this cannot wait." She put her mouth up to Molly's ear and spoke, slowly and clearly. "Uncle Beau is alive. He is here."

Molly's eyes opened wide. She blinked, trying to focus on Tess who held her hand.

"It is impossible," she mumbled. "My dearest Beau is gone forever. I must come to terms with it once and for all."

"He has a scar. On his right hand." Tess fought to keep from squealing, her muscles ached from the tension and excitement.

Molly struggled to sit. "I must see for myself. Nurse?"

The nurse folded her arms and shook her head. "You are in no condition to move at the moment. You had a frightening spell. It was irresponsible of you to while away the evening dancing in your condition."

Molly grabbed Tess's arm and leaned on her as they slowly walked toward the back of the hospital to Bert and the bandaged man.

Anna stood up from the chair where she had been waiting. "What is going on? Where are you taking Molly?"

"Tess thinks Beau is here."

"Tess, how could you mislead your aunt like that? Giving her a false sense of hope."

"I am positive it is Uncle Beau."

"I have to see for myself," said Molly. "What if it is him?"

They made their way slowly to the back room. Bert, Henry and Nellie watched as Tess led Molly to the man's bedside.

The man moaned and raised his hand, revealing a scar shaped like a scraggly 'M'.

Molly sobbed and grabbed his hand putting it to her cheek. "My Beau."

The man tried to speak, coughed, then whispered. "Water."

Tess poured water in a glass and gave it to Molly who held it to Beau's lips.

"Molly, my love," he said in a rasping voice. "I came as soon as I could."

"I am so pleased," she said, letting tears fall from her cheeks to his chest, laughing as one hit his nose. She wiped it away with her finger.

"Not sure why but Fred hit me. Next thing I remember I woke to find myself snagged on a stump in the middle of the river. Fought the current for miles trying to get to shore." He took a deep breath before continuing. "No idea how far from town."

"Don't speak. We want you well again. For me, and the baby."

Tess gasped. She gaped at her mother who merely smiled. "That was a baby blanket you were knitting all this time?"

Molly stared lovingly at her husband and nodded.

Tess frowned. Why had no one bothered to tell her? She clenched her fists and stormed over to the window.

The tops of the trees swayed, and the leaves flickered in the wind, instantly calming her. She didn't have to know everything that happened. Henry was right. Children were happier accepting what was and not worrying if something was wrong. Let the adults do the worrying.

"I'm going to have a cousin." Tess spoke the words to make them real, then smiled at her mother who stood next to her.

"I'm sorry we didn't tell you. There was concern Molly might lose the child. She was ordered to stay well rested. Last night's dance was too much for her but everything will be fine now that Beau is home."

ONE HUNDRED TEN

Two days later Beau sat at the head of the table for a private afternoon meal in the restaurant, his face lined with scratches and an angry scar ran along his cheekbone.

Chef Pierre made a fuss, giving him a plate with a giant slab of grilled steak and a pile of garlic roasted potatoes.

The restaurant had been busy for breakfast, lunch and dinner since news of his survival had spread throughout the town.

Molly sat to his right and Anna to his left with Tess between her and Clara. Henry and Bert sat across from Tess and Clara.

Clara's eyes grew wide, and she raised her hand to wave as Sergeant Roberts peered through the doorway. He waved to her with a heartwarming smile.

Beau stood to greet the sergeant, leaning on the table for support.

"You are a sight for sore eyes," said Sergeant Roberts, heartily shaking Beau's hand. He turned to Molly. "We caught Theo trying to board the steamship early this morning. Broke down and confessed to setting fire to the shed. Seems after I had a talk with him about Carl's stolen cigars he panicked, afraid he'd be accused of starting the fire at the mill, too."

"Did you find the gold?" Tess asked.

Sergeant Roberts shook his head. "When we questioned him on the subject he denied stealing it. Admitted he set the fire to create a distraction but found the box empty."

Beau frowned. "Gold?"

Molly leaned toward him. "Someone stole our gold from the music book box."

Beau laughed, placing his hand against his chest. "Ouch. I mustn't do that. I didn't get a chance to tell you, I moved the gold to the piano after I sent Theo on an errand last month."

"You suspected him, too?"

"He did his job too well, never left his post except to wander down the hall and stare into the parlour when no one was watching."

Molly's eyes widened. "Dear me, I almost gave away that piano. Thankfully I decided to keep it after seeing Tess trying to teach herself how to play."

"You are becoming such a lovely young lady," Anna whispered to Tess who rolled her eyes.

"It is interesting what people say and do when they think no one is watching," said Tess, winking at Henry.

Sergeant Roberts turned to Beau. "Turns out Fred's brother is a hardened criminal from out East hired to do his dirty work. Fred was not innocent by any measure. He planned to destroy your businesses. It didn't take much to get Earl to talk. The workplace accident was entirely Fred's fault. You were not involved."

"I was his partner and should be held responsible as well."

"While you were gone, he overworked those men and put them in jeopardy. The man fell into the trommel because he was exhausted."

"When I discovered what Fred was planning, I confronted him. He offered to buy me out of the dredge business so I could concentrate on the hotel with Molly, at a fraction of the initial investment. I refused, staying on to watch out for the employees. Fred did not like it, said I was too soft on the men, and we argued. He hit me with something and pushed me out into the current with his boot."

"You are lucky to be alive. The murder charge has been downgraded to attempted murder in that regard but Fred is done for."

Beau nodded solemnly. "I had hoped the decent man would emerge from under all that greed and arrogance but I was wrong."

ONE HUNDRED ELEVEN

One week later, Tess threw back the quilt and jumped out of bed as sunshine streamed through the bedroom window.

"What on earth are you doing?" Anna draped an arm across her face and groaned.

"Uncle Beau is going to show me how to pan for gold today. I want to get an early start." Tess pulled off her nightclothes and dressed, hopping across the floor as she tied her bootlaces.

"We are not leaving just yet. Chef Pierre will prepare a basket so we can have a picnic by the creek."

"Uncle Beau said the early prospector gets the prize."

Anna laughed. "Of course he did. I'll be downstairs shortly."

"I will check if Chef Pierre needs help," said Tess, closing the door behind her.

Moments later she peered into the kitchen.

Henry sat at the counter watching his father cut thick pieces of sourdough bread. They turned to greet Tess.

"Mornin' Sourpuss." Henry smirked, picking up a knife to spread butter on the bread slices.

"Good morning, Chef Pierre." Tess ignored Henry, abruptly turning away to check the ice box.

"French toast is warming in the oven." Chef Pierre pointed with his knife.

Tess grabbed a plate, opened the oven door and used a fork to spear a piece of French toast then dropped it on the plate. She headed toward the door into the dining room.

"Wait. I'm sorry. I won't call you that anymore."

Tess grinned. "At least not today."

"You know me so well." Henry pulled off a piece of her toast and popped it in his mouth.

"Get your own breakfast."

At that moment a woman screamed in the lobby.

Tess dropped the plate and ran out of the dining room.

Henry followed close behind.

Anna stood at the bottom of the stairs, both hands covering her mouth as she stared at the open door.

"I guess you did not receive my telegram."

Tess squeezed her eyes shut, afraid she was seeing things. In that split second she fear and hopelessness disappeared, allowing confidence and optimism to flow into her heart. The moment was perfect for wishes to come true.

James limped toward Anna and Tess using a wooden crutch tucked under one arm.

Tess almost knocked him over as she threw herself at him.

He leaned over and wrapped one arm around her. "My little Princess."

Tess hugged him and nuzzled her face into his jacket, inhaling the scent of tobacco and peppermint. "I am sorry for saying I hated you for leaving. Can you forgive me for being a selfish child?" As she took back the words she uttered the day he left an immense burden lifted from her shoulders.

James kissed her forehead. "Love softens the hard edges of words spoken in fear and sadness. I never doubted your love."

Anna fell into his arms and he held her in a tight embrace. They stayed like that for a long time.

She tugged on her father's sleeve. "We can stay in Dawson City, right? I know of a school in dire need of a terrific teacher. Don't worry I brought your grey wool sweater."

James turned his attention back to Tess.

"I like the sound of that. How's the sand up here?"

"Perfect. The Yukon River has no interest in destroying sandcastles so our family will stay safe. We can build one after we pan for gold."

THE END

Other Books by T.A. Leinemann:

Arcadia Deception (The Hover Chronicles, #1)

Flight Control (The Hover Chronicles, #2)(Sequel)

Both books are available from:

Amazon (Print book and ebook)
Kobo (ebook)

Visit T.A. Leinemann's website at:
https://taleinemann.wordpress.com

TESS

Made in the USA
Lexington, KY
28 September 2018